Le Balcon au Lac

THE BALCONY ON THE LAKE

P. Saville Monks

Grosvenor House
Publishing Limited

All rights reserved
Copyright © P. Saville Monks, 2024

The right of P. Saville Monks to be identified as the author of this
work has been asserted in accordance with Section 78
of the Copyright, Designs and Patents Act 1988

The book cover is copyright to P. Saville Monks

This book is published by
Grosvenor House Publishing Ltd
Link House
140 The Broadway, Tolworth, Surrey, KT6 7HT.
www.grosvenorhousepublishing.co.uk

This book is sold subject to the conditions that it shall not, by way of
trade or otherwise, be lent, resold, hired out or otherwise circulated
without the author's or publisher's prior consent in any form of
binding or cover other than that in which it is published and
without a similar condition including this condition being
imposed on the subsequent purchaser.

This book is a work of fiction. Any resemblance to
people or events, past or present, is purely coincidental.

A CIP record for this book
is available from the British Library

ISBN 978-1-83615-120-3

To my wife Sandra
who says she ought to
have been born French.

I should like to acknowledge that I have used some lines of the lyrics of 'Both Sides Now' (sometimes called 'Clouds') by Joni Mitchell as they seemed so appropriate. I have also used a dramatic recipe of the chef Marc Veyrat which I can thoroughly recommend. The photograph of 'Le Roc de Chère' and the mountains behind, including 'Les Dents de Lanfon' on the front cover was taken by my wife, Sandra. I should like to thank Julie Scott and Jasmine Damaris for their patience and help in getting this book to completion.

CONTENTS

Chapter 1   Jacques 1978–1999   1

Chapter 2   Catherine 1978–1999   27

Chapter 3   Jacques 1999–2001   64

Chapter 4   Catherine 1999–2001   97

Chapter 5   Jacques 2001–2003   122

Chapter 6   Catherine 2001–2003   155

Chapter 7   Jacques 2003   186

Chapter 8   Catherine 2003   202

Chapter 9   Jacques 2003–2004   211

Chapter 10 Catherine 2003–2004   241

Chapter 11 Jacques 2004–2005   268

Jacques 1978–1999

"Jacques."

"Yes boss."

"It's the fittings you've put on the schedule. We can't afford them. We need something cheaper."

"It can't be done boss. I know there is cheaper stuff on the market but in reality it just is not safe. You know that in those buildings near the canal the water can get anywhere. It would be OK for a while but that cheap stuff won't last."

"Well, we can't afford it and I need you to choose something quite a lot cheaper."

"I'll take another look but I don't think that it's possible if we keep to the safety standards."

"Do it Jacques. Just do it."

The boss gives a sigh and moves away. I carry on with my work. He leaves me undisturbed until the end of the day. We are rewiring a couple of flats in the old town area of Annecy. The buildings are very old and of course did not have electricity when they were built. The wiring has been added later and much of it appears to have been done on the cheap. Very often when a building changes hands, the new owner wants to replace the wiring. Any house or flat that is sold, legally needs an assessment if the wiring is over fifteen years old. The flat I am dealing with at the moment is on the second floor and does not pose much of a challenge. Often the ground floors and especially the basements are damp, with walls that tend to crumble. This evening, I am working till late, which I do happily any evening that I don't have a date with Sylvie.

Sylvie and I first got together about six months ago. There's a bar in the newer part of Annecy where I often go when I finish work, for a coffee or a beer. The cafés and bars in the old town are expensive as you pay for the atmosphere. It is better value to be in the newer part of the town. It is also the case that if I am working on a building in the old town, I find it difficult not to carry on thinking about the job if I have a drink just around the corner. It is better to be further away. I tend to go to 'le Bistro du Thiou' which is set back a little from the river. There is often a small group of young women in there. I'd been there several times when I caught the eye of one of them and she smiled back. That was unremarkable perhaps but on the way out she gave me a dazzling smile that made my whole body go weak. Then she was gone. A couple of days after, we were all there again. I determined that somehow I was going to approach her. This should have been a simple matter. She had shown me in no uncertain terms that she was interested. It is a strange paradox I find about approaching women. The more I want to do it, the harder it becomes. She passed my table. I have a feeling this was actually to help me make a move.

"I like your jumper" I said. My voice sounded strange to me.

"Yes, it is nice" she agreed. "It's cashmere. I bought it in Milan."

She casually sat down at my table. That was how it happened. I can truthfully say that she made all the running. She could not have made it easier for me. Why, I wonder do I find this sort of thing so difficult? So many men seem to have supreme confidence. We chatted about nothing for about half an hour and arranged to meet on the Sunday. That was several months ago.

Now it is the Sunday after the exchange with the boss about electrical fittings. I am on a ridge on the Roc de Chère overlooking Lac d'Annecy. I have come here to try and solve my dilemma, though in my heart I know there is only one answer. I am an electrician working for a building firm, although I do get a bit of freelance work which means that I am not entirely dependent on the job with the firm. I know that we are not doing well at the moment. Everyone knows. There are severe restrictions on building at Annecy and round the lake and the competition is intense. I got the job a couple of years ago and was delighted to be accepted. The boss at that time was an elderly man with a great sense of humour and an ability to turn any minor setback into something positive. He would always listen patiently to a problem and usually managed to find a simple solution. He had recently retired and the firm was now run by his son who was a jumped-up nobody who seemed to feel any problem was some-one else's to solve. Since he had taken over, the firm was going downhill and he wanted me to compromise on the quality of the electrics. I didn't think I could do that. It wouldn't be safe but I knew that if I stuck to my guns, my job would be on the line. Nobody likes getting the sack, especially when they feel that they are in the right. I had come to this place to sort things out in my mind.

The Roc de Chère is a nature reserve overlooking the lake and until this moment I had not realised what an impression it had made on me. I was born and brought up in Eymoutiers on the Vienne and when a kid, I have frequently gone to Le Lac de Vassivière with my family for a picnic or to swim. Le Lac de Vassivière is surrounded by land which is fairly flat. It's a beautiful landscape. There are plenty of trees and often one sees wild ponies running free but it did not prepare me for Lac d'Annecy. This is something else, magnificent, almost entirely surrounded by mountains; and the most beautiful mountains at that.

As I was brought up in Eymoutiers, I now need to tell you of my background and how I come to be in Annecy. Eymoutiers was an important town in the middle ages and has many beautiful buildings. As the population has been on the decline since then, it is not a place with a large number of new buildings and therefore retains much of its old-world charm. The river Vienne is very pretty and forms a gentle curve to the North of the town. This is somewhat marred by the railway and the station which separate the town from much of the neighbouring river. I suppose it is necessary for any town to keep up with the modern age and this is a small sacrifice to make for easy railway access to Limoges.

My best friend is Georges Barbier. We used to play together before school age and were in the same class throughout school. As young children, the place our mums most frequently used to take us was Le Parc du Pré Lanaud. There would be the six of us: Jules and me, Georges and his brother Gérard who was younger than Jules but older than Georges and me and of course our mums who were good friends. The park is a couple of acres. It is to the East of the town with access by a pretty little footbridge over the river Vienne. While you are in the park there is a walk along the river with a lovely view of the Church of St. Étienne. When we were older, we used to take the same footbridge to get to school. We would cut across the park to the North and take a path under the railway. Georges was not academically minded. He wanted nothing better than to leave school and have a straightforward reasonably well paid job. Georges instinctively understood money; supply and demand. He was very good at buying small things which were in fashion and passing them on at a profit; may be packs of playing cards or sets of poker dice, usually small easily manageable items. I was inclined toward science. Even before we were formally being taught any science, I was fascinated by the way a swing went to and fro or the way the sun changes colour throughout the day. Our different points of view on education did not cause any problem and we spent a lot of time together.

When I was 13 and my elder brother Jules, was 17, my mother was taken ill. She was taken to the Dupuytren hospital in Limoges. The hospital was almost new at the time, very large and slightly intimidating. My father for some reason which still is not clear to me, felt that I should go away while he and my elder brother could visit my mother in hospital. Of course I now realise that she was very ill and he felt that I was too young to see the consequences. It still makes me feel left out of a major event in my life. Jules was older at 17 and I can see that my father would not be able to prevent him visiting mum. His solution to what I feel was his problem, was to send me on holiday with an old friend of the family.

It was to the Diacres that I was being sent. Antoine and Anne Diacre have one child, a daughter Catherine; thirteen the same age as me. I had seen her name on cards sent from the family at the New Year or from holiday but knew nothing about her at all. It is a curious situation but my family, the Parisels, have a peculiar relationship with the Diacres going back many generations. They have never intermarried but in each generation the wife of one family has been introduced as the best friend of a member of the other family. So my mother, Françoise was the best friend of Marie Diacre, sister of Antoine and aunt of Catherine. The story which has been handed down in both families is that this has always been so and always will be. It can indeed be shown to be so for a period of over a hundred years. Over several generations this has made the families very close in some ways although actual contact has been limited. I had never met the Diacres although I had seen many holiday postcards. They had a house in Haute Savoie. My father arranged for me to go on holiday with them there at Écharvines near Lake Annecy. I had little say in the matter and if I had had any say, I would have objected vehemently. At 13 I just went.

Mum goes into hospital and I go to Écharvines to stay with the Diacres. Theirs was an old house with three very large bedrooms and an extensive area at the back with a couple of small barns. It was between a beautiful mountain 'Les Dents de Lanfon' and a nature reserve 'Le Roc de Chère'. Even though it was only a few hundred yards away, it was not possible to see the lake, although the mountains on the west side of the lake were quite striking. It seemed an idyllic setting.

A slightly odd feature of the house was a conservatory. It was not very large but had a highly intricate roof. It was a five sided pyramid with an apex so that there were five triangular panels. These slipped one behind the other so that up to four fifths of the roof could be opened. It also rotated so that the section which was not open to the sky could be altered. It seemed to be unnecessarily complicated. I asked Madame Diacre about it.

"Yes Jacques" she said. "It is complicated and it was very expensive. The reason we had it fitted is because of the hang- and para-gliders. It cannot be said to be their fault, but it is impossible to enjoy the sun in the garden without feeling, well, almost spied upon. On occasion there can be a dozen overhead. Of course the hang-gliders will not actually be looking at us but it is impossible not to feel intruded upon. This roof is complicated but it allows us to get the sun without feeling this intrusion as the section of sky where the gliders are can be blotted out."

I am not an outgoing individual. I am rather reserved and usually slow to make friends but Catherine and I hit it off immediately. Maybe as an only child, she found it exhilarating to have someone her own age under the same roof. For my part, she had an infectious laugh and a peculiar smile, hard to describe but a bit lopsided and thoughtful as if, yes life was fun but it did need thinking about. For whatever reason, we were inseparable. We went everywhere together. We took bikes and cycled for miles. The east side of the lake is mountainous, the roads are steep and cycling is hard work. The other side of the lake is much easier going. There is a cycle track which previously was a single track railway. As a result all the steep slopes have been levelled making cycling a real pleasure. We did manage to get that far one day but it is a long way from Écharvines and means going on the main road through Annecy itself which is much less fun. There is a plan to extend the cycle track right round the lake. For the moment however, cycling on the east side of the lake is tough.

We also walked a lot, rambling wherever Catherine wanted. She took me to all the places she loved best. There was a waterfall, the name of which I could not remember until I revisited it recently; La Cascade d'Angon. You can walk behind it without getting wet, or at least only a few splashes. I remember a pretty bridge across a little stream. The place we loved most was a certain ridge on the Roc de Chère which overlooks the lake and has an extensive view of the villages on the other side of the lake, including the magnificent Château de Ruphy which Cézanne painted. I fell in love with this little ridge. I named it 'Le Balcon au Lac' as you could see the whole area as if from a balcony. When I told Catherine's mother where we had been she was highly alarmed.

"It is very dangerous you know, Jacques. People have died jumping off the cliff there."

I looked at Catherine and grinned. "Yeah, Yeah," I thought. When we were alone Catherine admitted that it was true people had drowned there diving from the cliff edge. If you are in the lake, swimming or in a boat, from the water you can see memorials to some of the people that have died there and also a warning about snakes. I didn't let that worry me. I wasn't going to dive and I thought that the snakes would keep well clear of the open paths. Catherine thought 'Le Balcon au Lac' was a lovely name for it and we went there frequently during my stay. I was happy; life was great. Then catastrophe struck. My mother died.

Catherine's dad drives me back home to Eymoutiers. When we arrive, things are pretty traumatic. My father has fallen apart. He is slumped in an armchair. He seems unable to do as much as talk, let alone be constructive. Antoine Diacre remonstrated gently with his (well sort of) brother-in-law.

"Pull yourself together, Pierre, I know it's a dreadful thing to have to come to terms with but accept it you must. I'll help Jules make all the arrangements before I leave. You need to accept the situation and move on."

He stayed for a couple of days and helped Jules to deal with funeral arrangements as he said he would. Then he left. This was a cue for Jules to become very unpleasant to me.

"It's all right for you Jennifer" he started.

I knew immediately that there was trouble coming. He used to call me Jennifer when he wanted to wind me up. It's not that he is actually accusing me of being a little girl or wet. It's a corruption of 'Jeune Frère' which he knows annoys me. When we were much younger he could sometimes send me into a temper tantrum with it. I had long outgrown that reaction but the fact that he had brought the name back from the past meant he was going to have a go at me. There was trouble brewing.

"Oh yes" he continued. "It's been OK for you. On holiday in the Alps while I've spent the last month watching mum slowly die. You may deny it but oh yes, you've been enjoying yourself!"

I was devastated. He was being thoroughly nasty. I suppose he really had had a lot to put up with watching mum slowly going downhill but the worst of it was that he was right. The last month had been the happiest that I could remember and all that time my mother was lying in hospital dying. It was no good thinking that I hadn't wanted to go in the first place. Indeed I had not but once I got to Écharvines, quite honestly I had hardly given mum a thought. I felt awful. It was no good replying. There was nothing mitigating I could say. So I said nothing. The silence seemed to go on for ages. Then suddenly it got to him. He looked madder than I have seen him. Before I could move an inch he hit me; hard, just below the left eye. I was flung backwards against the wall by the power of it. Immediately he looked horrified, humiliated even. His face crumpled and he left without saying a word. The bruise sprang up straight away and looked pretty impressive in the mirror. Later, when asked what had happened, of course I had tripped and unfortunately fallen against the corner of the table. I think people believed this as there had never been any previous violence in our family. But dad; dad? He never even asked. He just sat there in his chair looking deathly white, doing and saying nothing. The next day Jules was, apologetic is too mild a word, he was horrified that he could have hit me like that. It never happened again. I assured him that I was all right. I pointed out that we were all under a lot of stress. I think just to keep the conversation going, he said how worried he was about dad.

"He just sits there day and night not saying a word. I think it would be better if he hit the bottle or started taking drugs to try and cope with it but he's just passive, a complete wreck. It can't go on like this."

It did go on like that. He went to bed. He woke up. He went to work. He came back. He sat in the chair.

He went to bed…Day followed day. Month followed month …Between us Jules and I had to run the house; all the cooking, cleaning and so on. Not only everything that mum used to do but also everything that dad used to do. He used to help mum quite a bit with the general housework and now he just sat in a daze. They must have been being very patient at his workplace because I don't believe he can have been doing anything constructive. A year goes by without any change. I receive an email from Catherine saying that her father, Antoine, has received promotion but it involves moving to Toulouse as he will be in charge of the firm's southwestern section. We kept in touch by email but only very rarely, perhaps once or twice a year. Jules was now sitting his baccalaureate. I was worried for him but I need not have been concerned. He managed to cope excellently. He passed his bac with flying colours and was admitted to Limoges University to study history. Limoges is a sort of middling university, hardly among the best but all right for all that. He would be near home and was excited to get the place. I was more inclined towards science. The Georges Guingouin College was getting good results at the time and my studies seemed to be going quite well. I was thinking of studying physics. Georges my best mate wanted to get a job as soon as possible and leave Eymoutiers for a big city. Perhaps not Paris but may be Marseilles or Lyon. Mostly he favoured Marseilles. As time went by, dad improved very slightly. He still looked terrible but was doing a little more and actually talking to us from time to time. Four years had passed since mum died and it was my turn to be coming up for the baccalaureate. On the morning of the fourth anniversary of mum's death, dad was not up at the usual time for breakfast. Jules went into his room and softly called me in. There was an empty brandy bottle on the bedside table and a large empty packet of sleeping tablets alongside. Jules took it very calmly. He made all the necessary arrangements.

I didn't think it would affect my school work but it did. My memory just seemed to fail me at odd times. When I took my baccalaureate, I didn't seem to be able to remember a thing and failed miserably. I can remember that the physics practical exam was a particular problem. Pupils were all given the equipment to measure the latent heat of ice. I had performed this experiment before and should have known exactly what to do. My mind was a blank. I could see all the other pupils getting on with the job but my memory just would not work. I knew the answer. The answer was 334 joules per gram but I could not remember the experiment. All I could do was scribble illegible workings on the paper and write an answer close to the correct one (I chose 329) at the end of the scribble. I did not expect to get any marks. No sooner had the exam finished than my memory came flooding back and I could remember exactly what I should have done. I found this incredibly depressing.

Catherine, being the same age as me, was also taking her bac. Soon after, she sent me an email. She'd got a place at the Sorbonne. Wow! That was some achievement. I congratulated her profusely. At the same time it seemed to accentuate my abject failure. My failure to get a place at university left me in a bit of a quandary. For some time I mooched around, uncertain of what to do. I didn't want to resit the bac, although I was sure I'd do well if I did resit. I just didn't have the stomach for it. After a lot of thought and discussing it with both Jules and Georges, I thought of vocational training as an electrician. I applied and was accepted for a two year CAP scheme at Limoges. It was near enough to home and seemed an excellent answer to my problem. Georges left school and almost immediately found a job with a firm in Lyon that bought up bankrupt stock. It was a very junior post but he found it right up his street and was confident that he could move up the ladder.

Other than getting on with the apprenticeship, very little affected me during my two year CAP scheme. The main thing was that Jules found a job teaching history at a school in Provence. This meant that I was alone in the house. While Jules and I were living there, we had mainly financed the running of it by using some of the money which the deaths of mum and dad had put at our disposal. Now that Jules was no longer living there, it would have been perfectly reasonable for him not to pay. However he willingly agreed to pay his share until I was earning. At that point we reckoned on selling the house and dividing the inheritance; in effect going our own ways. During this period while I was a trainee, Georges won the trust of the Senior Management in his firm and was appointed a junior manager with limited responsibility for buying in stock in some categories of goods. Catherine was still at the Sorbonne and judging from her occasional emails, she was loving Paris.

I was an extremely conscientious student. I was meticulous in everything I did. I took electricity very seriously, reasoning that it was dangerous stuff. It would be essential to form good habits as changing the way one does something one has learnt to do is very difficult. There are a large number of legal requirements for electrical installations and I learnt them all down to any footnotes or after-thoughts. Being an electrician is a practical business and I was careful to note the different ways that the people that I worked with, approached practical questions like dealing with inaccessible corners and working with very little headroom. I enjoyed the course immensely and came out with a qualification with merit. Jules was away. Georges was away. I felt very much on my own. I am a reserved individual. Although I obviously met a few people and I did have a couple of dates with girls, after two years I had no new friends. When my year's intake qualified there was, of course, an evening celebration which I went to but then I was on my own. I needed a job.

Then I had an amazing stroke of luck. There is a sports bar in Limoges which shows rugby. I am not an avid fan but I do follow the five nations. There is speculation that Italy might join and make it a six nations' competition. I'm all in favour of that. Anyway this weekend, when I have just finished my training, the sports bar in Limoges is showing the France-England match at Le Parc des Princes. I went there to watch and am sitting at a table with a carafe of wine. On a table close by I notice there is a man of about sixty on his own quite smartly dressed watching the game but at the same time seeming a bit pre-occupied. I did not think much of it at the time. I was just watching the game, which was in the final minutes of the first half. The scores were level at seven all. Then the French team carried out a beautiful move. There was a dummy scissors movement followed by the real scissors and a well-judged kick collected by the wing. Lots of the people in the bar were on their feet and I found that

I was also. At half-time nobody was really listening to the experts analysing what had happened. The man at the next table leaned towards me and introduced himself.

"I'm Claude" he said.

"Jacques" I replied.

"You were very enthusiastic about that last try" he continued. "Are you a rugby fan then?"

"Not really" I replied. "I keep abreast of the five nations but I don't support a club team."

"That's a bit like me" he said. "I enjoy the internationals especially with the southern hemisphere teams."

"Yes, the All Blacks are magnificent to watch" I agreed.

I offered him a glass of my wine and he gratefully accepted. He went on to ask me what I did and I told him about dad's death; how I'd ploughed the baccalaureate and had just recently qualified as an electrician. The conversation carried on but I began to feel a little uneasy. Rather than casual chit-chat, he seemed to be probing me; trying, if you like, to see what made me tick. Then the second half started and we watched the game. It was a good match. The French backs were better than the English but the English forwards had the edge. About halfway through the second half, they forced a try under the posts. It was an easy kick. 14 all; and that is how it ended. Disappointing, as it was a home game and we had led almost all the time. I got up to leave.

"Don't go yet, Jacques" said Claude. "I want to discuss something with you." That seemed strange but I sat down and listened.

"You see, I urgently need an electrician right now. I'm the boss of a small building firm in Annecy. It really is small. I only use one electrician. Olivier has been with me for ever but I've just had news that he's been involved in a car accident. He's in hospital in Geneva. They say he won't be able to work for at least three months and probably longer. He's the same age as me. We were at school together. I am pretty certain that he'll retire even if he could come back after three months. I've been impressed about what you've told me about yourself. Here we are fortuitously thrown together. You are an electrician and you need a job. I am a builder and I need an electrician. How about we talk?"

"Annecy!" I replied. "I spent a month in the region when I was thirteen. Certainly talk on."

"I can guarantee you three months. That is a good assessment period. If after three months or indeed even after that Olivier wants to come back, then you'll have to go. I owe him. If he doesn't want to come back and I think you're good enough, you have a permanent job. How does that sound?"

"Claude" I said. "You're a Guardian Angel."

"Jacques" he replied. "You're a life saver. By the way, how come you were in the Annecy area at thirteen?"

I told him the story without much detail but I did mention the Diacres.

"I knew them" he said. "They moved to somewhere west, Bordeaux I think."

"Toulouse" I agreed. "He was promoted."

"I did a rather complicated extension for them because Madame Diacre felt the paragliders were very intrusive if she was sun-bathing in the garden."

"That was you?"

"Yes, I designed it myself."

"Claude" I said. "I should love to work in your firm. Give me tomorrow to sort a few things, Monday to travel and I can start Tuesday."

"You'll need somewhere to stay, Jacques. You can stay at my place just for a while. We've a spare room. Only ten days say, because we keep it for when my daughter comes. You can stay at ours for ten days while you find somewhere." Claude and I parted on very friendly, first name terms.

Two days later I arrived in Annecy. Claude's house was in rue Capitaine Baud at Annecy-le-Vieux. His wife Marie was absolutely charming and made me as welcome as a son. The room that she had prepared for me was spotless and had a view of Mont Veyrier, one of the lower mountains that surround the lake. I knew that this was the room that they kept available for their daughter so I needed to find somewhere else quickly. I had no idea where would be best. Claude's company, Desplaces & Cie, had an office in the 'Romains' area of Annecy. For want of a better idea, I looked for somewhere in that area and very quickly came up with a studio flat. It was hardly more than a room really but had a shower and a cooking area, a bed and a table with a couple of chairs. Nothing much but I didn't need much. It was quite cheap being between the rue des Alpins and the railway line. I snapped it up before it vanished off the market.

The three months trial period passed very quickly. I was doing a good job without any disastrous errors. The change from learning to actually doing a job can be quite tough but I coped with the change very well. Olivier was out of hospital but not really able to get about. Claude visited him at his home. I therefore still had a job. A month later I came into the office one day and there was a man there with Claude. He was sitting in a chair with a walking stick beside him. It was one of those ones that, at the bottom, split into a little tripod of feet to give greater stability; the ones hospitals provide. I knew at once that this was Olivier. I didn't wait for the introduction.

"Olivier!" I said. "I'm so glad to meet you. I'm Jacques. How is the recovery going?"

In all truth I could see that he was in no fit state to come back to work. He was as white as a sheet and from time to time a grimace would cross his face as some unpleasant twinge hit him.

"Oh! It's coming along slowly" he said. "I'm glad to meet you, Jacques. Claude has told me a lot about you. I should probably let Claude tell you himself but he wouldn't. He is delighted with your work. He says that now he wouldn't let you go even if I did come back. I wish I could" he continued, "but I can still hardly walk. I'm well into my sixties. I must retire. It's common sense."

Now that I had a job in Annecy and Jules had one in Provence it was time to sell the house in which we had been brought up. This turned out to be very difficult, very much harder than I imagined. It held so many memories. Every room held items that we might not need but which we would miss. It was the idea of never seeing so much of our past life ever again; little things which I would never have thought mattered. The birdbath in the garden; the power shower in the bathroom; the view from my bedroom window, all of a sudden these things seemed to matter a ridiculous amount. However we got together one weekend and decided what we needed to keep, what we needed to throw away and what we hoped to be able to sell. Most of the furniture we put in store because one of us would probably need it. Things like the curtains we left, partly so that the house would not look bare when potential buyers came to see it and also because a buyer might well be grateful for some made to measure stuff that was not in too bad a shape. Dad's car Jules had already taken to Provence, as he had a ten mile journey from the place he was renting to the school. I took a couple of small pictures which would look good in my room in Annecy. In the loft we found a suitcase with the usual old photographs. On top there was an envelope that had a letter in it. This was dated about a month before mum went into hospital. It was to dad from someone called Henri Roussel. The name seemed slightly familiar but I could not place him. Jules wasn't sure but he thought that Roussel was a rent collector who came to Eymoutiers about once a fortnight to collect rent or otherwise inspect properties owned by a firm in Limoges. He knew dad was acquainted with him but didn't think that they were friends. This seemed borne out by the letter being quite formal.

Monsieur, (it started)

I must apologise for this intrusion, which I hope is unnecessary. Six weeks ago, I was in the supermarket and I saw your wife collapse. Naturally I went over to help but she recovered very quickly. She specifically asked me not to tell you and I agreed. That is part of why I feel so bad about writing this letter. The thing is that on both my last two visits I have seen her in obvious pain which appears to last but a short time. She has then gone into the Pharmacy. I imagine to buy pain killers. This is not my business and she has asked me not to tell you. However, I feel that I must as I fear she could be very ill and may be keeping it from you.

(Signed off with a formal French sign-off the equivalent of)

Yours faithfully,
Henri Roussel

Jules and I looked at each other, knowing what we both thought. Although we could not be sure, it looked as if the reason dad had taken mum's death so very badly and eventually committed suicide was that he felt responsible. He had received this letter, thought it was rubbish and ignored it. He then found that Henri Roussel had in fact given him a chance of possibly saving our mum, Françoise, which he had not taken. Watching her deteriorate must have been agony. Of course, maybe he did ask her about it and she denied it but would he then take it so badly that he felt obliged to kill himself? I do not think so. To me this letter explained the greatest enigma of my life so far.

Having sorted out the house and put it on the market, Jules returned to Provence and I returned to Annecy. It was a lovely old house and sold quickly for a decent sum which we split straight down the middle. Prices in the Annecy area are considerably higher than in Eymoutiers but I did find that I had enough for a healthy deposit on the purchase of a flat. There was a bit left over for the proverbial rainy day. Having only recently moved into my little 'Studio Flat', I was now on the lookout for something else. This was altogether a different question because whatever I decided to buy now was likely to remain my home for a substantial length of time. I had the advantage over the previous search for somewhere to live, that I now knew Annecy Town far better than when I first arrived. I took my time and after a couple of months, I found a good sized two bedroom flat with a parking space in an apartment block on the Avenue de Genève in the North of Annecy. It was on the fifth floor facing East. It caught the morning sun and had a balcony with a mountain view. Now I felt settled and spent enough of my remaining money to make the place really cosy.

Claude had a son Dominique. He was generally around the place watching what happened and officially had a job in the office. Unlike his father, he was not a friendly type. I had been with the company about a year when Claude announced that he was thinking of retiring and that Dominique would take the helm. To me personally Claude said that he was in his late sixties and although he still enjoyed the job, he thought it was time to pass it on to his son. I can't say that I was happy about this. At base however, it was none of my business. Claude had been very good to me and if he wanted to pass his business on to his son, that was up to him. I call Claude by his first name in spite of him being my boss because that was how it happened when we first met. His surname is Desplaces. Once he was in charge, Dominique would put up with being called Monsieur Desplaces but preferred to be called 'Patron'. So I called him 'Boss'; anything for an easy life. Nevertheless life was not easy. It became awkward, as he perpetually found fault with something, usually the price of the materials. He also seemed to expect me to work on very late, which I was doing voluntarily anyway.

Six months after Claude retired, I met Sylvie. On our first date, a Sunday in May, we had a meal at 'Le Jardin de l'Auberge', a restaurant overlooking the Thiou where it is really more like a canal. We had a table overlooking the water and chose Pierrade de Boeuf. It is a dish which is great fun. You cook the strips of beef at your table on a heated metal plate. Sometimes it is charcoal powered, although the modern ones are electric. Sylvie has made all the running up to this point. I decide it might be the right time to take a bit of a risk. She may not be ready for this sort of thing. I take the nicest of the little strips of beef that have already cooked and using the cutlery provided, place it between her beautiful lips. It is amazingly sexy to feed your girlfriend like this. When she returns the tribute, it seals a bond. I feel a breathtaking sense of togetherness. Feeding and being fed like this also brings us very close together without any actual contact. I can detect the gentle fragrance of her perfume. It is delicate. She has not overdone it. It is trying to draw me closer but I have to resist it. It is too early and not the place. After dinner we take a walk along the lake through Les Marquisats Park. At the end of the park she turns to me and I take her in my arms. Her body seems to melt into mine. I kiss her lips and am utterly lost in the sheer wonder of her.

Sylvie was born and brought up in Annecy. She knows every café, every food shop and certainly every chic clothing boutique that there is. Restaurants come and go surprisingly fast in Annecy but for recommendations, she would beat any holiday brochure. When she was young the family were in a top floor flat on L'Avenue d'Albigny overlooking the lake. I cannot say that I like them from the outside. The view from the top floor down the lake, however, must be superb and owning a place like that, does suggest money. Sylvie having seen it from a young age, was not hugely impressed but had to admit that it was a lovely view. She now has a job as a Junior Manager of a jewellery shop in rue Carnot. Rue Carnot is the main shopping street in Annecy. It used to be the start of the main road to Geneva but is now a pedestrian precinct. When Sylvie was eighteen, her mother and father moved to a bungalow in Annecy-le-Vieux. This was partly determined by a couple of unfortunate power cuts that left everybody having to walk up numerous flights of stairs; a distinct disadvantage of a penthouse! It was at this time that Sylvie moved into her present flat in Chemin de la Croix Rouge with her friends.

We saw each other almost every evening after that first date, often repeating the same walk along the lakeside. A fortnight later we became lovers in my cosy little flat on L'Avenue de Genève. Life was great. I was ecstatic. She was beautiful. She was fun. Holding her in my arms was a delight. I was well and truly smitten. Yes, I was very much in love with Sylvie. She was sharing a flat with three other young women, the group that she was with when we met. It was close to where Le Chemin de la Croix Rouge crosses the remains of the single-track railway. It was rather unfortunately concrete from the outside but very well appointed when you were in it. It was very smartly furnished but anything but private. Any time we wanted a bit of privacy we needed to go to mine. Being with Sylvie meant that I was no longer prepared to work all hours and Dominique, 'Le Patron', didn't seem to see the justice of this. He and I did not get along. That was for sure.

I have now filled you in on my life up to the point where I am on my favourite ridge on the Roc de Chère trying to sort out what to do about Dominique's desire to use cheap material, the fitting of which will be my responsibility. Sylvie has gone to Chambéry for the day to visit her sister. From Le Balcon au Lac, there is a little path that goes steeply and a bit dangerously down to the water's edge. There is just about enough flat ground at the bottom to put down a rug and have a picnic. In July and August someone has nearly always taken a boat along the lake and moored it there for that purpose. Today it is free and this year there is a sideways-running branch of a tree at just the right height to sit on. So I do just that and am deep in thought when I hear voices on Le Balcon above me. Then there is a laugh. A laugh that I would know anywhere, even though I have not heard it for years. Catherine! I leap to my feet and scramble up the slope.

"Catherine" I call.

"Jacques" she replies. "What on earth are you doing here?"

"And you" I say. "I thought you were in Paris."

"Jacques," she says, "this is my fiancé Jean. Jean this is Jacques, a friend from childhood whom I haven't seen for years."

"Hello Jacques" says Jean. "Welcome. Any friend of Catherine's is a friend of mine. Isn't this a beautiful spot?"

"We call it Le Balcon au Lac" Catherine and I say in unison. We then laugh at just the same time. Then we both get the giggles. It is embarrassing. I am so pleased to see her again after so many years. Catherine has brought Jean to Annecy for a short break to show him where she lived as a child. They are at the end of their stay and need to go back to Paris tomorrow.

I bought one of these new-fangled mobile phones the other day. They've come down a lot in price recently. Sylvie already had one when I met her. It still seems odd to see people walking about apparently talking to themselves but now I am joining that group. I give Sylvie a quick ring to see if she is on the way back from visiting her sister. She is. I suggest that we four have dinner together. We don't go anywhere posh. We go to Le Bistro du Thiou where Sylvie and I first met. They serve a good fairly-priced meal and there is always a friendly atmosphere. Catherine and I have a lot of catching up to do but have to keep it to a minimum or we'll both be ignoring our partners. The conversation goes very well but is mainly kept to subjects that we all know something about. Catherine and Jean are thinking of getting married next summer. They'll probably get married in Paris but Toulouse where Catherine's parents live is still a possibility. They have not made their minds up yet.

Jean is a keen skier and paraglider. He was brought up in Pau in the Southwest, so his skiing experience was largely in the Pyrenees mostly at Cauterets but he had a skiing holiday in Denver. Since he moved to the North of France, he has let it drop. He tells us about a couple of guys that free-fell from a plane over Mont Blanc, landed by parachute and skied down a large section before paragliding into the valley. He makes a very good story of it; a natural raconteur. His eyes are bright and he looks very much alive. He is very keen to have a holiday skiing in the Alps this coming winter. I wondered what Catherine would think of that. As far as I know she has no skiing experience but she looks highly enthusiastic. She mentions Le Grand Bornand, which is quite close to Annecy but he seems pretty stuck on Chamonix and Mont Blanc. Neither Sylvie nor I had any experience of skiing at all and did not share Jean and Catherine's enthusiasm.

Then Catherine asks me about my best friend Georges. I tell her he has a job in Lyon but much more importantly a light bulb explodes in my head. Georges! Why didn't I think of him before? It probably won't come to anything but if anybody can get me some high quality electrical fittings on the cheap, that person is Georges. I must contact him first thing tomorrow. I force myself back to the present. They serve a marvellous mango sorbet at Le Bistro du Thiou and we round the meal off with that and a cup of coffee. Catherine and Jean need to catch the early morning train back to Paris so we all call it a day. I am overjoyed to say Sylvie does not go back to her flat. Sylvie decides to come home with me.

Catherine 1978–1999

I'm Catherine Diacre. I'm 20 years old and I'm studying law at the Sorbonne. I have a fiancé Jean Montaut, several years older than me who qualified in Law from the University of Lyon. He is fast becoming a world expert in International Law. I was brought up in Écharvines, a small village in Haute Savoie on the east side of Lake Annecy. I am an only child. While I was young we lived in a large old house. It had three bedrooms but being old it did not really fall very well into the modern classification of houses and flats. The rooms were big. There were largish grounds outside the house and several small outhouses or barns. One of these we used as a garage. We had a rather strange extension to the house which mum had wanted. It allowed her to sunbathe without being overlooked by paragliders. I thought that it was a complete waste, although I did see her point of view. Sometimes at weekends the sky seemed to be filled with them but so what? My family on my father's side had lived there for generations, owning a few cows and making their own versions of Raclette and Reblochon cheeses. My father worked for a furniture making company. While I was young, he was a local manager at the Industrial Estate of Grand Epagny to the North of Annecy. This meant that we did have some rather lovely furniture.

The dining room was fitted out in Louis Philippe style. It was very elegant with a beautiful mahogany sideboard. My father was born in this house. He has an elder, unmarried sister Marie, who lives at Aixe-sur-Vienne in the Limousin and a younger brother, my Uncle Robert. He moved to Provence and married my Aunt Nicole while they were still teenagers.

Their daughter, my cousin Aurélie, is a couple of years older than me. Everyone says we look alike. We do, although I think Aurélie is much prettier than I am. When I was small my mum and I used to go and visit them in Grasse for a week or two in the summer. Aurélie and I used to love dressing the same. We would persuade our mums to buy us the same summer outfits so that wherever we went people would say 'I can tell you're sisters'. We would giggle as if the fact that we were cousins, not sisters, was some sort of secret. Aunty Nicole took us to some very lovely places. I particularly remember a visit to the little Beach at Bauduen on the Lac de Sainte Croix. One thing that I did not think odd at the time, was that dad never came with us down to Grasse where they lived. They were his relatives not mum's. I imagine that he was trying to demonstrate his work ethic to the furniture firm because it was when I was about ten years old that he was promoted to manager. About the same time Aunty Nicole had a surprise late baby Léo and our visits to Grasse stopped. I was sad not to be seeing any more of cousin Aurélie. I think Aunty Nicole may have found a late and probably not really wanted, baby a bit of a handful. I only ever saw Léo when he was a babe-in-arms. Aurélie and I do keep in touch in a rather casual way. She passed her Baccalaureate and has just qualified as a doctor at The University of Aix-Marseille. Currently she is doing an internship at Marseille. The Medical College goes back to the fifteenth century as part of The University of Provence but for some reason the government seems unable to leave its administrative structure alone. The original University of Provence has been combined with newer ones then divided into two; restructured into three and there is now on-going discussion about recombining all three back into one. Aurélie says that its medical institute dates right back to 1409 and all this reorganisation makes no difference to it at all.

I went to the local school at Menthon St Bernard. I do not want to boast but if I am telling you about myself, I must be truthful or there is no point. I am bright and was always top of the class. I get this largely from my mother. She was an only child as I am. She was born in Chambéry and qualified in law at the University of Savoy which has a campus at both Chambéry and Annecy. She married my father soon after qualifying and was pregnant with me almost immediately so she had never practised law. I have certain qualities that other people call hang-ups. I love patterns. When I was very little, I used to play with bricks. I had a push-along trolley with 50 of them. By the time that I went to school, I already knew that if I made a triangle with one side of three bricks, one side four bricks and one side of five bricks and formed them into squares using the other bricks, this used up all my 50 bricks. Half my bricks made the five brick square and the other half made the three and four brick squares. I was less than four years old and already understood Pythagoras without ever having heard of such a thing. I was not much older when looking at a chess board which is eight squares by eight. I could imagine taking one column off and putting it back on as a row. There would be one square left over. 9 times 7 was one less than 8 times 8. If you did it again (10 times 6), there were 4 squares left over. Years later at school, we were taught in simple algebra $a^2 - b^2 = (a + b)(a - b)$. I already knew this just by looking at a chess board, although maybe I had not thought of it in quite the same way. So I'm bright and I'm a nerd. Luckily, unlike a lot of nerds I get on with people OK. There are other facets of patterns are so much more interesting than the maths. When I am very happy, I see beautiful shapes which I can never reimagine when they have gone. I see colours that are not there. That is to say I only see them when I am very happy. They vanish almost immediately. It is as if a person could not see colour at all except when very happy. When I was young, I remember seeing an old film called, I think, 'The Secret Garden', which was shot in black and white except for the scenes in the secret garden which were shot in colour. That is the peculiarity I have. I see all the normal reds, blues, greens etcetera all the time like everyone else but when I am very happy I see colours and shapes that I cannot describe. I usually keep quiet about this as people give me a funny look and call me a weirdo.

I was thirteen when one day my dad said to me:

"We're going to have a young boy to stay with us for a while. He's called Jacques and he's the son of old friends of the family. He's thirteen, same age as you. His mother's got to go into hospital. His father would like him to stay with us while she's not at home. You may have seen the odd picture of him on holiday snaps that they send us from time to time."

"Yes I think so" I replied. "There's one of four boys and two women with the background of a lake that I've seen."

"Right! That's Jacques, his mother and elder brother Jules with some friends at the Lac de Vassivière. I don't really know much about Jacques but I've said we'll put him up. I do hope you get on together."

I must say, I was apprehensive about this. Being an only child you get used to not having other kids around. While it can be great fun meeting someone new, sometimes it can be difficult to find your own space. To have another child in the house all the time might not work out at all. I was quite concerned. How would I react? How would he react?

I need not have worried. When Jacques arrived, he was lovely. We got on well together immediately. He was so interested in everything that I showed him; so enthusiastic; so prepared to go along with anything that I suggested. He loved Le Pont des Fées, the little 'Fairy Bridge' that led to the waterfall. It was school holidays. We were together all the time every day. We went cycling a lot. My mum and dad are keen cyclists, they went everywhere on bikes before they were married. We have several bikes in one of the outhouses so Jacques actually had a choice of them. Cycling is tough in the Menthon area. It is the Alps so you can imagine. I was used to it and I wondered how Jacques would fare. He came from somewhere near Limoges. It's a lot flatter in that region. He managed fine. In spite of the fact that I was used to it, he could beat me up the steep slope from Talloires. I suppose boys are just stronger than girls. The place that enthralled him most was a little ridge on Le Roc de Chère with a beautiful view over the lake. He called it 'Le Balcon au Lac'. I liked that. From then on, it was 'Le Balcon au Lac' for both of us.

Then the worst thing that could possibly happen, occurred. His mother died. I could hear dad telling him something in a serious voice. There was a curious gurgling sound and a door slamming. I rushed into the room to ask dad what was going on. He told me. How terrible, how awful, how would Jacques cope?

"I know where he's gone" I said. "I'll go and comfort him as best I can."

I went as fast as I could to Le Balcon au Lac. I knew he'd be there. There he was indeed, sitting on the ground with his legs dangling over the edge, his eyes red from rubbing away the tears. I sat beside him and put my arm round him. He said nothing. We were like that for a long time. I said nothing. There was nothing to say. Nothing would make it better.

Finally he said "Thanks Catherine" and we walked slowly back home. The next day dad drove him back to his home near Limoges.

About eighteen months later, Dad got promoted to regional manager in the firm. This involved a move to Toulouse where the company had its main office for the southwestern region. We let the house long-term through an agency and moved to Toulouse. Mum and I were upset at leaving. If he was too, dad did not show it. I think he was very pleased with his promotion which meant a good hike in salary and this trumped any sorrow at leaving the house, even though that had been in his family for generations. Moving to Toulouse meant a new house and a new school. The house was very different from the one I was used to. It was in rue Biot in the Minimes area of the town, modern with four bedrooms. There was not much garden and only a single garage. The rooms were smaller. At Écharvines there was plenty of space. We had two cars. Mum had the classic Deux Chevaux Citroen which she had bought before they were married and dad had a swanky new Peugeot Estate; useful if he needed to transport a bit of furniture. At Toulouse mum decided to sell her Deux Chevaux. I could see that she was very sad at that. She was very attached to it. She would always use it in preference to the Peugeot. It was however, very seldom that we had used both cars at the same time. So it was unnecessary. The thing that is very nostalgic about selling a car is that you may well see it again. Toulouse is a big city but mum did see her old car from time to time. On every occasion it made her sad.

My new school is the General High School of Saint-Sernin. This is an easily walkable distance of just under a mile. I settle in very quickly. Immediately I am top of my class, a position that I have come to expect. A couple of the boys, Emile and Thierry, who have been there for years and are also very bright, seem to resent this. It looks as if there might be trouble. What seems to diffuse the situation is that I have made friends with a couple of girls, Janine and Louise. They are both stunningly good-looking (and quite aware of this). There is no doubt that the boys who are resenting me, fancy Janine and Louise in a big way. They can see that it is not the best way to make a hit with a girl to be thoroughly unpleasant to one of their friends. So thanks to my two beautiful friends and boys' overactive adolescent hormones, I am inviolable. As we get to know each other better, their resentment fades.

When I am sixteen, mum feels that it is time for her to get a job. It must have been very frustrating for her to qualify in law and immediately have a baby to look after. I know that she feels very strongly that it is a woman's job to care for her children, being at home for them all the time until they are old enough. We both agree that at sixteen I am now old enough; that I do not need her to be constantly available. The first thing that she does is to take a quick refresher course. In any country the law will have moved on in sixteen years. Then she finds a job helping the poor who need legal assistance. She finds a job with the 'Aide Juridictionelle'; The Legal Aid System. I can see her blossom. It is such a delight to see my mum so happy, actually being able to use what she has learned to help people in need.

As we become a bit older I begin to worry about Janine. She seems to be boy-mad. Every week sees her up close and cuddling with someone different. Louise is much more mature. Sure she has boyfriends. She told me she went the whole way with one of them but you could see that she was in control. She is not going to get herself into trouble. We girls are luckier than those of previous generations. There are several forms of birth control, which are tried and tested and on which we can rely. If we feel that we must have sex, we can remain in control to a large extent. I could see Janine was going off the rails. Louise and I both had a quiet word with her but to no avail. Perhaps my hormones were late developing or perhaps it was just my personality for although I had a few dates, the occasional kiss never did anything much for me. I didn't find myself wanting more and it certainly didn't make me want to risk my whole life by falling for a baby while still a teenager. I think, in fact, that when you're 16 or 17 this is a huge advantage; not to have rampant hormones. It lets you concentrate on other things in life.

Eventually the inevitable happened. When she was a couple of months past her 17th birthday Janine fell pregnant. I think the boy was Thierry but Janine never let on so I can't be sure. Janine had used a pregnancy test. She knew that she was pregnant early on. She dithered about, wondering whether she should have an abortion or not. Louise and I knew full well that before she was pregnant she said that if it ever occurred she would have one. She now wasn't sure whether to keep the baby or not. It seems that the desire to have a baby can be very deep rooted. I suppose that is what you would expect on evolutionary grounds. The limit for legal termination here in France is early by some country's standards. She was coming right up to the limit when she had a miscarriage. There were those that reckoned she had the pregnancy terminated but either Louise or I had been with her almost all the time. We both thought it was natural.

The experience of pregnancy, then a miscarriage changed Janine's personality drastically. She went from being a friendly happy-go-lucky type to a miserable whiner. She was unable to take the simple little setbacks in life that previously she would have laughed at, grinned and got on with things with a 'that's life' approach; very little things, like the shop being out of eyeliner, just missing the bus by a few seconds or the mobile phone being inexplicably flat. These little irritations would either send her into a flying rage or a whimpering, self-pitying wreck. It was very hard being with her. Louise and I were her friends and we stuck by her. More and more we needed each other's support to do so. It was a strain especially with the baccalaureate coming up. We organised a support rota for Janine. We divided the part of the day that she was not at home with her parents into three sections. As far as was possible Louise would be with her for one section, I for another and both of us together for the third. It was awesomely wearing. We certainly did both need that third section; the part of the day when we were all three together; Louise and I supporting each other as well as supporting Janine. We calmed her. We cajoled her. We pampered her. We spoilt her. On occasion we even scolded her. The main effect did not seem to be on Janine although she did get a little better. The main effect was on Louise and me. We became the best of friends. We are so close now that we tell each other everything. After those few months I would die for Louise and I'm sure she feels the same for me.

When at home, I concentrated on my work to the extent that both my mum and dad thought that I was overdoing it. They told me to relax a bit, take some nights off the studies. I told them that because Janine needed so much care during the day, my home work was just about all the work that I was getting done. I became very tense and concerned about it. I started having bad nights and waking up exhausted. I am glad to say that when the bac came along, my mind was totally clear. I was in fine fettle. I found it an absolute doddle. Everything seemed so easy. It was a pleasure to see how much I had learned; how well my memory served me. I applied to the Sorbonne. I was delighted when I was given a place. Louise passed well and even Janine scraped through. I think Louise and I deserve a medal for Janine's pass. She would never have made it without us. Jacques sent me an email. He'd ploughed it. I felt so sorry for him. First his mother dies, then his father kills himself just as he is coming up for his baccalaureate. I do not know whether I could cope with that. I found Janine hard enough to deal with.

Now I need to go to Paris and find somewhere to live. It is exciting. My state student allowance, 'La Bourse sur Critères Sociaux' and my housing assistance grant have both come through. It is difficult to imagine that they would be enough for living in Paris. I am lucky. My father has given me a good allowance for while I am a student, which should keep me clear of financial worries. He seems to have money to burn after his promotion to Senior Regional Manager. I understand that he is so highly thought of that he was co-opted onto the board, as a non-voting member, to give his view about certain strategies. He has hopes of actually getting onto the board of directors. His generous allowance means that, in spite of Paris prices being sky high, I can afford to rent a very nice one bedroom flat. I find just what I am after in the 13th arrondissement; a flat on the 6th floor of a high rise concrete monstrosity. It is in the Avenue de Choisy, right close by to Place d'Italie metro. That made it within easy reach of the Sorbonne and most of the places that I would need to go. Although expensive for what it was, my generous budget could cover it with enough to spare for life's other necessities. The one bedroom of the flat was actually quite large. It easily took a double bed.

The sitting room had one of those windows that go down to the floor with, not really a balcony, but just enough room to stand outside the window with some railings to stop you falling out. It faced East and caught the morning sun. Now I felt pretty good. I had a place at the Sorbonne. I had a flat very much in the centre of Paris. All I have to do now, I thought, is to enjoy it.

Louise had been given a place at the University of Toulouse where she was due to study Biology. She is mainly interested in the biology of plants. Toulouse University is large with over a hundred thousand students, but well thought of. I missed Louise very much. We were so close after the problem with Janine. As soon as I was settled in, I arranged for her to come to Paris and stay with me during the winter vacation. Neither of us had ever been to Paris as children. During my first semester, I deliberately did not go sight-seeing at all so that when Louise came, it would be fresh for both of us. The first term went by very smoothly. I fell in naturally with the rhythm of university life. I made friends with a couple of other law students, Marie and Jeanne who were on the same course as I was. We went for a coffee break together and discussed the course and politics as if we could have any influence on either of them. They made good friends but I looked forward to the end of the term when Louise would visit. The train from Toulouse arrives at Paris Montparnasse which is a bit too far to walk to my flat, although Louise had one of those cases on wheels which are so common these days. We took a taxi. I was so pleased to see her. She looked very well. Much better than the tired and drawn looking Louise who took the bac! I must have looked very similar at that time. The Janine saga certainly took its toll on us both. Louise was very impressed with the flat.

"Can you really afford this, Catherine? In Paris?" She asks.

I have to admit to a very generous allowance from my father. Louise settles in. We have coffee with a slice of cake. We then just look at each other happily for a bit. It is so nice to see her. The next day and over the coming days we explore Paris to the full. Occasionally I am sorry that I have not been to places before to prepare the way for our joint visit but on the whole it has been a good idea not to see anything first. We both come to Le Louvre and other attractions fresh and therefore laugh together, groan together and just enjoy everything we see together. When we get back to the flat after the first day, the sunset through the window to the West is the most amazing I have seen with colours that just do not exist on any artist's palate. I am so happy, so very, very happy. I only have the one bed. We both go to sleep in that. When we wake up we find that we are both hugging each other. There is nothing sexual about it. We are just both so happy to be together that in our sleep we have drawn together and hugged. These periods of serenity pass and Louise has to go back to Toulouse. I feel that I should as well. I should see my parents. We take the same train South and part at Toulouse station after a very happy, brief though it seemed, week together.

Mum and dad were delighted to see me. Mum looks so much younger since she took that job with the legal assistance people. She obviously feels that it justifies all her hard work and the expense of training her in the first place. There is obviously something a bit daft about training a group of people to do something and then finding that they go off and do something else. For many situations you could make it a condition of the training that somebody works a couple of years before going on to anything else and some courses do that. As far as women and pregnancy goes, however, there does not really appear to anything that can be done about it.

I stayed with my parents for about a week. It was, to be true, a bit of a bore. They were both at work on weekdays as the university vacation did not coincide with their days off work. We went to Narbonne on the coast on the Saturday. Dad's swanky Peugeot makes very light work of a trip like that. In winter though, Narbonne is a bit of a dead loss. We took a (rather chilly) look at the med, had a (very nice) lunch at a bistro in the centre of town and returned home. I love my parents but I was quite relieved on Sunday, to take the train back to Paris and my lovely little flat in the 13th.

So I was back to the round of coffee with Marie and Jeanne and the interesting legal course that I was pursuing. Just after my 20th birthday in April, there was a lecture advertised. Jean Montaut was due to lecture on the difficulties of trying to get the nations in the European Union to have the same laws. It was entitled 'A Common Law for All EU Countries?' He was a young lecturer, not at the Sorbonne. He had an appointment at Lille but he must have made sufficient of a name for himself to have been invited to speak on the subject as a Guest Lecturer. I decided to go along. It is obviously a bit strange if you live at a frontier that every time you cross the border, the law changes. The United States had a huge problem with that in the prohibition years because the individual states have differing laws. I am not the type of student that sits in the front and holds their hand up all the time to ask a question. He had intrigued me with a certain point. I waited to the end of the lecture and managed to have a word with him before he left. He had mentioned that the EU regulations said that any state which thought that a law passed by the EU parliament was against its national interest, might repeal it. I knew at that time that the United Kingdom had a large group of politicians who were whinging that there were laws being passed in Brussels about which they could do nothing. I wanted to be sure of the position.

I managed to corner him on his way out, complimented him on the lecture, saying how clear he had made it but... and asked him about the potential for individual states to repeal laws made by the EU.

He said: "Shall we go and have a cup of coffee instead?"

I was taken aback. 'Instead?' I thought, - but he was wandering off so I followed. There was indeed a café very close. We sat down. He immediately apologised.

"I'm sorry" he said. "When I said 'instead' I meant instead of standing around in the hall; not instead of answering your question. I am still quite new to being a guest lecturer. I find most of the questions are either prepared to make the questioner look intelligent or are on a subject that the lecture was not intended to cover. I like to get out of the building before I'm cornered." He grinned. "But in your case I didn't make it in time. You probably know I'm Jean, what's your name?"

"Catherine" I answer. "There's no problem. It's just a misunderstanding and misunderstandings are the reason for a lot of law suits."

The waiter comes and takes our order. We both ask for a white coffee.

"I like your question, Catherine" he says, "partly because it is something that I did deal with in the lecture and partly because it has more than one answer. Question: Can member states revoke a law passed by the Parliament of the European Union? The straight one word answer is 'Yes'. In reality the answer is 'With a great deal of difficulty'. The caveat in the actual law namely that it has to be against their country's national interest, is not the hard part since only that country can decide what is against its interests. The difficulties are first that most countries have a backlog of intended legislation to pass. Parliaments have become overburdened. The use of the Filibuster in the USA is an example of how a small minority is able to prevent or significantly delay a bill. The result, of course, is to delay all other bills as well. A new bill is therefore difficult to fit into the schedule. Then there is the psychological fact that the bill has already been passed by the EU. Unless the parliament of a country is massively in favour of revoking it, the fact that a large number of other countries have already agreed it gives a considerable credence to those who do want to accept it. Therefore the reality is that it seldom happens."

At this point the coffee came and we both took a sip.

"Thank you for such a full explanation" I said. "It always seems to be the case that nothing is cut and dried. I love the song 'Both sides now': 'I've looked at clouds from both sides now from up and down but still somehow it's cloud illusions I recall'. It describes so much of life."

I can sense a subtle change in Jean at this point. I think he may actually be becoming more interested in me than the question I put.

"You are so right" he said. "Everything can be looked at from different points of view but seldom is. History is the classic; seen from the point of view of the victor. But everything that we are taught in school is taught from a single point of view. There just is not time to do otherwise and unfortunately a majority of people learn better if they are told something as a certainty even if the reality is that it only one of several possibilities."

I have taken to Jean. He is very much on my wavelength. All through my school days I could see the tunnel vision approach that education has; the algebraic way of looking at what I had seen as a pattern change for example; the total Darwinian approach to evolution when so much of evolution does not actually fit it. Sure, natural selection is undeniable but it does not explain everything by any means. I realise as I have told you that I am a nerd but I think Jean is a person who understands nerds. He is looking thoughtful.

"Catherine" he says. "It may be that some people would say that to give a lecture and ask for a date from a girl who has attended it, is bad practice. I cannot really see why and anyway that is what I am going to do. Can we meet up sometime? I really would like to get to know you better."

I know my answer but I keep him waiting just a little. I admire his clean-cut looks, the angle of his jaw and his general air of being very fit. I like his easy smile. Already I think I know that we have a similar outlook on life.

"Yes, Jean, I would really like that."

We arrange to meet at the café we are now in, as we both know where it is, at midday on Sunday in ten days' time.

The next week seems to drag. Slowly, slowly move the everlasting spheres of heaven. Marie and Jeanne, through no fault of their own, are suddenly exceedingly irritating. I have to bite my tongue on several occasions, knowing the fault is with me not with them. At last it is Sunday. I rise early, skip breakfast, have a good long shower and then think about what to wear. Everyone wears jeans these days. That would be OK but I want to look special; not ultra-special. I don't want to overdo it. I choose a smart fairly plain dress. It has a bit of a tight waist which gives me a nice figure and is three-quarter length, so it is far from provocative. I look in the mirror. I know that I am no beauty; not like Louise who is stunning. I think I have made myself look, not stunning, but nice, presentable, someone you would like to be with. That is good. I leave exactly the time that I think it will take to get there by noon. I am not a girl who thinks that one should keep people waiting just for the sake of it. I arrive dead on the dot of twelve. Jean is already there and has managed to get a table sitting outside. His face lights up when he sees me and I know mine does the same on seeing him. This is a good start. We are both already enjoying each other.

"You're spot on time" he says. "It is so good to see you Catherine."

"And you, Jean. Doesn't this café look different in the daytime? I was a little doubtful that I had come to the right place. I hadn't noticed that there were so many trees around here when it was dark."

This is true but maybe a little odd. We are in rue des Médicis, opposite Le Palais de Luxembourg. It is a pretty tree-lined street which I know quite well because it is close to the Sorbonne. On a sunny day in May, it is lovely to be sitting outside. We linger over our coffee, talking about nothing very much. Then we wander slowly up Le Boulevard St. Michel to the river. A walk along the river is always relaxing. We cross to the other side of the river and take the footpath next to the river, along the Quai du Louvre. François Mitterrand died a couple of years ago and there is a move to change the name of this street to honour him. I have nothing against him but I am a traditionalist in these respects. I do not believe in changing the names of places except in exceptional circumstances. We just keep walking slowly along the river, not talking that much. It is surprising how far one can wander aimlessly. Jean suggests a spot of lunch. I suddenly realise that I am ravenous having skipped breakfast. We find that we have reached Quai Louis Blériot. There is a lovely little bistro on the corner of Boulevard Murat exactly where we need it. Again we sit outside in the May sunshine. We make lunch last an absolute age just enjoying each other's company. The sun goes in. It is getting a bit cold. I decide it would be a good idea to quit while we are still warm. I tell him how much I have enjoyed the day.

"I'm getting a bit chilly" I say. "I think perhaps it is time to go home. You have to get back to Lille don't you and that takes a couple of hours."

Then I do not wait for him to ask me.

"Can I see you again Jean?"

"The sooner the better for me" he says.

"What about Friday evening?" I suggest.

"That would be excellent, Catherine. I can leave Lille a bit early and be here in time to see a show. Would you give me your phone number? I'll book something for the evening and let you know where it is best to meet."

"Thank you, Jean, I look forward to that." We swap phone numbers, walk to the nearest Metro and go our different ways.

The first date has gone very well. Waiting for the second date I am no longer a bundle of nerves. I am confident that we will enjoy whatever Jean decides to book but more importantly, we will also enjoy each other's company. Marie and Jeanne are suddenly lovely people once more. How could I have ever found them irritating? Our second date is on the Friday evening. We are going to the opera. Jean has tickets for the dress circle of Le Palais Garnier, the opera house in Paris. Puccini's La Bohême is showing. When it comes to 'Your tiny hand is frozen', Jean takes the opportunity to gently hold my hand. A bit corny? Not for me; he always seems to get the timing right for me. We hold hands for some time without it disturbing the flow of the opera. Afterwards we walk towards the Seine and down the steps at Le Quai des Tuileries. Unlike L'Île de la Cité, it is almost deserted at this time of the evening. The Seine is flowing gracefully beneath us. We walk a few steps and then the moment that I have been longing for happens. Jean takes me in his arms and kisses me on the lips. For the very first time in my life, my dormant hormones spring into action. I feel an immense rush of desire. 'So this is the force that drives people to lie, cheat and kill' I think. I had never experienced anything like this. After a few moments we part and I can see the ripples in the Seine forming fascinating patterns in indescribable colours. There is the expression 'I was blown away'. It describes very well what I feel. I am completely absent for several minutes as the vibrant unique colours slowly fade and the miraculous shapes return to being mere ripples in a river. This lasts too long for Jean.

"Are you all right, Catherine?" He asks, looking very worried. "Should I not have done that?"

I do not feel that I can explain the unimaginable colours, the fascinating shapes of the ripples on the Seine or indeed the overwhelming pleasure I feel. Those weirdo effects that show my total happiness and have rendered me completely absent also make me a bit of a nutcase in most people's mind. Not yet; it is too early in our relationship. But Jean is more than a bit put out. I must do something. It seems to me that there is only one answer. I turn to him, and kiss him passionately, longingly on the lips. This one lasts a long time but eventually we part. I think he is reassured. We stroll slowly along the Seine, parting at L'Île de la Cité to go our separate ways; he to the North, I to the South.

We saw each other regularly after that. I would have loved to drop my studies, go to Lille and stay with Jean. This happens to some girls. They go to Uni with the intention of getting a degree and using that for something useful, whatever it was meant for. They fall madly in love and opt out. That is not me at all. I am desperately in love with Jean but this is finals year for my degree. Here again I seem to be different from many young people, boys and girls. It is frequently the case that being in love disturbs the ability to learn or to think concisely. I found the opposite. I found my thinking was pellucidly clear. I get a first class honours degree from the Sorbonne. I am an LL B! I feel very proud of myself. That is an achievement. I am determined to become a notaire. That is going to take another four years but I know I can do it. With the long summer holidays coming up I shall relax and concentrate on my relationship with Jean.

With that in mind, after several more dates, I invite him back to my place one Saturday, for dinner. I say to arrive at about half past six. I am a good cook. Not first-class perhaps, but as an only child a lot of the time that I might have spent playing with brothers and sisters if I had had any, was instead spent helping my mother prepare meals. So from an early age I was competent. As I grew older, I used to get one of the meals on Saturday or Sunday as I didn't have any homework at week-ends. This meant that instead of having only one or two dishes that I felt I might prepare, I had dozens. Choice is usually regarded as a good thing to have but the trouble with choice is that it means making a decision. Decisions are not always easy to make. I am uncertain to what extent I want to show off. Do I produce a wonder meal or a homely straight forward tasty dish? I decide on two courses; a starter and a main. I shall make the starter, the smaller dish, a humdinger; a real surprise. The main is to be more homely. I know just the dish for the show-off starter. It is one of chef, Marc Veyrat's, specials. Marc is owner and chef at a restaurant in Veyrier du Lac just along Lake Annecy from where I was brought up. I think he probably has as many Michelin stars as it is possible to get. This soup of his is amazing. It has contrasting textures and colours as well as contrasting temperatures. It can also be described as if it were nothing worth mentioning. It is 'Pea Soup'. You take fresh peas; purée them; add half their weight of water and add a little salt with an option of some herbs. You bring it gently to the boil; make a raft with little sticks of a hard cheese like Gruyère; pour the soup; float the raft and add a scoop of a homemade berry sorbet on top - myrtle or raspberry work best and there you are. You have the hot soup, the room temperature cheese and the frozen sorbet. You have the green of the peas, the yellow of the Gruyère and the red of the raspberry with the contrasting flavours and acidity. It is a masterpiece and really not difficult to prepare.

I am having a harder job thinking of what should follow. In the end I decide on Lemon and Garlic Chicken. It is a dish that takes two and a half hours to cook, making the chicken very tender, but all the preparation is at the start so I shall be free and cool as a cucumber, when Jean arrives, not dashing about in the kitchenette like a headless chicken. The headless chicken will already be in the oven. For wine I know my mother would have chosen Chignin Bergeron when we were in Savoy but it is said 'not to travel' so I probably wouldn't be able to buy it in Paris. I am choosing between Petit Chablis and Sancerre and eventually go for the Sancerre. The water from the tap is fine in Paris but I am regarding this as a special occasion so I decide on the softly sparkling Badoit rather than the salty Vichy St. Yorre or sharply sparkling and slightly acidic Perrier. I review my choice and I am happy. This meal will rival anything but the very best and almost certainly hugely expensive restaurant. I start thinking about what to wear. I want something just a little bit sexy. Something that will encourage without making me look cheap. I have seen just the thing in a boutique off Boulevard Haussmann. When I get there they still have it. Oh joy! It is a little black skirt that is maybe just a shade short at the front and the very slightest bit shorter still at the back. It is in a very nice soft expensive-looking material with a delicate pattern, not in-your-face leather or even worse cheap plastic. 'Go for it' I think to myself. It is a bit pricey but this occasion has become important to me. I know that I already have just the blouse to go with it.

The day comes and I am surprisingly nervous. I know that I'm a good cook. I know that I have chosen the dishes with great care to get just the balance I want. However anyone, however good a cook they may be, knows that on the actual day anything can happen. You can forget to preheat the oven. You can drop the soup on the floor. There may be a power cut and the meal undercooks. I stop myself thinking of everything that can go wrong and relax. I am looking forward immensely to this evening. Jean arrives at 6.30 as arranged. It seems that we are compatible on the punctuality stakes too. I have arranged the meal so that it wouldn't matter if he was early or late but it is reassuring when he arrives exactly as planned. I offer him a beer but we settle for coffee. As I get it, he sits on the sofa so I join him there with the coffee. Everything is very relaxed. We get on so well together. I would like to hug and kiss him there and then but I have got a meal to serve. After we have had our coffee, I prepare the soup which only takes a few minutes and does not require any angst. When I serve the soup, he is really taken aback.

"Catherine, this is marvellous. Just look at it. It is beautiful."

"Yes it is a pretty soup."

He tastes the pea soup. There is no doubt that fresh peas really make all the difference. I have, in the past, made this soup with frozen peas but it reduces it to the mundane and makes the sorbet look a bit silly; trying to be something that it isn't. Jean gets the picture; the different colours, the different temperatures, the different flavours. Yes I have surprised him. One of the great things about the Lemon and Garlic chicken is that although the recommended cooking time is two and a half hours, it cooks at a relatively low temperature so ten minutes or more either way doesn't really matter. There is none of the 'Oh I've got to serve it this very second' or 'Oh dear I've burnt it'. I take it out of the oven and serve it casually with no hassle. Of course Jean is impressed. This is a first class meal served with ease, casualness and panache, as if it were a tin of baked beans.

"You're a marvel" he says. "Where did you learn to cook like this?"

"At my mother's knee" I reply and it is true.

We are back on the sofa with the last of the Sancerre. We cuddle up close and it is very sexy. I know my little black skirt did its work when he was on the sofa before dinner. I served the soup bending over the table just a little and I could tell he noticed. After some minutes, I can see that he is as aroused as I am. I expect him to suggest that we move into the bedroom where this would be even more enjoyable. That does not happen. I am perplexed. I have arranged this evening. It has gone well. I think I would look a bit pushy if I make a move myself and suggest the bedroom. It might blow our whole relationship but it does not look as if Jean is going to do so. This would be my first time so in some ways I am unsure of what I'm doing. I'm running on instinct and natural feelings alone with no experience to back them up. I'm confused and feel I need to leave it there; regroup and think. We have a gentle hugging session with a bit more kissing and Jean leaves. I was expecting him to stay the night so I have a lot to think about. I am sure that I love this guy. What on earth am I going to do? Marie and Jeanne are no good for a question as important as this. I need to talk it over with Louise. She has far more experience than me. I think her advice would be to let him go. I am not at all sure I can do that; at least not now. I can give her an outline by email or on the phone but I want a face to face heartfelt talk. To be honest I am a bit desperate. I ring her mobile. Louise comes up trumps. I knew she would. She is reassuring, kind and sensible. She says she'll come up to Paris anytime but she imagines I would like her to see me without Jean.

"No." I say. "I should like you to meet him, Louise. Of course I want you to meet him. You're my best friend. You have to meet. Can you come up next weekend? I'll tell him that you're my best friend and that I would like him to meet you. I'll arrange to see him in the flat. He'll know he's not expected to stay because you'll be staying. After he's gone we can talk about it and you can tell me what you think."

Louise is a real sweetie. She agrees to come up to Paris and see me next weekend. We ring off. I give Jean a call. I can tell that he is very pleased to hear from me. Does he have a feeling that he might have messed up rather badly yesterday? I don't know but I am glad to know that he still wants to see me. So it is arranged for Saturday. We all meet for lunch at my flat. I serve up fresh sardines on toast with a variety of herbs. It is easy to do and I don't want anything elaborate now. The day goes very well. Jean enthuses about me to Louise saying what a marvellous meal I dished up. Louise is very complimentary to Jean and talks me up just a bit; not really enough to be noticed. We all get on very well. We go out to a bistro for the evening meal and after that Jean leaves for Lille. Louise and I wander back to the flat. I make coffee. Louise sits in the chair and I take the sofa.

"Right" she says. "Let's get down to business. First, you've got an absolute dish there. Don't let him go unless you feel you have to. I think all will come right in the end. Several things come to mind. I think perhaps you made a mistake not making that crucial suggestion. It's your place. He, I imagine, hasn't even seen your bedroom. It might be an absolute tip filled with stuff you've chucked out of this room to make here tidy for when he came. But I do see your point and anyway it's done now. This would be your first real sexual encounter and you say that you are a little bit lost. I have a strong feeling that this may well be his first encounter as well. He may also be uncertain how to proceed. I imagine that you have put yourself on the pill but he doesn't know that. Even if he has been thoughtful enough to bring a contraceptive, he may well find it awkward thinking about how he is going to put it on. So I think that there are very many reasons why what didn't happen, didn't happen. So the question is 'where do you go from here?'"

I stare at Louise in amazement. She is so positive. She makes me feel that what happened was the most natural thing in the world. She even makes me feel a bit foolish for making such a fuss. I have never felt happier feeling foolish in my life. But I am still at a loss about how to proceed.

"Go on Louise" I say. "You're being so helpful."

"OK. Because of the other night, your place here is out. Equally I don't think you should expect to be able to force the issue so to speak, at his place. We must arrange something on neutral ground. I think I may just be coming up with an idea."

She pauses and we both take a sip of our coffee. It is getting a bit cool by now.

"Jean was genuinely impressed by the meal. He kept coming back to it with almost reverence in his voice. You certainly did a good job there, Catherine. I saw in the paper that Saumur on the Loire is hosting a festival in early July. It is a wine, mushroom and herbs festival. Of course it will feature Saumur Champigny and St. Nicolas de Bourgeuil and expect there will be a number of the Loire whites as well. The Saumur region is famous for its mushrooms. He knows now that you are a culinary wizard. You can say that you're interested in the mushrooms and herbs. Suggest you go to this festival together; that it will make a really nice weekend. He'll agree. Why wouldn't he? You book a double room for the two of you and tell him that you have done so. I don't think there will be any doubt what you intend. This time if he seems reluctant, you can come on strong but if he doesn't respond quite quickly, back off or you might not get another chance."

I give Louise a big hug. It is lovely to have a plan. It makes perfect sense.

Louise goes back to Toulouse. I mention the Saumur festival to Jean and he seems keen on it. Before he can say that he'll make the arrangements, I say that I know just the hotel so I'll do the booking. I do know a good hotel because I have already looked some up. I book the Hotel Anne d'Anjou. It is a lovely 18th century building overlooking the Loire with a beautiful staircase and some very nice rooms. I book a double room for Friday and Saturday night. On our next date, I tell Jean. His grin is lovely to behold and he gives me a long delicious kiss on the spot. This looks as if it is going to work out fine.

When the first week in July arrives, we take a train from Montparnasse. It is about two and a half hours to Saumur. The railway line approaches the Loire at Tours and follows much the same course as the river following the right bank to get to Saumur. There are some great views of the river on the way. When we arrive at Saumur, it is about a mile to the hotel. It is a mild evening so we walk. L'Île d'Offart is situated in the middle of the Loire at Saumur. Almost all of our walk is on the bridges which span the river, on the island or the road overlooking the river on the left bank. There are great views all the way. There is a perfect view of the castle which is almost exactly over the top of our hotel. We arrive very relaxed and ready for dinner. The hotel is one of those that seems not to have its own restaurant but has an arrangement with one that is virtually on the same site. From the guests' point of view it is hard to tell whether it is part of the hotel. I have booked for half past eight. We are a couple of minutes late from dawdling on the walk from the station but not enough to upset anyone.

Thinking of the festival that we are going to tomorrow, we have a mushroom starter followed by mullet and herbs. Jean orders half a bottle of Petit Chablis to go with it. I take this moderation to be a good omen. The mullet has been freshly caught that day from the river close by. The meal is superb. Jean smiles at me "...but not as good as yours" he says. I smile back, pleased at the compliment. I'm not sure though. It is a close-run thing. There is always a touch of anxiety when eating a meal that you have cooked yourself. I certainly enjoyed this one as much. We have a coffee after the meal. It is now about half past ten. We go up to our room. Jean then surprises me with a suggestion.

"We check that we have the same number of items of clothing on. Then let's undress each other one garment at a time" he says, "like strip-poker without the poker. I think that will be a great deal of fun."

Now there's an idea. I go first and slip his jacket down his arms while kissing him on the lips, my breasts pushing into his shirt. That is sexy but does not compare to him sliding his hands down the inside of my thighs to take off my tights. The last thing to come off is my bra. He turns me round to undo it from the back then pushes me firmly over the bed. Things get very close and personal after that. A little later as our bodies merge, I get a sharp pain. It mingles with so much pleasure that they blend like the perfect vinaigrette. 'Is this the sensation masochists are after?' I wonder briefly. Then I hold him tighter, tighter, tighter until he bursts.

The next day we go to the festival. Last night has changed our relationship. Every word, every touch, every smile has an enhanced meaning. We enjoy the mushroom snacks, the occasional taster of wine and of course, these festivals always attract a heap of stalls of goods not specific to the type of festival; paintings, bric-a-brac and so on. We walk hand in hand, occasionally pulling a little closer together. I buy a kit for growing your own mushrooms at home. It suggests that you grow some herbs with them in the same soil. It is claimed that the flavour of the herbs becomes incorporated in the mushrooms. The herbs are provided in the kit. It is ridiculously expensive and I know that it is going to be rubbish. Mushrooms like damp conditions with moderate cool and dark, they are unlikely to grow well with herbs but I want to buy something here, just for the memory and, who knows? It might just work. In the evening Jean orders a full bottle of wine to go with the meal. We have a liqueur after with the coffee and we go to sleep in each other's arms without any of the drama and passion of the night before. So it is back to Paris for me and Lille for Jean. He is due to give a lecture during the vacation period. It is a slightly odd idea. He says that it means that students from other universities can attend. The oddity is that almost all the people attending are from relatively far away as they are unable to attend except during the vacation.

Although it is holiday period, Jeanne, Marie and I often still meet for coffee several times a week. It has become our custom.

"The traffic is so much less in July....." I start but I see that Jeanne is grinning all over her face.

"What is it Jeanne?" I ask.

"So he came across with it OK did he Catherine?" she says. I am at a loss. I have never discussed Jean with Jeanne and Marie, yet it seems as if Jeanne knows exactly what has happened. Can she really tell? Just like that? I stammer something that is inaudible and probably doesn't even make sense.

"Catherine" she continues. "You've been as tense as a pressure cooker for the last few weeks. Far more tense than you ever were with finals coming up. Today you come in perfectly relaxed and absolutely glowing with health. I can put two and two together. Some tension has suddenly been released and ten to one it has something to do with a man."

I laugh out loud. "You should be a detective, Jeanne, not a lawyer. Yes, you are quite right, I had no idea it was so obvious. We spent the weekend at the Saumur festival and it really brought us together."

"Who is this guy, Catherine?" asks Marie. "Is it anyone we might know?"

"You might just. Do you remember there was a Guest Speaker from Lille University earlier in the year, talking about how difficult it is getting the countries in the EU to have the same laws?"

Jeanne looked blank but Marie remembers "Oh yes, I went to that. A young guy, wasn't he dishy?"

There was a slight pause, then realisation. "Oh no, Catherine. You're not dating him are you? You lucky devil!"

"Yes I am a lucky devil. I do think I am. I have really fallen for him."

So life continued. Jean and I saw each other at weekends and occasionally during the week, usually in Paris. There is much more to do in Paris than in Lille and my lovely flat was better than the bed-sitter that Jean had in Lille. Without me realising it a whole year had passed since I met Jean. Then one Sunday in July, Jean surprised me by saying that he wanted to take me to church. I am not religious. Neither my mother nor father went to church. The subject seldom came up at home but the general feeling was that although it was remotely possible that there was a God, it did not seem likely. Certainly the abundance of different religions suggests that no-one knows what they are talking about: the fact that the number of conversions to a new religion is very small and almost everybody follows the religion of their parents, suggests that 'faith' is a result of brainwashing in childhood. 'Faith', after all, is believing in something for which there is insufficient evidence. To my mind 'God' falls into that category. Jean had never previously mentioned church or even religion. I wait for some explanation. I am getting used to Jean's sense of humour. It is a little like a cryptic crossword clue. The words that he uses sound as if they mean one thing but turn out to mean something completely different.

"There's a church near Rambouillet that I'd like you to see" he says but explains nothing more.

Well I'm happy to go. I suppose there's something special about the architecture. Jean is not opening up. We get there and it is quite a nice little church but I can see nothing about it to make it worth a special visit.

"Come inside" Jean says. We enter and walk up the aisle. The choir stalls and altar are up two steps and at the top of them is a life size statue of a boy with his hands clasped together in prayer looking upward towards the stained glass window over the altar. He is down on one knee with a beatific expression on his face. He is quite cute but hardly a Michelangelo. Jean gets down on one knee imitates the boy's ridiculous expression and looking up at me adoringly he says:

"Catherine, will you marry me?"

What a way to propose. I laugh out loud. Then I feel perhaps I shouldn't laugh as we are in a church. So I pause. Jean has not moved. Oh dear! I have to tell him about my hang-ups. I should have done this already. How stupid of me to wait this long.

"Jean, before I answer, I've got to tell you something about myself" I say.

He looks very puzzled and a little concerned. I tell him about what happens to me when I get an overload of happiness.

"You remember our first kiss?"

"Of course I do" he says.

"How I was sort of away with the fairies for a couple of minutes?"

"Yes, you were a little strange."

"When I have a moment of extreme happiness, it seems that a part of my brain overloads. I see impossible shapes and colours which rapidly fade and are no more. It almost incapacitates me for a minute or so. I feel that I need to let you know this; that you should know I'm a nutcase before making any long-term commitment to me."

"I've read about something like that" he said, "but not quite the same as you are describing. There are some people who see colours round small numbers or small words. Others can get the same effect from voices or music. Some of those colours are said to be ones that don't exist in so-called real life. It is called synaesthesia I believe. It sounds very similar to what you are saying. It's odd isn't it" he says, managing I'm glad to say, to avoid the word weird. "I don't see that this makes you a liability. Rather more I think it makes you even more fascinating to me. I cannot really see why you feel the need to tell me about it so seriously as if it were a fatal condition. Something like that is not going to stop me loving you. It is certainly wonderful to know that you had an overload of happiness when I kissed you."

I suddenly realise that Jean is still down on one knee waiting for an answer, although he has lost the silly beatific expression!

"Jean, for heaven's sake get up. Of course I'll marry you" I manage to say. I would like to fall into his arms but again the church restricts me. I look up at the stained-glass window. Sure enough, it is filled with unimaginable colours. The pillars of the church are arranged in what must be four-dimensional interlocking curves. I am tongue-tied. Again I have an overload of happiness. Happiness, I realise, is quite different from passion. Passion is aggressive, almost painful; perhaps it should even be avoided. Happiness is quietly comfortable like a log fire on a winter's night. Our passion may fade but I hope our happiness will last for ever.

It is getting towards the end of the summer holidays. For the last two weeks in August, Jean has no commitments at Lille. We can be together 24 hours a day. This is the ultimate test of a relationship and it is working well. I suggest that we take a trip to the Alps so that I can show Jean where I was brought up until I was a teenager. Jean is a keen skier but he has not been to the Alps. He has done most of his skiing in the Pyrenees. He is interested to see what the mountains of the Alps look like and is wondering whether we could take a week's holiday in winter in an alpine ski resort; Mont Blanc of course is what he fancies. He readily agrees to a trip to Lake Annecy. My family home is being leased on a long term rent so we cannot stay there although I certainly intend to show it to Jean from the outside. There is the question of where to stay. If I want to show Jean all my favourite childhood places, we need to be able to get around easily.

Although Jean has a driving licence having passed the test some years ago, he does not have a car at the moment. Lille, like Paris, has a good public transport system and exorbitant parking charges. A car tends to be more of a liability that a help. I have not taken the driving test. I must get round to it some time. Annecy itself, the town that is, has quite a good bus service but the service to places round the lake, although it exists, is rather sketchy. Some services are only two or three times a day. The parking charges are very reasonable. Several car parks within walking distance of the centre are actually free. The answer that we decide on is to hire a small car. We can take the TGV to Annecy if we are prepared to get up early in the morning. Otherwise there are slower trains later on. There are several Hire Car firms close to the railway station. If we hire a car, we can get around very easily. It also makes the choice of where to stay much easier. Jean leaves it to me to choose the hotel as I know the area. I decide on L'Auberge du Lac at Veyrier. It is midway between Annecy itself and Écharvines where I was brought up. It is at the lakeside and the rooms have a view over the lake to mount Semnoz on the other side.

I take Jean to all my childhood haunts. I show him the house where I was brought up. It still belongs to my mum and dad but I do not want to be intrusive and disturb the family who are living there. From the road, I show Jean the odd extension that my mum had built. I point out the (wow, it is worse than ever, there are twenty) paragliders in the air above the house. On the day before we are due back, I take him to see 'Le Balcon au Lac'. We leave the car and walk along the little unmade up footpaths of Le Roc de Chère. It is peaceful and calm. When we get there I point out some of the more interesting features on the other side of the Lake. Jean says he thinks the colour of the water must be one of those amazing colours that I see when I am very happy. I laugh at this and suddenly there is a shout from below us and a figure is scrambling up the steep path from the lakeside.

"Catherine" it shouts.

Good heavens, it's Jacques. I haven't seen him since we were thirteen. That must be seven or eight years!

"Jacques" I reply. "What on earth are you doing here?"

"And you" says Jacques. "I thought you were in Paris."

I introduce Jean and Jacques. Jean says what a great place this is. Jacques and I answer together. We keep talking in unison and end up having the giggles. It is very embarrassing. He is delighted to see me after all this time and indeed I am very pleased and surprised to see him. He has recently acquired a mobile phone. It is new and obviously his prize possession at the moment. He rings his girlfriend and arranges for us all to have dinner together. Dinner is at a bistro close to the river. It is new to me and perhaps it wasn't there seven years ago. The meal is a great success. The four of us get on very well. Jacques is obviously completed besotted with Sylvie. It wouldn't surprise me at all if there were wedding bells in the offing there. We don't make a late night of it as Jean and I have to return our hire car and catch the train to Paris next morning.

Jacques 1999–2001

It is Monday morning and I send Georges an email. After the usual pleasantries, I tell him what I need for this next job and what the price requirement is. I say that I realise that this is probably quite impossible and explain the tension that undoubtedly exists between Dominique and me. I also give him the number of my new mobile phone. I feel rather proud of it. A year ago they were well out of my price range. Then I get on with my own work. This second floor flat in the old town is quite straightforward. I have completed the new wiring. All it now needs is a new fuse box. The modern fuse boxes have trip switches or circuit breakers that will turn off an individual circuit before the fuse blows. This means that the frequency of having to change a fuse is much rarer. All one needs to do is reduce the circuit load and flip the switch back on again. They also have a circuit breaker for the whole installation. If the amount of current being drawn goes above a certain point everything goes off; the fridge, the cooker, the lights, everything. If it is evening the place is plunged into darkness. This can be a little annoying so when I am installing a new fuse box, for example in the hall, I exempt the nearest light to the box. I give it its own circuit and its own circuit breaker so that it alone will remain on if the maximum amperage is exceeded.

LE BALCON AU LAC: THE BALCONY ON THE LAKE

Just as I am finishing the job, the owner arrives. He is delighted to see that I've finished and I take him through what I've done. There really isn't any need. It is all straightforward. But it is good public relations. I show him the light in the hall which will stay on if the flat's allowable current is exceeded. He looks pleased with that and asks if I have a card. I had some run off the other day when I bought my new phone. I rather liked an old German script.

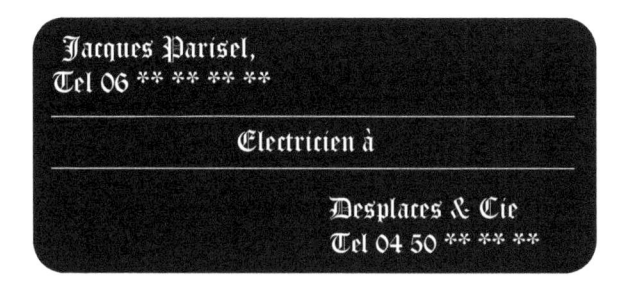

> Jacques Parisel,
> Tel 06 ** ** ** **
>
> Electricien à
>
> Desplaces & Cie
> Tel 04 50 ** ** **

He tells me that a couple of friends need an electrician and he will pass the cards on. I thank him and return to the office in Les Romains. Dominique is there looking as if he owns the place, which of course he does. I must not let this guy annoy me when there really is no reason: keep it for when there is a reason. That happens often enough. In fact today he is being quite pleasant.

"Ah hello Jacques" he says cheerfully. "You've finished the rewiring of the flat have you? Good work man. I'll send the bill out right away. They'll be pleased to have had it installed so quickly. Great stuff!"

"Thanks, Boss. Yes it was all straightforward. There weren't any problems. It's a nice flat. I wouldn't mind living there myself but the old town stays very noisy till late and I think one wouldn't get much sleep."

"Yes you are right about that. Oh by the way, any news on the fittings for the next job?"

"I've put out feelers but I am not hopeful. I'm afraid I cannot see myself agreeing to fitting sub-standard stuff."

He looks a bit annoyed but keeps his cool.

"Not substandard Jacques, just cheaper. We'll have to wait and see what is available. Won't we?"

I change the subject.

"What would you like me to do for the rest of the day?"

"Guy and Michel are starting on the extension for that house at Sévrier, the one a bit up the mountain with the beautiful view. I can't remember the address. You could go there and assess what you'll need for that."

"OK boss, I'll do that."

I go the 'work pending' drawer and find the address. As I do, I happen to see the latest accounts on his desk. Of course I cannot see the detail but they look disastrous to me. Dominique was not being very helpful saying 'the one a bit up the mountain with a beautiful view'. There are many houses in Sévrier that are a bit up the mountain with a beautiful view. However, I can see that there is only one on our books. I make a note of the address. It is on Le Chemin de la Grotte. Then I leave. It is less than a mile from my flat to the office. If that is the first place I'm going in the day I usually walk. It takes about 15 minutes, often less. Depending on where I am working, I either walk or take my little Vespa scooter. It is very practical being quite easy to get off the road if there is no parking. Of course, if I need to take a lot of equipment, I take one of the company vehicles. The centre of Sévrier is over 3 miles. This house is a bit further and then part way up the mountain. I'm not, certainly not, walking there. I walk home and collect my Vespa.

It doesn't take long to get to Sévrier on the Vespa. The N508 is nearly always a jam for cars although it keeps moving slowly. It is the only main road between the lake and Semnoz, the mountain to the West. It is the route to numerous ski resorts in winter and they are also quite popular in summer. The main international airport in the region is Geneva. So most people coming in by air to ski at resorts like Tignes or Les Trois Vallées have to go along it. Also, as Annecy is the main town in the area for shopping, anyone from the South has to use it to get to Annecy. I have heard a lot of foreigners criticize French car drivers but one thing they willingly do is make way for motorbikes and scooters. The Vespa gets me to Sévrier in no time, cars take a bit longer. When I reach the house, I find that it is just high enough above the others nearer the lake to have a stupendous view. The mountains behind Écharvines, where I stayed with the Diacres are a lovely formation but if you are on the east side of the lake, you are too near them to see their real beauty. Yes, the view from this house of both the lake and the mountains is truly outstanding.

As I arrive, Guy and Michel are measuring out the extension. There is apparently a bit of a problem with the soil under where the last foot or so of the proposed room is due to be. It abruptly changes to very loose sand. Michel is assessing how deep the foundation will have to go to reach bedrock. Guy is sitting on a low wall puffing at a Gauloise. Michel is wondering whether that last foot or so of proposed extension is going to cost a whole lot more for the owner. Michel is about 40. He is a friend of Dominique's and has been with the firm for a long time. He seems settled and happy in the job. Guy is younger, a few years older than me. He joined the firm about six months before I did. I know that like me, he isn't satisfied that Dominique is going to manage to keep the firm going. The idea is forming in my head that Guy and I might manage to form a loose informal team, quit Desplaces & Cie, and work for ourselves. After all many an electrical job could benefit from the availability of a bricklayer and vice versa. Michel is going to have a word with the owner about the difficulty he envisages. I chat to Guy as he finishes his cigarette. I suggest we have a beer at Le Café de la Boule in Sévrier when we finish. There is a huge concrete ball outside it which is designed to be surrounded by water but that never seems to be the case. The café may be named after what I regard as a bit of a monstrosity but the coffee is good and the service is very friendly. Guy is happy to join me there.

Now we are sitting at a table just inside the café. Michel has taken the company van back to the office. I have a coffee in front of me and Guy has a Bière Blanche. They are brewed near Mont Blanc. I like them. They are flavoured with herbs from the mountains. I am now finding it difficult to broach the subject. I decide to start in the opposite direction from my real thoughts and talk Dominique up a bit. Give him some credit and see what happens.

"Dominique was in a good mood earlier" I say. "He complimented me on a job well done and was positively beaming."

"That makes a change" he replies. "Most of the time he looks like a wet week. He always finds something to grumble about. I look back to the days when his father was the boss and I wonder how everything has managed to change so quickly. Old Desplaces certainly knew how to run a show like this. It's a shame he retired. He was still quite up to the job."

"Yes." I take the bull by the horns. This is commitment. If I don't leave the company after this I shall lose a lot of face "I'm thinking of chucking it in and trying to make a go of it working for myself."

"Wow!" he says. "That's a bit of a gamble isn't it?"

"Perhaps, but you have to take a risk now and then. The last couple of jobs that I've done, the people have asked for my name. The last one took a couple of my cards specially to give to friends who need an electrician. You do a little bit in your own time don't you. If any of the jobs I get need any masonry I'll recommend you. If you've got any cards, give me a few. If you haven't got any yet, get some printed. If it goes well you might even manage to break with Dominique yourself."

"It sounds very tempting" says Guy. "Thanks for the offer. Let's see how it goes."

Guy lives in Sévrier, quite close. I give him a lift on the back of the Vespa. That went better than I expected.

Next I get a call on my mobile.

"Jacques Parisel" I say. I can hardly keep the smirk out of my voice. I never thought having a mobile phone would be such fun.

"Hi Jacques, it's Georges. I thought I'd give you a ring about that electrical stuff you were after. I think you'll be pleased. I have found one of our warehouses with a limited amount. It's most of what you wanted. It is slightly more expensive than your bottom line. My firm allows me a ten percent reduction for something I buy for myself. If I throw that in for you, it will be only be a touch above your figure for almost all of what you wanted. I wouldn't be able to use my staff discount for you again; at least not for a long time. It would get noticed and anyway it wouldn't be right."

"That's marvellous Georges. I'll get payment out to you right away."

"Thanks Jacques. There's another thing. It doesn't take long from Lyon to Annecy on the motorway. I can run the stuff over to you myself next Saturday afternoon and we could have dinner together."

"Brilliant Georges that will be great. See you then."

We ring off.

Just before he decided to retire, Claude gave me the power to make payments for electrical goods up to a certain limit. As the amount is within this, I immediately arrange for the payment to go out. I tell Sylvie that Georges will be coming and she is quite excited to meet my best friend. I book a table at Les Jardins de L'Auberge. I remember the Pierrade de Boeuf with a touch of wistfulness but this meal is not going to be along those lines at all. Georges arrives on Saturday afternoon in a small company van which fits nicely into my parking space. I introduce him to Sylvie. After they've said 'Hi' to each other we go down to the van and I take a look at what he has brought me. He has almost everything I asked for. Amazing! Only Georges could have managed that. The goods are high quality at only slightly over the budget that Dominique has set. Sylvie has made coffee while we were downstairs. We make ourselves comfortable. Georges and I have a lot to catch upon and Sylvie seems really interested in Georges' job. The conversation runs smoothly but to my mind Georges seems a little reserved with her. I wonder if I am imagining it. He has just had a journey and that can be stressful, although Lyon to Annecy with the motorway doesn't take long, under two hours. Or maybe I expect everybody to be as enthralled with Sylvie as I am.

At the restaurant things seem to have relaxed. Everything goes well. We have Fera, fish from the lake with a bottle of Roussette Altesse, a Savoy wine that goes very well with fresh fish. This is followed by Rum Baba. Georges stays the night in our spare bedroom. I say 'our' because Sylvie is spending most of her spare time here now although tonight, I suppose because she knows Georges is staying, she goes back to the room in her old flat. Before we retire, Georges looks a bit serious and asks me for any advice I might have. He has seen a girl he fancied and managed to get round to asking her out. They'd had a date which seemed to go OK. They had been to the cinema. A couple of weeks later he asked her out again and she'd said no. This, he said, has happened twice now with different girls. I said it was no good asking me. I was hopeless. The same sort of thing used to happen to me until this wonderful girl took a fancy to me, made all the running and I'd have had to be deaf, blind and stupid not to have asked her out. All I'd done was sit at a table looking lonely and pathetic. I could recommend that.

"Otherwise" I said, "arrange the second date while still on the first before they realise you're a waste of space."

"Oh! Very funny" says Georges. "God only knows what a girl like Sylvie sees in you!"

He goes back to Lyon after breakfast.

On Monday I go into the office managing to take most, but not all, of the equipment Georges brought, on the back of my Vespa. I show it to Dominique saying what good value it is. I expect him to be either enthusiastic because of the quality or relieved because of the price. However, he is annoyed.

"It is still over budget Jacques. I'm rescinding your right to buy equipment. I didn't think my father should have allowed it in any case. So that has to stop."

"There is a certain quality of equipment which I am happy with. If the quality is below that, I will not use it."

"We both know what happens then" he says grimly.

Indeed I do. I almost hand in my notice on the spot but I decide that there is one thing that I need to do first. I need to have a word with Claude. I think that I owe it to him to let him know what is going on. I shall be careful what I say. I am not trying to put father against son. I want to help save the firm Claude has built up during his working life.

I should have given Claude a ring and made an appointment but I didn't. I just turned up and rang on the bell. Madame Desplaces answered the door.

"Hello Jacques."

Before I can reply she calls loudly through to Claude.

"It's Jacques, Claude."

"Well, let him in, my dear" comes the light-hearted reply. I go through and am disconcerted to find that Olivier is ensconced comfortably in an armchair. There is a walking stick alongside the chair but he has changed the hospital model for a very handsome rather ornate one with a tiger's head at the top. He looks much better than when I saw him at the office all that time ago. We make the usual greetings but I am a bit nonplussed. I should have thought of this. I'm not at all sure that

I should be discussing this with Claude while Olivier is present but now I have to start.

"I wanted to talk to you about the firm, Claude."

He immediately sees my problem.

"Look Jacques" he replies. "Olivier and I go back a long way; to early teens. It may nominally have been my firm but in reality we ran it together, didn't we Olivier? If you want to talk to me about anything to do with the firm you can say it in front of Olivier."

I take a deep breath. "Claude, however this conversation goes, I am handing Dominique my resignation tomorrow. I am going to work on my own account. I want to give you the reasons. I'm afraid your son does not have much of a clue as far as running the firm is concerned. I got a brief glance at the figures the other day and they looked dire. Dominique wants to buy cheap electrical equipment that is not going to be safe in the ultra-damp state around the lake and the Thiou. He has taken away my ability to buy in what I need. I do not want to cause any friction between you and him but I wonder if you were in the position to be able to return in some kind of capacity to help him. He needs you back at the helm or the firm that you; and Olivier" I add in view of his previous comment, "have built up is going to sink. This does not in any way affect my decision. I have made up my mind already but I am prepared to see the next job through as my friend Georges managed to get me almost all the equipment for that job at a knock-down price."

Claude sighs. "I see." There is a pause while he thinks. "Yes" he says at last. "I can say to Dominique that I find that I am bored with retirement and that I miss the office. Would he perhaps let me come in for a couple of mornings a week, on an unpaid basis of course, and see if I can be of any help. That might let me give him some advice without him feeling any loss of face."

That is so Claude. He has this ability to solve problems with the minimum of friction, prepared to take a degree of blame for a situation when the reality is that it is none of his fault.

I go straight back to the office. I intend to be as pleasant as I can as I hand in my notice. Dominique looks a bit puzzled.

"Hello Jacques, you back? I thought you were going to make a start on that job now you've got the equipment."

"I shall do that piece of work, Monsieur Desplaces and then I shall leave. I am handing in my notice now. As I said, I shall complete the new job. I have told you that I will not work with substandard equipment and you keep ignoring that. I have managed to get an almost unbelievably good deal through a friend and in spite of that you have removed my right to buy my own equipment that your father gave me when he was boss. That is too much."

"But Jacques, you will leave me without an electrician."

"You'll have a while to find one. If you can't, I might be prepared to do some work for you as a consultant but that would be on my terms."

He looks a bit white but what can he say. I repeat that I shall do the current work, then I leave the office.

In the evening I tell Sylvie that I have handed in my notice and am going to work freelance.

I have not often seen Sylvie look annoyed with me. There is no doubt that she is now. She keeps her voice very calm and measured but her face shows that something is up.

"Is that wise, Jacques?" she says. "You've always said that the competition here in the Annecy region is intense. I hope you've made a good decision."

I explain about Dominque's attitude to the equipment Georges managed to get me and his intention to buy cheap materials. Sylvie doesn't say anything but the irritation on her face remains. Since we met, Sylvie has very seldom seemed to be annoyed with me and then only briefly over minor things. I feel bad. Seeing her like this makes my heart churn over and over. I find it very hard to take her being annoyed. I can't see why she is. I put on some of her favourite music and keep the lighting subdued. Over the course of the evening her face softens. By the time we go to bed she seems to have forgotten about it, I am glad to say. We snuggle up very close and everything seems all right.

To my surprise, my freelance days start with a bang. The cards that I gave out immediately result in two enquiries to me on my number and one to Dominique on the firm's number. Not only am I in business, I am still helping Desplaces & Cie get business. One of the jobs is in the old town on a ground floor flat. The brick work outside is in poor condition and certainly needs repointing. I mention this to the owner without pushing it, just as a casual comment. He is taken aback.

"Yes, it is in bad condition, isn't it?" he says. "I hadn't noticed. You don't do pointing do you Jacques?"

"No, I'm afraid not" I say, "but I do know someone who will do very good job. I can recommend Guy Oudart."

I give him Guy's card. This is going well. Over the next year, the work keeps coming in. Guy and I have got this loose partnership of helping each other. It is working out well for both of us. We are keeping our independence but putting work each other's way whenever we can. I am having to work into the evening a lot of the time now and don't get home till late.

One day when we are working at the same place, Guy says to me:

"Oh Jacques, I met your girlfriend Sylvie yesterday. I was wanting to buy some jewellery for my mother. It is her fiftieth birthday soon and I was looking for something suitable."

"Oh good" I say. "What do you think?"

"She's unquestionable stunningly beautiful" he says. "She had an assistant there but she came over herself and she couldn't have been more helpful. You know the tendency in any shop, if you mention a guide price, they immediately go over it. No! She stuck below it and I came away with exactly what I had in mind at a good bit below what I expected to pay. We got chatting a bit and I said how well our loose ended agreement seemed to working out. How on earth did a div like you make out with a girl like that?"

"Oh just natural charm" I reply. But he has a good point. I just cannot believe my luck.

The millennium is coming up. Earlier this year, I was thoughtful enough to book a table for two at the Imperial Palace Hotel for the millennium. It will cost an arm and a leg but millennia do not come up every day and I hope it will show Sylvie how much I love her. There is a lot of talk about aeroplanes falling out of the sky because of computer failure. The idea is that many computer programs which involve the date have only been set up to recognise 1900 until 1999. When the year 2000 comes, they won't cope, the thinking goes. Computers are going to imagine that it is 1900 and act accordingly. Interest payments on investments will stop because no interest is due for the year 1900. All sorts of things like that. Sylvie says that she can believe this because when her grandmother had to go into hospital two years ago, she was 75 years old but because somebody had not put her age on the form it was filled in automatically by the computer as 97 because 1997 was the year at the time. If that happened she could see there might be trouble ahead. There is a great deal of talk about 'new starts'. We are used to that at the beginning of each year with 'New Year Resolutions' but the idea of new millennium resolutions has taken a hold. I think this is a little odd. I see that authorities have decided that the new millennium starts on 1st January 2000. Anyone with a hint of maths would think 1st January 2001 was the correct date for the new millennium as that is when 2000 years would have passed. The world today cannot wait for its kicks so the celebrations must be one year early. I hear that some countries are actually thinking of changing their time zone so the millennium will start on their soil. How mad can the world get? I am happy to have thought of booking a table well in advance because everywhere is going to be booked up.

It is a great event at the Imperial. There is a casino in the same building. I am unsure whether they are connected financially or not. I have never had a bet before in my life. Sylvie and I decide it would be fun just this once. We get 200 francs of chips each and decide to have a competition. We must use exactly the 200 francs by betting on as many different games as we wish but must never use any winnings. At the end we can see who has the most money. It is good fun. We put small stakes on so that the money lasts. We try roulette and blackjack. We keep away from slot machines as there is not much fun to be had there. There is a horse racing game which is good. Because of the time the 'race' takes, one loses money slower! At the end of us spending our 200 francs each, I have 100 francs of winnings so am 100 francs down. Sylvie has 250 francs. She has definitely won. She is fifty francs up. Between us we have only lost fifty francs and it has been great fun. We go back home for the first delicious love-making of the next one thousand years. For me it is as amazing as the very first time almost two years ago. Sylvie is everything to me. As our second anniversary is coming up, I am wondering what special surprise I can think of.

Then at the end of February, the bombshell exploded that threatened to end my whole life. It was a Monday. I was late getting back home because of the job that I was on. It was complicated. I was working in very cramped conditions and there appeared to be a differential voltage between the earth in the kitchen and the earth in the bedroom. It was a problem that needed to be sorted out before I could safely continue. I came through the door and immediately slumped in a chair. I was dog-tired and ached all over from the cramped conditions that I had been working in. Sylvie comes in through the bedroom door. She has her coat on.

"I'm leaving you, Jacques" she says.

Several things happened to me at the same time. I couldn't have heard her right: it was a joke: I was so tired I was imagining. But no, I had heard right. My mouth opens and shuts but nothing comes out.

"I don't want any recriminations. This is a clean break. It is best that way. I do owe it you to say why and I shall be brief. You never ask my opinion about anything and that hurts me intensely. The most important time was when you handed in your notice. You never discussed it with me at all. You never gave me any inkling that you were thinking of doing that. It may not have affected me as much as it did you but it did affect me quite a lot. You were bound to be late in the evening far more frequently. Our joint income to live on was bound to fall even if only for a short time, yet you never even mentioned the possibility to me. The point is that you never discuss a thing with me. You just go ahead and do it. Then you tell me later. There are lots of minor occasions which are not much in themselves but add up to what can only be called an insult to me. It is a problem with the way you regard me. I met someone called Guy in the shop the other day. He recognised me as your 'girlfriend' because you had told him a lot about me, including where I work. He said you and he were co-operating together in a loose partnership that was turning out rather well. You never told me the slightest thing about that. You barely mentioned Guy; just enough for me to know who he was when he introduced himself. You told him about me but you never told me about him. You changed the bedside lights in the bedroom the other day. It is your flat. Of course you can change your bedroom lights but the emphasis is on 'Your' lights. I had nothing to do with it. You just did it. I actually like your choice but I have come to the conclusion that we are together, from your side, only for the sex. I admit that for me, you are really good in bed. You do it for me every time. That is why I have stayed with you as long as I have. But that is not enough at the end of the day. I need to be somebody whose opinion is valued. I've already packed. I'm off. If you get the chance of another relationship, remember what I've said. I wish you well but I've had enough."

My mouth is dry. It is still working up and down trying to say something but as I don't know what to say the result is that nothing comes out. Sylvie manages to give me a slight smile as she leaves and the door closes quietly. I am left alone in the still of the evening unable to digest the enormity of what has happened to me. There is a half full bottle of cheap brandy that we use (oh no, no, that we used to use) for cooking. By the end of the evening I have consumed all of that and the best part of a bottle of wine. The next day I have a hangover to beat all hangovers. I cannot possibly go to work. I stay in bed all day. I eat nothing. I am thoroughly miserable. Effectively, I feel my life is at an end. I realise, however, that I have to get over this. I am not the first man to be thrown over by a woman. I ring the owner of the job that I am on. I apologise profusely for not working yesterday and claim an upset tummy is responsible. This is actually quite honest. Sylvie's departure and my hangover have left me emptied in more than one respect. I go back to work. Here my earlier determination to be first class in everything I do as an electrician pays off. Although I am almost incapable of thinking anything at all, I carry on doing exactly what I have always done. Automatically, I carry out all the safety checks, use all the best materials and so on. The only downside from the point of view of the work is that I am now very slow. I have lost all motivation. I move like a zombie and must have a face that looks as if the apocalypse is arriving right now. All the same I am at least doing the job. Without the huge desire to get back to Sylvie as soon as possible, I work even later and this makes up to some extent for the slow rate at which I am now operating.

At the weekend, I take my Vespa to Le Balcon au Lac. It is the place I need to be to analyse my feelings. I think about what Sylvie said. I conclude that she is right. Furthermore I compare the situation to the time when my mother died. Then Jules was so incensed with me that he hit me very hard below the eye. Why? Because he thought that I didn't care about mum. I draw a parallel with Sylvie. She is saying that, when it came down to it, I didn't care about her. She has hit me far harder than Jules, although the bruise is not so obvious. The hurt I am feeling now is a hundred times worse. I am still not sure that I shall survive it. I remember Catherine's mother saying that people have been killed diving from here. I even wonder whether to dive now myself but I realise that in reality it is by no means a certainty that it would be fatal. Probably I would just break a leg and end up in hospital. If I want to follow my father's path and top myself, it needs to be a certainty. Even in the absolute depths of my despair, I do not actually think that it will come to that. As I sit on the rock with my legs dangling over the edge, I realise Sylvie's accusation that I was with her just for the sex is not true. I loved listening to the music that she played, often light classical or country and western. I loved the way she hummed to herself as she made us coffee after dinner. I loved the way she came from work with interesting little stories of how her day had been. Why didn't I tell her more about my day, the stories associated with some of the quaint old buildings in which I often work? There were interesting stories.

Some time ago there was a top flat that I was doing some work in that was rumoured to have a ghost. I am fairly sure that I have seen this ghost, although in the stories that are handed down, one does not receive precise information about what others have seen. I was there late one night when there was a full moon. There was a floor to ceiling built-in cupboard on one wall. A ghostly figure appeared to come out of it and then fade and vanish. It was very spooky. I am not a believer in ghosts, although I do know that there a number of sightings that seem to be inexplicable. I think that they are hallucinations that occur in the brain of normal people, by which I mean people without a medical diagnosis to explain hallucinations. I think they occur when conditions are rather spooky in the first place and even though a person may not consciously feel spooked, their subconscious does. This results in a hallucination. So I took a careful look at the possibilities. Old glass tends to flow and can produce the equivalent of a lens, even a distorting lens rather like the distorting mirrors in some fairs where you see yourself with a very large head or with tentacles for arms. The glass of the window in this room of the flat had two distortions which I thought might throw the light of the moon onto the shiny cupboard door. I was back the next evening to see. Sure enough at a certain point the light from the moon projected one small oval of light on the door and immediately below it was a larger oval of light producing the effect of a head and body like a small child might draw on a piece of paper. As the moon moved the 'ghost' moved then suddenly faded and vanished. I recall my delight at having solved this mystery. But I don't think that I ever told Sylvie. I bring myself back to the present. It is winter and I am freezing. Freezing to death is a relatively painless way to die, they say. Shall I give it a try? I give myself a wry smile; return to my little Vespa. It doesn't let me down. Our love is mutual. I return home.

In June I receive an invitation in the post for Sylvie and me to attend the marriage of Catherine and Jean in Toulouse that August. I accept for me and forward it to Sylvie at the flat she still shares with her friends. I don't imagine that she will come but if she is invited I need to let her know. Then only a month later comes a cancellation. The wedding has been postponed because Catherine's mother Anne has been taken very ill with flu. She is failing to get completely better. I can see that the mother of the bride is an important person at a wedding and in this particular case, the main reason for having the wedding in Toulouse. These days when so many engaged couples are already living together, the timing of a wedding only becomes important if the bride is pregnant. I send an email to Catherine asking how her mother is and giving my phone number. All this email communication, I think, is a bit silly now I have a mobile phone. In spite of me sending my phone number, Catherine replies by email. It is short. Her mother has the A(H3N2) strain of flu. It is sometimes called swine flu. It is a strain which has a relatively high incidence of people taking a very long time to get completely better. It is prevalent in Spain at the moment and seems to have spread from there to southwest

France. It seems to be spreading even though winter is long past.

The loose partnership that Guy and I had formed was working better than we could have hoped. It works because we are both meticulous in everything we do. We tidy as best we can before leaving everyday even when working in an unoccupied flat. It takes a little longer but you never know when the owner is going to look in to see how the work is progressing. Tidiness impresses the clients and they mention us to friends. Word of mouth can be a very effective way of building up a business and it costs nothing at all in advertising. Several months have now past since Sylvie left me. Guy now has to bring me to heel.

"Jacques" he says. "I know that you are still very cut up about Sylvie, but you're going about the place looking completely miserable. That is all right when no-one else is around but dealing with the people whom we hope are going to recommend us, looking like death is just around the corner is not going to help our cause one bit."

"Of course you are right Guy" I admit. "I shall really give it a try to be more cheerful; as you say especially with the clients."

I do manage this during the day while working but at home in the evening I just sit there like a statue thinking of nothing but Sylvie. Guy is still working for Desplaces & Cie. He says that Claude, 'Old Mr. Desplaces' is what he calls him, comes into the office just one or two mornings a week and chats to Dominique and anyone else who might be there.

"It's remarkable" says Guy, "how the old boy, using a memory of some previous job, can weave a relevant suggestion into the conversation, something pertinent to some current bit of work, looking as if he is merely reminiscing about the past. Then he will leave without having made any suggestions, leaving the present boss to think of the solution for himself. He is amazingly subtle."

We laugh. We both appreciate the worth of 'Old Mr Desplaces'!

September brings some surprisingly hot weather. This 'Global Warming' that everybody is talking about is becoming a real problem. It seems to be accelerating and, of course, in one way or another, it affects the whole world. The world needs a unified plan. It is obvious to anybody thinking about it seriously that the rich nations have to pay. They have the resources and they cause the pollution. So ultimately they will have to cash out or the whole world will pay the price. But back to the present. I am finding working indoors in cramped spaces very uncomfortable. I start to wonder why, when I ploughed my baccalaureate, I decided to become an electrician rather than resit the exam. This is the first time that I have had this thought and I realise how hard it is to recall the precise reasoning for a decision taken years ago. I am ruminating uselessly on the problem when a call comes in from a care home in Seynod to the northwest of Annecy. They have had some problems with their electrical equipment and would like me to check it over. They have a number of beds with electrical controls so that their elderly residents, who do not have much strength or mobility, can control the position and tilt of their bed by using a control panel. They can sit themselves up to read or put a slope so that the foot of the bed is a little higher than the head end to bring down ankle swelling. The care home has had a problem where one of their residents received an electric shock when touching the control panel. This reminds me of a problem that occurred a while ago in a hospital in the United States. The patient had a pee in a bottle and when trying to put the bottle back on the side table, spilled some over the control panel. This broke down the resistance of the box. The electric shock he received stopped his heart. He was lucky that this was a very advanced hospital for the time. It had a monitor recording the heart of each patient at the central control desk. When his heart stopped an alarm was set off and a member of staff immediately leapt into action in order to resuscitate the patient. As soon as he touched the patient, he was also incorporated into the electrical circuit, receiving a nasty shock as well. They were both lucky to survive. So I am surprised at what has occurred at this care home. I know that a lot of improvements have been made to these beds in the last ten years.

When I get there, I see that the beds that they have are quite old models probably much older than ten years. This is the only reason that it could occur these days, I think. When I set to work, I find that the panel which the patient uses to control the bed is wired up at mains voltage. These days it would be low voltage or more probably remote controlled using a battery powered device. I check the offending bed and it works perfectly well now. The incident has not caused any damage to the bed or the motor. The switch has dried out and the problem has disappeared. The reasons for the issue in the first place are that the switch that is used to work the motor of this bed is not waterproof and the current running through it is at the mains voltage of 230 volts. As long as it keeps dry there should be no problem. If it gets wet the insulation breaks down giving the potential for a 230 volt shock. I take the lid off the compartment where the motor that operates the bed is housed. There is room in that compartment to place a transformer. That is a relief because a transformer is what is needed to sort this problem. The lid of this compartment is obviously designed to fit different models as it has some unused housing for screws. That is an unexpected bonus and makes life a lot easier. If I can find the right size of transformer and the right size screws (both these should be easy) I can insert a transformer. This gives two possibilities. I can either fit a low voltage lead to the same type of switch that the bed had before the problem occurred, not the same actual one as it isn't waterproof, or I can fit a remote control. I go to the manager's office. The door says 'Madame Thierry' I explain the situation and ask her which she wants. I point out that the battery operated remote is marginally safer as it is completely separate from any electrics that come from the mains but it is slightly more expensive.

"Make it the low voltage wired switch," says Madame Thierry, "not because it's cheaper because I don't suppose that there is much difference. No, the reason is that in a place like this, the remote is going to get lost. Someone will wander off with it and forget where they have put it. The low voltage switch is actually connected to the bed so nobody can walk off with it. I think that one is going to be the better bet for us."

I see her thought. "I can see that" I say. "Another thing is that if you are wanting all these old beds converted, the remotes would undoubtedly get muddled up and if any two beds were reasonably close, you'd find that one person would be controlling the nearby bed."

So that is quite a nice little contract. There's nothing in this for Guy however. On the way home on my Vespa, I think about the way Mankind so often makes life harder than it needs to be. Look at the calendar. September to December are obviously meant to be the seventh to tenth months but they have nevertheless been placed ninth to twelfth. It stands to reason that there should be seven months of 30 days and five of 31 with one of the 30 day months taking an extra day in leap year. But no, life must be made harder. It is mains electricity that started me thinking like this. Across the world, mains electricity is 50 or 60 Hertz (Hz or cycles per second). This is the most dangerous frequency range that there is. It takes less flow of current to stop the heart at 50 to 60 Hz. than any other frequency. With direct current (0Hz) it takes five times as much current to stop the heart and at very high frequencies the current becomes so safe that surgeons can use it to stop bleeding by coagulating the blood with heat (diathermy) with no risk to the heart at all. The reason for making mains voltage 50 to 60 cycles per second is that it is 3000 to 3600 revolutions per minute and that is a convenient and cheap speed at which to run generators. Never mind safety; it's money again.

In October, Guy and I have a couple of jobs in Sévrier. In the evening we begin to get into the habit of having a beer at Le Café de la Boule. The weather is mild for the time of year but not really warm enough to have a table outside. Several nights in a row we see a couple of young women at a table with what looked like Diabolo Grenadines. On the third evening, without asking me what I think, Guy goes up to them and says:

"Can we join you?" The girl nearest Guy looks at her friend questioningly. I thought perhaps a little positively rather than not. The girl opposite me looks me up and down. In a tone that I can only describe as resigned, she says:

"Why not?"

Guy introduces himself and me. The 'resigned' girl introduces herself as Diane and her more 'positive' friend as Eugénie. We sit and chat for an hour or so. We get on quite well in an unremarkable way. Then I get up to leave to go back to my flat in Annecy. Guy lives in Sévrier. He seems to be enjoying himself and stays behind with Diane and Eugénie.

The next evening, we again make for the café. Diane and Eugénie are there, sitting at a table by the window, so naturally we join them. It is obvious to me that in my absence last night, Guy has made a play for Eugénie. There is definitely a flirtatious repartee going on between them. Fair to say, Diane has lost her dismissive, resigned attitude and seems to be enjoying seeing the flirtation. I agree it is fun to watch. The fact that Guy and Eugénie are flirting away, sort of makes Diane and me accessories to the play and we join in, just for the fun of it. At about nine, Diane and Eugénie get up from the table move to the door. Outside the café, they start wandering up the hill to the church. If you don't know Sévrier, the church is at the top of a little hill which then falls steeply down to the lake edge. From alongside the church, there is a magnificent view of the lake from a grassy area with a few trees and a couple of benches. Because of the mountain to the West, the sun sets early on this side of the lake. Tonight there is an almost full moon. We amble up the hill and everything is very relaxed. Guy takes Eugénie's hand and they go up together hand in hand. Diane and I follow a couple of paces behind. Looking at Diane, I can see that she has a lovely profile. I hadn't noticed in the café. When I look back in front of me, Guy and Eugénie have vanished. Perhaps they have gone round the side of the church but they are nowhere to be seen. It is certainly a beautiful view in the dull evening light with the moon casting its light on the lake and we can see the outlines of the Alps to the East.

Diane turns towards me and her right breast pushes into my left side then she kisses me on the mouth. I immediately think of Sylvie which is disconcerting. Diane has got my lower lip between her teeth. Not biting but just hard enough that I cannot pull away. She is running her tongue, very slowly across my lower lip, gently to and fro. She certainly knows how to do this. It is a sensational feeling. I feel a need to hold her tight and at the same time a reluctance to do so. She relaxes my lip but carries on with the kiss and just as I feel that I must respond she moves away the merest trace, kisses my ear and whispers a few mock words of nonsense into it, still holding herself gently to me. My mixed feelings leave me at a loss. There is no doubt I enjoyed that immensely. All sorts of bits of my body are telling me that. Somehow though, I am not yet over Sylvie.

"You can certainly do that again" I say.

"Yes, but not this evening."

I smile at that. I decide that I certainly like Diane a lot.

"Where do you live" I ask. "I'll give you a run home on my Vespa."

"OK" she replies. We walk hand in hand back to my Vespa. "It's along here" she says pointing back towards Annecy. Then she gets on the pillion behind me and puts her arms round me kissing me on the back of the neck below my crash helmet. I hope I shall be able to concentrate on the road. We go under 200 yards.

"It's here" she says with a little laugh.

"What already" I say.

"Sure" she says. "I only got on as an excuse to put my arms round you again. Thanks for the lift."

She disappears down a little alley and is lost from sight. I am at a loss. She has made a huge impression on me but half of me is still saying 'she's not Sylvie'.

Guy and I have several more days on the work at Sévrier and each evening follows the same pattern. We have a drink. We wander up the hill to the church. Guy and Eugénie miraculously vanish and Diane and I have a session of hugging and kissing. I remain a bit ambiguous about it. Sylvie is still getting somewhat in the way. I notice that my thinking is changing a bit. I am seeing myself as being stupid but it is difficult to alter one's feelings at will. Diane seems to be happy with this arrangement. Either she is being very patient or her needs are being fulfilled.

We finished the Sévrier jobs today and I realise that this means a decision. We, meaning the four of us, have not actually been making dates. We have just turned up at the Café de la Boule each evening and met as if by chance. Now, if I want to see Diane again, I shall have to arrange a meeting. For Guy, living in Sévrier, the problem is not so clear cut. I decide that I enjoy Diane's company. She is very relaxing to be with. She never pushes the situation. There is no doubt I enjoy her kisses and the physical contact. It is, as they say, a no-brainer. My next piece of work is back in Annecy. I make a decision. I hope it is a wise one. I suggest we meet at Le Bistro du Thiou where I first met Sylvie. I feel that meeting Diane there will exorcise the ghost of Sylvie. Diane is amazingly laid back about it.

"Yes I'd like that." She says as if she had never thought of an actual 'date'.

We arrange to meet at 6.30 the next day which is a Wednesday. We arrive together, meeting at the door. Diane has made a bit of an effort. She is not dressed to the nines but she has a smart blouse and a new-looking tight pair of jeans, under-emphasised make-up and just a hint of perfume. I have turned up from work and must look my usual scruffy self. I feel a little ashamed. We go into the restaurant. Sylvie is not there but two of her flat mates are and they wave me a desultory greeting then carry on with their conversation. Le Bistro du Thiou do serve a good meal. We had filets de perche from the lake with a bottle of Apremont, pretty much the standard Savoy wine. Some have won prizes and are excellent but most are pleasant without being spectacular. Then we finished off with their signature mango sorbet. Sylvie came to mind. It was with Sylvie, Catherine and her fiancé that I last had mango sorbet but I could dismiss Sylvie now with a shrug. Thank heavens, the agony was truly over. I suggested that we went back to my flat.

"Yes, I'd like to see that" said Diane. She had arrived on a scooter similar to my little Vespa so we go, both on our own two wheels back to my flat on L'Avenue de

Genève. I make a coffee and we both sit on the sofa, nice and close. I cannot get over some aspects of Diane. She is so natural about anything she wants to say. Now she is quite blunt.

"I don't have to get back home tonight, Jacques" she says. "It would be fun to spend the night here with you."

My brain is completely taken aback by the simplicity of actually saying what we are both thinking. I manage to keep cool.

"In that case" I say, "I shall show you round the flat."

It is two bedrooms, kitchen, and bathroom with a separate loo. Naturally we end up in my bedroom.

"This definitely looks like the best place to be" she says.

She comes close and before I know it she has my lower lip between her teeth like the first time. It renders me completely useless. She is right up close, meaning I can reach none of her; like when boxers get in a clinch together and cannot punch. I cannot move back without tearing my lip. She is stimulating me with that deliciously slow to and fro movement of her tongue across my lip and her understated perfume is promising heaven. I try to force my hands down the back of her jeans onto her buttocks but the jeans are too tight. The only way I could do anything effective would be by real force. I suddenly understand how a man can do that but I stay completely under her spell. This is heaven and hell combined. Suddenly she releases me and is out of her jeans in a second. Now I am able to move. I have her where I need her in a trice and we climax together. I am absolutely drained physically and emotionally.

"Jacques" says she. "You certainly know how to keep a girl waiting."

Six weeks pass. We are seeing each other almost every night. I know I do not love Diane. I loved Sylvie and this is completely different. Diane fulfils a need for me. I imagine that I do the same for her. She fulfils that need superbly; she is fun to be with, but I don't feel the same as for Sylvie. I realise what Sylvie said about knowing about what one's partner is doing and being involved in any decisions. I see that I know nothing at all about Diane. I dropped her off nominally near her home once but it was just an alley and she disappeared. She might have had her scooter round the corner and gone anywhere. She is in absolute control. It is really no surprise to me when she says:

"Shall we arrange something special for tomorrow night? It is the last time that I shall see you. My husband comes back the day after tomorrow."

She is the second woman to leave me gaping with my mouth opening and shutting with no sound coming out. This time I am not as taken aback. I get the picture. I recover from this bombshell with remarkable speed.

"I'll book a meal at L'Impérial" I say. "We can have a little gamble at the Casino after and see who comes out best."

Diane laughs as if she is fit to bust.

"You're on" she says. "I have never known anybody take it like that. Jacques, you are something else. Let me tell you just a little about myself, I owe it to you after that. I met a man when I was 18 and I thought that I fell in love with him. May be I did. Love has so many different facets. He was 26, so eight years older than me. His job and indeed his hobby is as a wildlife photographer. He is very good at it. Some of his photos are amazing. I was brought up as a Christian in a Catholic community, although I never really understood what it was all about. My future husband and I kissed and cuddled a lot but the idea of sex before marriage was taboo. I was still a virgin when we were married. Henri, my husband was very loving in most respects but seemed to find it difficult to consummate our marriage. These days that is thought of as one of the reasons for living together before getting married. I would be aroused by foreplay and nothing followed. I found it frustrating. So I read books and articles. There were heaps of suggestions. Lots of them ludicrous, I thought, as I could never have carried them out. I learned about the kiss that grips the lower lip and makes your partner completely powerless and effectively entirely at your will. You can stimulate his lip while natural pheromones take things to another plane. It worked a treat and I was over the first hurdle. My husband has a far lower requirement for this than I do, so although life was much better, I was still a little disappointed. Then he got a job that fascinated him, going to all the outlandish places on earth, photographing the wildlife. Typically a trip is three months and then he will be home for three to six months before finding some other interesting place to go. It is a bit like being married to a sailor. I don't know if I am wicked or whether my solution is just common sense. I took a decision. When he is home I am entirely faithful. I see no-one else. I tend to his every need. When he is away and the opportunity arises, I have a relationship with someone else; in this case you. I go from being a gentle angel to a scarlet woman. You have been lucky enough to have had two months of the scarlet woman in me. I can tell that you enjoyed it. I am now 32, I have been doing this for twelve years and it keeps me sane. Because of my husband's low demands, I have learnt to be very patient. I must admit you tried me almost to the limit with your obsession with a previous relationship. I could see her in your every move or indeed, lack of it. My husband comes back this weekend. He will be home for: I think it is 4 months this time. If you are still available at the end of that time, I am certainly prepared to think about taking up with you again but I usually find that time has passed on." I say that I see her point of view and indeed I do.

We go to the Casino. I lose 200 francs. Diane wins 300 francs. Such are the vagaries of the laws of chance. I shall probably never see her again. So ends my second deep relationship with a woman. This time I take it in my stride. I am lucky enough to have two women throw me over without any acrimony, periods of unpleasantness or hard feelings. Few men are that blest. The more I think about it, the more I appreciate Diane. With Sylvie, I was so in love it hurt me, especially when it finished. With Diane it was gentle, humorous fun all the way; a gentle loving. I knuckle down to my work. Then in the January of 2001, I received an unexpected call from Catherine. It was the first time that she had called my mobile and she was distraught.

Catherine 1999–2001

It was so surprising, coming across Jacques like that at Le Balcon au Lac yesterday. The meal with Jacques and his girlfriend, Sylvie was the perfect ending to this holiday. I have been showing Jean all my childhood haunts. This has made me see that the brief spell when Jacques stayed with us is among my fondest memories. Jean and I just managed to catch the early morning TGV back to Paris. When I woke I was tightly held in Jean's arms and train or no train, there I wanted to stay; for ever would be too short a time for me. Jean was more practical.

"Come on Catherine we've got the rest of our lives to hold each other like this. The main priority this morning is to get the hire car back to Avis in time to catch the train."

"Spoilsport!" I said. Of course he was right and we caught the train by the skin of our teeth. We are now having a coffee at La Gare de Lyon and in spite of the journey being over 300 miles, it is still quite early in the morning.

This has been an exhilarating time. For the whole of this holiday we have not had a single cross word; not so much as a single sigh of irritation. It has been idyllic. Now we must each introduce the other to our parents and make arrangements for our marriage. Initially we were thinking that Paris would be the best place. My current friends Jeanne and Marie are here. It would also be convenient for a couple of Jean's friends in Lille too. On further reflection though, both Jean's parents and my parents are in the Southwest of France, in Pau and Toulouse. It is traditional to marry where the parents of the bride live. I suppose that is because, in the past, it was usually where the bride herself lived as well. Brides tended then to go and live in the same area as their new husband's family. For the bride and her parents, it could be a fond farewell. All things considered, we come down on the side of Toulouse. When sitting comfortably here in Paris, it is easy to think of Toulouse and Pau as being almost next door to each other because they are both far away in the Southwest. In fact they are 125 miles apart and the journey by road used to be very tiring. A motorway, the A64, was opened last year but I understand even though it makes the journey very much easier, the journey time is still over two hours.

I have to try to keep my feet firmly on the ground. I am only half way through my way to becoming a notaire. It is very important to me to finish that. I realise that I am heading in the direction of following in my mother's footsteps. She qualified in law, was married and had a baby all within a year. That was then followed by not using her law degree until she was middle-aged. It is a sobering thought that even my overwhelming happiness, my utter love for Jean, might be viewed in some ways as spoiling the purpose of my life. Drop the philosophy Catherine, I think to myself, 'just hang on to this happiness'. I laugh out loud. I have forgotten my surroundings musing like this. I come back to earth to find myself sitting in front of a cup of coffee in La Gare de Lyon. My fiancé is looking worried but not too worried. He is getting used to me being away with the fairies on occasion.

"What is it, Catherine?" he asks.

I tell him the truth. "I'm just so happy and I was philosophising about it in a rather grandiose fashion until I felt utterly stupid."

He says nothing. He gently takes my hand over the table and squeezes it. We sit in silence, quietly at peace.

We arrange to see both sets of parents in December during the Universities' winter break. After that Jean wants a skiing holiday. We are going to be in his usual haunts and it would be logical to go to a Pyrenean resort. Jean, however, is determined to go to Chamonix. He wants the experience of Mont Blanc.

"I've done the Pyrenees" he says. "The Alps are a different sort of mountain. I found Denver was a different experience from the Pyrenees and I expect the Alps to be different again, especially if we go to Chamonix. I mean Mont Blanc is iconic isn't it? I think the appreciation inside you of where you are at the time something happens alters your actual perception of the event. It is simple really. Everyone would feel differently about a glass of champagne in a bar overlooking a beautiful bay in the sunset than they would about a glass of champagne at an office party. It automatically tastes different." I think most wine experts might well not agree with that but I let it go. I do know what Jean means.

Back on the law course, I am again seeing a lot of Jeanne and Marie, who have also decided to take at least the next two years. Marie was very doubtful that she would be accepted. To start with I thought them a bit dull compared to Louise and Janine. Although neither of them can compare with Louise as a friend, or with Janine as (I find that I am at a complete loss to describe what I feel about Janine: a friend: a compete pain in the neck; someone who needed help: someone who might have ruined my life and aspirations: I am going to settle for:) an interesting person. I am nevertheless, coming to appreciate them more, especially Jeanne. She was remarkable the way she could tell what had happened between Jean and me without having been told anything about him. She carries on showing an immense level of intuition. I wonder if it is a striking level of observation she has, or is it largely guesswork? Either of these would give her a real edge in court if she becomes a barrister. She is obviously well in control of the course whereas Marie, I think, may be floundering a little. I shouldn't get complacent. So far I have found any challenge requiring intelligence to be well within my capabilities but this is something it is now unwise to rely on. I have a degree with first class honours from the Sorbonne. Anyone, but especially a Frenchwoman, should be very proud of that. However, there is one of those 'this is a joke, but yet it is true' laws, 'Peter's law of Ultimate Incompetence' I think it is called. You get a job and you do it well so you are promoted. You do the new job well so you again get promotion. Now you are in above your head, you cannot cope so you don't get promoted but stay in that job until you retire. Ergo, almost everyone ends up doing a job that they are incapable of doing properly. I must watch that I never, ever start falling behind. When I am in my lovely flat in the 13th arrondissement, I can sit there for ages just thinking how lucky I am. I see the ordinary ornaments in the room take on the strangest shapes and acquiring unbelievable colours which slowly fade into the sheer peace of happiness. It would be so easy just to sit there, loving it and doing nothing. Then I think "That is probably just what heroin does to you: leaves you with a false dream of the ultimate happiness."

December comes. We think we might spend three days with each of our families and have one day in between to do what we want. Jean would like to show me Bagnères de Bigorre which was one of the places he loved as a child. It is only slightly off the direct route from Toulouse to Pau.

"The thing is Catherine, we could stop off at Lourdes. It would mean almost exactly the same amount of diversion from the new A64 but Lourdes is completely commercialised. It is famous but no fun. Everything is given over to making a profit from tourists. Bagnères de Bigorre is relatively unspoilt. It has a history going back to Roman times with thermal baths, lots of old buildings and several streams running through it. Not as many as Annecy that you showed me but a lovely place all the same."

We decide to see my parents first. Jean suggests that he should formally ask my father for my hand in marriage. I can hardly stop laughing. It is just so anachronistic. Apart from that it is sexist in the extreme. A man asks another man if he can marry a woman even ignoring the other woman, my mum, who might have some interest in the situation. I laugh because I know it is because Jean loves the idea of the long tradition, not because he personally is sexist. However, I do see him taking the point on board without me even having to say anything.

"No, perhaps not" he says.

Mum is delighted to see me. She is so proud of my law degree. It is very nice that she sees it as even better than her own. She is still enjoying her work giving legal assistance to the poor. Even in countries with a legal system which is fundamentally fair, and there are not too many of those in the world, the poor always come out with a rotten deal. Dad seems to be in a different world. I am, of course, only getting a snapshot but my parents seem to have drifted apart in the last few years. May be it is because Mum is perpetually seeing how the poor are being treated while Dad, it must be said (and he is still giving me a generous allowance, so I can't grumble) is getting a fat cat income. I hope they don't split up. They were so very close when I was small. They both take to Jean straight away. So that goes OK. They have given us separate rooms. I ought to have been prepared for that but it came as a surprise. We don't want to cause any embarrassment, so we go along with it.

While we are in Toulouse, I arrange for us to see Louise. We meet at one of our old haunts from schooldays, La Gazelle in Avenue des Minimes. Louise has been in contact with Janine. She has moved to Carcassonne but is going to make a special effort to come and see me. I am very touched. We used to be very close in early teenage. I am so close to Louise now that I shall have to be careful not to seem to cut Janine out. Janine has a job in a shop and a boyfriend called Davide who is very keen on her. Louise is unattached at the moment and says she is saving herself for a rainy day! There are a lot of guys out there missing a real gem. She is still at Toulouse University. She got a degree in Biology with 2(1) honours and is now studying for a higher degree. She is concentrating on Plant Biology, hoping to research the way plants might be modified to fix carbon dioxide more quickly. This could have two major effects on the world. Food could be grown more quickly and carbon dioxide levels in the atmosphere might fall, stopping the worst effects of climate change. She says that this is not so hard in principle. There is apparently a part of the photosynthesis pathway where sometimes an oxygen molecule gets in the way of taking up carbon dioxide. I probably don't have that quite right but Louise is very excited by the prospect. She thinks that genetic modification of the pathway might solve a lot of the world's problems. I am sceptical. I think people are the world's main problem.

Jean and I book one night in the Hotel de Béarn in Avenue Charles de Gaulle in Bagnères de Bigorre. We hire a car in Toulouse for two days with an arrangement that we can drop it off in Pau. Then we drive to the Hotel de Béarn. We visit the Thermal Baths and the Traditional Market, Les Halles. It is a calm relaxing day. We then move on to Pau to visit Jean's parents. Jean's mother Émilie is very sweet. She fusses around us offering us, coffee, biscuits, cake and so on. We settle for coffee and say we are all right without cake or biscuits. I am surprised at how old Jean's father, Louis, is. He looks to be about eighty. Jean lets me know that he is actually seventy. I had not realised that Jean had such elderly parents. I knew he was an only child like me but his mother was 35 when he was born and his father was 44. Louis has not aged well. I am afraid that he has some sort of dementia. He keeps losing the thread of what he is saying. Many older people do this a bit but he also keeps calling me Caroline in spite of Jean perpetually correcting him; his voice becoming crosser each time. I whisper to Jean to let it go. It really doesn't matter and Caroline is a nice name anyway. Again they have given us separate rooms. Oh well! Emilie is easy to get on with, if fussing over us too much but Louis is difficult because he keeps forgetting who I am. I mean not remembering that I am Jean's fiancée as well as calling me Caroline. We manage to get out so Jean can show me some of the sights. The view of the Pyrenees from L'Avenue des Pyrenées is stunning as is the château. It is far more impressive than Annecy's château and prettier though not as impressive as the one we saw in Saumur. Thinking of Saumur, I find myself blushing a little with the memories. The round of our parents now completed we take the four and a half hour journey back to Paris in the TGV.

It is the millennium coming up. I feel that we should do something. All the restaurants will be heaving, probably overbooked, overpriced and under staffed. It does not make an appealing picture. I suggest that we give a small party. We try counting up. There could be us, Jeanne and Marie; I know that Jeanne is unattached at the moment but Marie has a boyfriend called Luc who has been hanging around for a while. There is also a girl called Colette on our course whom I know well enough to invite and she is unattached. If Jean can invite couple of unattached friends from Lille or even pairs, we can give a small party of eight to twelve people. Jean says he'll invite Davide and Françoise who are an item and he has two unattached friends Marcel and Robert. My flat is just big enough for that and it would probably be as cheap as going out. We make a list:

Men:	Jean	Luc	Davide	Marcel	Robert
Women:	Catherine	Marie	Françoise	Jeanne	Colette

I get a letter from Aurélie. She is half way through her medical post at Marseilles. The reason that she has written is because her current boyfriend comes from Bauduen, a village on the Lac de Sainte-Croix where we used to go sometimes in the summer when we were very young. She doesn't say much else. She just says it brought to mind how much we enjoyed being together when we were kids and we must get together sometime. As a result, I decide to invite her as well but she says that she cannot make it, which is a shame. I haven't seen her for years. The party list works out well. They can all come. We get in the drink and I cook a lot of stuff that can be stored in the freezer and then defrosted and eaten cold. I reckon on making a straightforward carrot and coriander soup on the day but nothing else. We are not expecting this to be an all-night party although it will obviously run past midnight because that is the whole point of it but we expect it to pack up about 2 or 3 a.m. We reckon the flat can sleep six at a pinch so we book a room in a nearby cheap (for Paris) hotel for the other four. Perhaps it will not be needed. In the event the party goes with a swing. Everyone lasts until breakfast time. I serve gallons of hot coffee and Jean goes round to the boulangerie for fresh croissants. Jeanne and Robert seem to have got on especially well. I shall watch this space.

The second week in January, we are in Chamonix in a small one bedroom flat slightly out of town. I never realised how expensive skiing is; hiring the equipment, ski lift passes and, for me, beginners ski lessons. Jean is immediately out on the black runs while I am learning to snowplough to a halt. I keep falling and am not taking to skiing at all. When we meet for lunch, Jean is all hyped up. His eyes are shining and he is hopelessly animated. He cannot stop talking about how beautiful the high slopes are. It is lovely to see him so excited while I secretly nurse my bruises. By the end of the day we are both exhausted and after dinner immediately fall asleep. The next day I suppose I am a little more proficient but I am still falling a lot and am definitely one of the worst in the beginners group. At lunch Jean is again completely hyped up. After dinner, Jean holds me tight and starts to undress me. Then he sees my hips and thighs.

"Catherine" he says. "I'm so sorry, I had no idea. Are all those bruises from falling over?"

I nod rather disconsolately. He is embarrassed. He has been so hyped up that he has not been aware of how poorly I have been progressing. He has hired a guide for the next day and is going to ski off-piste. I am relieved that he has hired a guide. There are so many stories of people injuring themselves by skiing off-piste on their own or with a friend who also doesn't know the area well. By the end of the week, I can ski on a gentle blue run and snow-plough to a stop. I am pleased with this achievement but it is the first time in my life that I feel that I have failed miserably. I am afraid that I am not a fan of skiing and I realise that Jean is going to want to do this every year. I can manage a week's skiing per year for his sake, I'm sure.

The next term at university follows the usual pattern, but Marie is wondering whether to chuck it in. She has a degree. She is asking herself if she needs a higher degree. Jeanne is encouraging her to stick with it. She points out that there are only a few more months to go before we take our Masters 2 exams.

"If you'd pulled out last year that might make sense but…"

However, I am not so sure. She could get a well-paid interesting job with the degree that she has. If she feels that the course doesn't suit her, my feeling is that perhaps she should jack it in even if there are only a few more months to go. It is certainly not a decision to be taken lightly. I am not sure so I say nothing. That of course doesn't work. They both see that I have said nothing. Jeanne asks me directly:

"Well what do you think, Catherine?"

"I really am not sure." I turn to Marie "I think the way to approach the question is to ask yourself what career you would have if you left now: what career you would have if you complete the course: which of the two would you prefer: what is the likelihood of, for some reason, being unable to do your preferred option anyway."

"That is good thinking, Catherine" says Marie. "I shall go away and think about the question within that framework. I think you may have been very helpful."

I ask Jeanne if she is seeing Robert.

"Not now" she says. "We had a couple of dates but in the end we didn't click." That is a pity. They seemed to get on so well.

Jean and I have definitely decided to get married in August in Toulouse. We send out the invitations. Almost immediately there is a problem. My mother falls ill with flu. It is not your common or garden flu. It is a virulent A(H3N2) variety, sometimes known as swine flu. It has been widespread in Spain last winter and now, even though winter has passed, it has reached southwest France and is spreading surprisingly quickly there. It is one of those types of flu that can result in a long lasting recovery period of up to six months with the victim feeling well below par. It seems stupid to hold the wedding in Toulouse largely for the sake of my mother and to have her feeling quite incapable of enjoying it. Jean and I are already living together as much as we would be able to if we were married. We both want to get married but precisely when seems quite unimportant. That is unless I fall pregnant but that would cause a whole heap of problems anyway. We decide to postpone the wedding. We both want to be married in summer when the weather is warm. It is so much better for the reception if guests can be outdoors at least for some of the time. We postpone it until August next year. We send out postponement notices but do not actually mention when the new date will be; just some time next year.

Marie has carefully weighed up the pros and cons. She has come to the conclusion that she has had enough of being a student, even a post-graduate student. There are some good jobs with reasonable salaries listed. She has put out feelers and has found a couple firms interested in having a lawyer on their Human Resources team. There is one firm in Rouen which is offering a remarkably good salary. Marie thinks this could be the answer but she is a little suspicious of the salary. She wants to find out why it is significantly higher than other posts which on the face of it look similar. She rings the firm and manages to speak to a director. She is pleasantly surprised at this. So many firms make it almost impossible to speak to somebody with any seniority. Marie says that she would like to apply but is suspicious of the salary. Why is it so high? The director thinks this is funny.

"Oh dear!" he says. "I never thought that a high salary was going to dissuade people from applying. We could always" he jokes, "pay a little less if it helps. But seriously the reason for the high salary is that we have very high standards here. We want the very best people to apply and the board has agreed in advance that there will not be an appointment made unless the candidate is of a very high calibre."

"That is very reassuring" says Marie. "I shall apply because I am of exceptionally high calibre."

The director laughs. "And what is your name" he asks.

"Marie Monet" she replies. "Like the artist."

"Where's your degree from?"

"La Sorbonne."

"I shall remember you, Marie" he says and rings off.

Marie puts in an application for the post. Two weeks later she finds that she has been short-listed. She has put in a great deal of research looking into the firm. It is large and it seems as if their head office is in Rouen because they do a lot of business with the United Kingdom. Rouen is rather nicely placed if Senior Managers need to visit the UK.

Marie says that they have told her that there will be two interviews, both on the same day. One is a social interview to sus out what type of a person she is. How well she is likely to relate to the rest of the team and so on. The second interview is more like an exam where they intend to test her legal knowledge in the areas that they find affect them most. This gives me an idea. Jean is getting close to being a world expert on International Law. He is very highly thought of. As a lecturer he is also brilliant at getting his message across within the hour or so allocated. The interviews are in three weeks' time. I wonder if Jean would give Marie a couple of tutorials on points likely to arise if they are dealing with French and UK law. Marie is excited about that prospect. Jean readily agrees and the next two Saturdays they have two hours closeted together discussing points that are likely to come up.

We are all on tenterhooks as the day dawns; not only Jeanne and I but also Jean as he now has an interest in the result. Have the tutorials he has had with Marie been worthwhile? Marie looks really smartly turned out in a well-fitting beige suit, its skirt just below the knee and a 20 denier pair of tights with a scarcely discernible motif on them. She has had her hair coiffured at a top Paris hairdresser in the 1st arrondissement. They have done a first class job. I bet that cut cost Marie a fortune but she looks just right for an interview with a top firm. I am amazed. Marie usually looks a bit dowdy. The transformation is impressive. Jeanne and I wish her well and off she goes on the train to Rouen. I have invited Jeanne over to my place for the evening and we have told Marie that when she gets back from Rouen she must call in at mine and tell us all about it. I have got in a couple of bottles of pink champagne and we can drown her sorrows or celebrate her success as the occasion demands. I have also baked some navettes, those Marseille biscuits which look like little boats. They are associated with Candlemas but I think they go rather nicely with champagne. It is ten o'clock when Marie finally arrives. She is rather bedraggled because it has come on to rain quite hard and she does not have an umbrella. The hairdo looks a bit the worse for wear too. But far more importantly she has an immense smile on her face.

"I got it" she whoops. "They don't normally tell you right away but they said there was no doubt at all in their minds so why wait."

I give her a towel to dry herself off and I sit her down in the armchair.

"So tell us all about it" says Jeanne as I open the champagne with a loud plop. Of course one ought to open it quietly but it is so much more fun to make a big bang if one is celebrating. I pour the glasses and sit on the sofa next to Jeanne.

"The first interview was a sort of trial by party" she begins. "The candidates were given a choice of a glass of wine or a fruit juice and then circulated round the board. There were eight of them, all men standing in twos. The four candidates circulated round the pairs of board members. I was the only woman candidate. I think that might have been a little helpful as it made me stand out. They wouldn't have any difficulty remembering which candidate I was. When I got to the third pair, one of the men gave me a great grin and said 'Glad you could make it Marie'. I could see he was impressed by the way I was turned out. 'Can you tell us why you want to join our *exceptionally high calibre* team?' I knew he must be the director that I had talked to on the phone. He was quoting my own words back at me. It was quite obvious that I had already impressed him and that gave me a lot of confidence. In the second interview, I had all the luck in the world. Three of the things that they asked me, I would have known nothing about when we finished the degree course last summer but one was the subject we were dealing with on this course only last week and two of the other subjects had been covered by Jean in his tutorials with me. That was your idea Catherine. I really cannot thank you enough for that. It is very likely that those tutorials are what got me this job. I'm due to start in one month, at the beginning of April. Yay, Yay, Yay!" She says. I could tell she was pleased.

She came round to the flat the next Saturday with a bottle of champagne for Jean to thank him for the tutorials. That was nice but Jean was so delighted to hear that two of the points he had emphasised actually came up that I am sure that fact was reward enough in itself. We had a pleasant afternoon relaxing with the champagne. Marie's course is paid for until the end of the academic year so she is now a free person who can attend any lectures that she thinks would be really interesting or useful to her and can ignore anything she chooses. She becomes very relaxed. She used to have a lovely smile on her face most of the time during our basic degree course and the first year masters but she lost it when this year got under way. Now it has returned. She is a joy to be with. She often comes round to my flat in the evening, though after that first Saturday with the champagne, she generally avoids the weekends as she knows I shall be with Jean.

The Masters 2 exam comes up. Jeanne and I both find it pretty straight forward. There is always some tension in taking an exam. There are so many stories of people failing because they didn't read the question properly or their mind went blank. We both sailed through. So we are now LL M – masters in law. The next stage in become a notaire is a two year apprenticeship to a law firm. Not only do we have to do the apprenticeship but we continue taking frequent exams during the two years.

Mum is taking a very long time to recover properly from the flu. She is managing to go to work now but finds it difficult to concentrate. She is worried that she is not doing a good job and may be letting her clients down without realising it. She is very depressed about it. I do not think this is the sort of depression which is almost part of the disease; a direct result of the virus. I think this is just the sort of depression that any conscientious person might feel when they are unable to do their job well. At the summer break I say to Jean that I want to go and visit my mother for a couple of weeks. He is quick on the uptake.

"I don't suppose you would like me to come because I expect you want to take your mother out and about a bit to try and get her out of herself. I'll come if you want."

"You're right, Jean. I think that I would rather go by myself. It's easier to do exactly what I feel mum would enjoy without having to think of how it would affect you." So in early August I go back to mum and dad in Toulouse for a fortnight.

If I am going to leave Jean and all the comfort he brings me for a whole fortnight, I intend to conduct this visit like a military campaign. I have tactics and I have strategy. I arrive on a Wednesday while both my parents are still at work. I buy fresh herbs and all the ingredients for some of mum's favourite meals. I intend to do most, if not all of the cooking for this fortnight. I shall start with some simple dishes that I know mum likes and progress through to the cordon bleu which I know she used, on occasion, to do herself. That is for the weekdays when mum and dad will both be at work and back in the evenings. At weekends I shall take her out to see a show of some sort; cinema, theatre; a fair; whatever. I shall not take dad along. In the back of my mind,

I suspect he may be part of the problem. Let us see how it progresses, I think. The result is in the hands of fate.

When mum gets back in the evening, her face lights up at seeing me and we have a long hug. I am encouraged by this. I have read somewhere that people with depression as a disease do not respond like this. The sun shines but they still look glum. The birds sing and far from making them feel better, it worsens their depression because it emphasises to them that they do not have a normal response. I regard even this pleasure of a mother to see her daughter as a positive sign.

"While I'm here mum" I say, "I shall do the cooking and the washing up afterwards. You go and find some of your favourite music. I've bought a bottle of sauternes. I shall pour you a glass but do not feel obliged to have it."

"I don't think that this is going to help" she says, "but thank you anyway. You're a good girl Catherine."

I smile innocently. I am actually thinking that considering my attempt to seduce Jean in my flat and the subsequent scene in the bedroom in Saumur, many people would regard me as a very naughty girl indeed. I am not however, about to tell my mother about my exploits. I pour her a glass of dessert sauternes. She puts on some Johnny Hallyday. It takes me right back to being a very little girl. She used to play Johnny Hallyday a lot. I am about to go in and say how it brings back memories but as a I start to do so, I can see through the door that she has tears in her eyes, more than that, she is quietly crying. I back off and start getting the meal. A bit later, I check cautiously to see if she has recovered and then go in.

"This is lovely Catherine" she says. "I don't know why, but I haven't listened to Johnny for years."

I notice that she has not touched the sauternes. I have mixed feelings about that. It was an expensive bottle but it shows that she is not need of that sort of crutch. A bit later dad comes back. He is pleased to see me.

"That's nice of you to get dinner for mum, Catherine" he says giving me a hug.

Then he goes into his study with a pile of papers. I chalk up this event in my mind. Things are beginning to take shape.

The first Saturday I take mum to see 'Beau Travail' at the cinema. It stars Denis Lavant and is all the rage at the moment. It has hardly started before I am thinking 'what have I done?' It is about the French Foreign Legion but that is not really the point. It is about how one person can quite irrationally hate another, to the point where they are prepared to kill them: and, I suppose, the consequences of that hate. I found it thoroughly depressing. Mum came out, like a small child with candyfloss.

"Wasn't that brilliant?" she says. "That Denis Lavant can certainly act can't he?"

I have to change my glum depressed expression very quickly before she notices. On Sunday I take her to see another film that is very popular and advertised everywhere. It is 'Rosetta' starring Emilie Dequenne. I ought to look up the plot before deciding where to go. This one is so depressing I can hardly watch it. It is a tale of Deprivation, Drugs and Teenage Angst. I close my eyes in horror to avoid seeing the mother and daughter actually descend to physical fighting. I come out worse than yesterday, thoroughly depressed. I am actually feeling sick. This is doing me no good at all. Mum is jabbering at me like a wild thing.

"I've got a case just like that at the moment" she is saying. "A mother on drugs, living in a squat and her teenage daughter. The daughter is torn between saving her mother or following in her footsteps. Of course, they both often break the law usually in rather minor ways. They need my help. They need all the help they can get. It brings it so vividly to light. Oh Catherine I'm so glad you took me to see this."

So there you are. The more depressive I find the film, the more mum is exultant. She is so pleased to have seen both of them. Quite frankly I have had enough. I am going to research what we do next weekend very carefully. I could not stand another depressing film like the two I have just seen. All the same, the therapy is certainly working with mum. Johnny Hallyday and two films, and she is already so very much better.

I cannot help laughing at myself. I'm not going to see another performance that is depressive. Did I say that? No? - 'La Bohême' is on at Le Théatre du Capitole, Toulouse's opera house. I remember my first proper date with Jean. 'La Bohême' in Paris. It is of course another depressive story where a young girl dies essentially from deprived circumstances. But I cannot resist it. I must see it again. I take mum. She is now really looking forward to the weekend shows. When it comes to 'your tiny hand is frozen' my memories of Jean taking my hand are so vivid that I get one of my attacks. The performers are all dressed in surreal colours. The stage is the shape of some four dimensional spaceship and I am out of action for at least two minutes. I have only once, when a very little girl, told mum about these episodes. She said "Don't be ridiculous Catherine" and I have kept quiet ever since. I wonder if she notices. No, she has loved the performance. She hasn't seen an opera for she cannot remember how long but certainly not since moving to Toulouse. My scheme is working wonders on mum but I am wondering if I am beginning to fall apart. Thank heavens there is something really light showing at the cinema on Sunday. Astérix! Yes it is 'Astérix et Obélix contre César'. I can't go wrong with that. And so it proves. At last something that we both enjoy without any fuss and drama. So my fortnight is coming to a close. I feel that I have had a lot of success with mum. She is certainly better than when I arrived but will she revert as soon as I leave? There is one last shot I can try but I am nervous.

The Tuesday night, my last supper, I cook exactly the same meal that I did for Jean on the night of my failed effort at seduction; pea soup starter followed by Lemon and Garlic Chicken. Mum loves it. She remembers both recipes.

"That soup's a Marc Veyrat isn't it?" she says, "I remember I often made the Lemon and Garlic Chicken when we had friends round but you've added some fresh coriander and a touch of mint as well as the thyme that was in the recipe, haven't you, Catherine? I had forgotten that you could cook like this. I remember teaching you from such a young age, from even before you went to school."

She really is delighted. So far so good but now comes the hard bit. I am very nervous. Possibly even a little frightened. What I am about to do, I have never done before. I corner dad in his study. He is looking over some papers. This seems to be what he does most evenings.

"Dad" I say. "I want a word." He looks up, his expression encouraging me to speak. "It's about mum. You can see that she is quite a lot happier since I arrived." He nods. "That," I say winding myself up to say it, "is because someone, me in this case, is caring for her. It doesn't have to be me. It could be anyone. I'm suggesting that it should be you."

He looks first surprised and then annoyed, very annoyed. That is what I have been worrying about. However, he doesn't say anything so I carry on.

"I have invested a full fortnight of my time to mum" I say, "but I have other commitments. I am still training to be a notaire and I have a fiancé. I am suggesting to you that you invest the same amount of time that I have done; one fortnight. I know you cannot do that as a single stretch. We will make it one weekend day – either Saturday or Sunday, for three months. You arrange to take her somewhere; a film, the theatre, a car boot sale. I don't mind where, just take her somewhere. Those are my terms, is it a deal?"

I am shaking inside as if I'll fall over. I have never spoken to my father like that. I am amazed that I could even do it. I'm surprised to see that he has stopped looking annoyed. He is looking half way between embarrassed and penitent.

"Catherine" he says, "you are quite right. I admire you for what you have achieved in the fortnight that you have been here. Anne is certainly a great deal better for what you have done and, yes, I suppose I have been neglecting her. The job is very busy but nothing excuses ignoring one's wife. I agree to your terms as you put it. I shall take Anne out somewhere one day a week for three months and if it works out, I fully intend to carry on in the same vein."

I breathe a sigh of relief. I need to be alone. I go to my room, the one I had in this house as a teenager, and I sob into the pillow. It seems like for hours. I am absolutely exhausted. The next day I return to Paris. Jean and I have missed each other. The fortnight has seemed a very long time. The next morning I have a smile on my face but I am still exhausted.

Now that I have my higher degree, I become apprenticed to a firm of notaires in the rue Racine. There are two principals; Maître Jean Favre and Maître Antoinette Dubois. I am pleased to be in a firm with a woman principal. Women were first admitted as notaires about 50 years ago and it is only recently that the number has started to grow significantly. The next few years are going to be harder going I think than I have had so far. That is because I am a fast learner. When it is a matter of learning something in my own time, I do not take very long. Now, however, I am going to have to be present whether learning anything or not.

Jean is planning our next skiing holiday. I must admit that it fills me with dread. I did not get on at all well last time. I still remember the bruises from falling and the aches and pains caused by the overwork of muscles unaccustomed to having to do very much. The muscles on the side of the leg that have to produce unexpected force when I snow-plough. The ache in the knees, caused I think just from the tension of waiting to fall over. This is going to be a penance for my love of Jean. He has now decided that this year we shall go to La Clusaz and Le Grand Bornand for a week skiing. That is nice because Le Grand Bornand was the resort I suggested last year. Jean says that they are both smallish resorts but it is possible to get one ski pass that covers both and there are dedicated buses that run between the two, making them effectively one large resort. He suggests that we stay in a hotel this year. He has found one in St. Jean de Sixt which is between the two resorts and served by the ski bus. It's called Hotel Chez Pugein and looks very well appointed. Jean wants me to be in an intermediate class this year but I assure him that I shall be happier redoing the beginners class. This time I shall be much better and when it comes to doing the blue runs I shall probably actually enjoy it. He books us in for Saturday 15th January for a week.

I decide that my beginners' course will be at La Clusaz rather than Le Grand Bornand. This is because I know that there is a skating rink at La Clusaz. I have been ice-skating there several times as a child. If I still don't feel comfortable with the skiing lessons, I might have a go on the skating rink. The first two days Jean comes with me on the bus to La Clusaz, we part at the bottom where my lessons are held. He goes up to the high slopes he likes best. The next two days, he goes to Le Grand Bornand. I am a little bored because we do not meet for lunch but I have lunch with a couple of other girls in the beginners' group. On Tuesday Jean books a guide for the next day to take him off-piste in La Clusaz. We part as usual at the bottom of the Ski lifts. The lesson has just finished when there is a commotion where the ski lifts are. Someone is saying that there has been an unexpected avalanche. There has been an accident but the details are not yet known. Someone has rung from a mobile phone, so rescuers will be able to go straight to the right place. My heart is in my mouth. There is no reason to suppose Jean is involved but it has to be someone. A whole crowd is milling around. Everyone who has a member of their party up the mountain is there and very many people are just there to gawp. Hours go by. Then the ultimate pain; Jean is brought down dead. I collapse to the ground, out to the world.

It is not for long. I soon recover and there are far, far too many people trying to help me. They fuss around until my head spins. I know they are all trying to do their best. I make a huge effort to regain some control of myself. There will of course, be lengthy formalities to be gone through. I cannot take this on my own. I need someone with me. I return to the hotel. All my family and friends are hundreds of miles away in Paris or The Southwest and I need someone now. Then I think of Jacques. He is in Annecy. He can be here today, may be within an hour. Shaking in every limb, I get out my phone and ring his number. I have never rung him before; always used email. He answers but I can't talk sense. Somehow he knows it is me.

He says "Calm yourself Catherine."

I pull myself together and somehow manage to give him my address. I cannot tell him what has happened.

"I'll be there as fast as possible" he says.

I lie on the bed. I cannot sob. I cannot think. I wish I did not exist. It seems like an eternity later, Jacques arrives. Reception has given him my room number and must have told him of the calamity. I am sitting on the bed. He comes in and immediately can see that I am utterly distraught. He sits beside me and puts his arm around me. We stay like that some time. It calms me a little.

I say "Thank you Jacques."

Even in my pain and misery, it takes me back to when we were thirteen. I did the same for him when his mother died.

Jacques 2001–2003

When Catherine rang she was distraught. She couldn't even tell me who she was. I'm not sure how I knew. Since we first met I've always had a sort of empathy with Catherine. She managed to give me the address of where she was; Chez Pugein at St. Jean de Sixt. I say that I'll be there as fast as possible. It is what she must want to hear, but I may well be some time. First I must wrap up really warm. The Vespa is fine but it is wide open to the wind. This is mid-winter and it is literally freezing outside. Also the Vespa is not the most stable vehicle in icy conditions. Catherine is in a skiing area. There is likely to be snow. It is about a twenty mile journey to St. Jean de Sixt. The last quarter to a third of it, when I get past Thônes, is probably very icy indeed. From Thônes the road rises steadily to reach the ski resorts. If it has snowed there today, the roads may well be covered in snow. The main roads are cleared frequently but that cannot be done instantly. My Vespa, lovely as it is, is not the vehicle to be on when the roads are snow-covered and icy. I put on my warmest clothes, check that I have enough fuel. Luckily the dial is registering close to full. I have taken down the address Catherine managed to tell me, Chez Pugein, on a bit of paper. I take that with me just in case I forget. It is not a hotel I have heard of. I have no idea where Chez Pugein is and will have to ask when I reach St. Jean de Sixt. I mentally check that there is nothing else I need. I have my phone though I can't see why I would need it. Ah! A torch would be a good idea. The Vespa has lights of course, but it is difficult to point them in any desired direction. I have a really bright torch. It is one of those with a powerful rechargeable battery which is ideal when I am working in dark corners. I go and get it. Then I'm away.

As I thought, it is plain sailing until just past Thônes. Then it starts to snow. The roads have been recently cleared but the new snow is settling fast and it is starting to come on hard. My windscreen is starting to clog up. The wipers are doing their best but I can only just see in front of me. I am just past Les Villards-sur-Thônes with less than three miles to go when I skid and come off the Vespa. I curse myself for an idiot. I must not hurry. I know Catherine will want me there as soon as possible, her voice was desperate but I won't be able to help anyone if I don't arrive at all. My left ankle was under the bike when we fell. At the moment it feels as if I've sprained it or broken a bone. I inspect the damage to my Vespa. There is a nasty dent in the mudguard but it does not seem to be touching the wheel so the machine should still be functional. It is. Phew! Stuck out here with a broken ankle in the cold and snow, I might not even survive. That, I think, is what I might have needed my mobile phone for. I get back on the Vespa but slow down to a crawl. I can hardly see ten feet in front of me with this snow. My ankle is hell. Those last three miles seem to take hours but eventually I reach St Jean de Sixt.

Naturally enough there is no-one around. I shall have to decide who to knock up and ask. I go a little further and just past the main cross-roads there is a bar.

I give a sigh of relief. I hobble across the road. Mercifully, painful as it is, I can tell that my ankle is not broken or sprained. It is just badly bruised. That does not stop it being very painful indeed. Inside, yes, they know where the Hotel Chez Pugein is. It is a further mile and a half. Furthermore, it is not on the main road, so the road will not have been cleared. They tell me that there is no street lighting along it and it has a number of sharp bends. There is a fork in the road about halfway. Their advice is simple. 'In this weather, don't do it.' I know that I must. Catherine is relying on me. They draw a sketchy map for me and I set off once more. I have gone about three quarters of a mile when the division they warned me about appears. The right hand fork is the one that I must take. It is narrow. I think it may well be nothing more than a dirt track but with several feet of compressed snow followed by the present snow-fall which is now pretty much of a blizzard, it is impossible to tell. The whole surface is uneven and very slippery. My little Vespa, bless her, is not going to manage this. She is all over the place. There is nothing for it. I do not want to end up with a flat battery so I turn off the Vespa's lights. Guided only by the torch that I was prescient enough to bring with me, I walk the last three quarters of a mile in the dark pushing the Vespa, with an ankle that feels as if it is being pierced by a red hot poker. I arrive at Chez Pugein, soaked through with the snow, chilled to the bone and totally exhausted. I may have made it but can I possibly help Catherine in my present condition?

I leave the Vespa under cover outside the hotel and go in. I ask for Catherine Diacre. The woman at reception shakes her head.

"No" she says. "There is no-one here of that name."

For a moment, I can't think. Then I get it. They will have registered under Jean's name. What was it? Mon…. something - Montaz? No, Montauban? No, not quite.

"She may be registered under Jean Mon… something" I say.

There is a sharp intake of breathe from the receptionist followed by an ear-splitting silence.

"What's up?" I say.

"Jean Montaut was killed this morning in a freak avalanche" comes the terrible reply. "He was with a guide who escaped the fall and immediately phoned the emergency service but Mr. Montaut was dead when they arrived."

Poor Catherine. How must she feel? Poor Jean too of course, but his suffering is over. I know Catherine wants me there as soon as possible but I cannot see her like this. My outer clothing is soaked and I am frozen. The receptionist is very kind. She tells me where I can put my wet clothes. She orders me a cup of coffee and shows me where I can warm my hands in a basin of hot water.

"Make sure it is only luke-warm or you'll get chilblains" she warns.

I am starting to feel a little bit better. I go up to Catherine's room, Room 11. It is on the first floor at the front of the hotel. I knock but do not wait for a reply. I just enter. Catherine is sitting on the bed. She is not there, if you know what I mean. There is absolutely nothing behind her eyes.

"Jacques" she says.

It is not a greeting. She is just registering the fact that I'm here as an automaton would. I sit on the bed beside her and put my arm around her. We sit in silence. Eventually she says:

"Thank you, Jacques." There is now just the slightest bit of awareness in her voice. It takes me right back to when I was thirteen and my mother died. Somehow a wheel has come full circle. I snap back to the present. This is going to be best dealt with in a business-like way.

"Have you contacted anyone?" I ask. She shakes her head. "If you have a book with the names of family and friends, I'll contact them all and let them know. Did Jean have a book like that? I'll contact those people as well."

"Jean's stuff is all in that grey suitcase over there or in the bottom drawer of the chest of drawers. I'll get you my book."

A little more feeling has crept into Catherine's voice. That is a relief. I did not like zombie-mode at all. I work methodically through Jean's book first. His parents are in Pau. I cannot see any brothers or sisters. There are a number of people in Lille and one woman in Dieppe; only ten or so in all. Two do not answer; a man in Lille and the woman in Dieppe. I write a list of the people on a piece of the hotel's paper with whether they answered or not. I start on Catherine's contacts. She has more than Jean. I hate to fuss Catherine at all. I would like to do the whole thing without bothering her but I realise that I have to know one thing.

"Catherine, do you want to talk to anybody on the list if they want to talk to you? Your parents?"

She shakes her head, "No, Jacques, nobody. Pretend I'm somewhere else."

I start with her parents. I stayed with them for a month when I was thirteen but this will not be a time to reminisce. Her mum, Anne, answers the call. She is shattered.

"He came to stay for a few days with Catherine when they first got engaged" she says. "He was such a nice man. How is Catherine taking it?"

This sort of thing shows you how difficult it is to be natural: how hard it is to cover up even the smallest of lies. If Catherine were really somewhere else, I'd tell her mother exactly how she was taking it. How she was completely vacant and hardly recording anything when I first saw her; how she has improved very slightly now I'm here. I am after all talking to her mother. But Catherine is here. She will not want me to be telling her mother how she is hardly coping with the situation at all and doesn't even want to speak to her. Catherine is my first priority.

"Oh! As you would expect" I reply. "Sorry Mrs. Diacre, I have a lot of people to phone."

I carry on down the list copying on to the hotel paper those whom I have contacted. Louise, Janine, Jeanne, Marie, Colette. Then I catch myself doing a stupid thing. Normally I would have laughed and told Catherine but I don't think that she is in the mood to hear this sort of thing. I am halfway through ringing a number, when I realise it is my own number. I have started to ring Jacques Parisel to let him know the bad news without even realising that this is me. I am obviously on auto-pilot. If, when I rang someone, the phone was not answered, I didn't leave a message. I don't think it is the way a friend should hear this sort of news. I have completed the lists. It is now late. I am not going back to Annecy to-night in this weather. I go back to reception. I ask if they have a room that I could book for tonight. I am very touched. This darling receptionist has spoken with the manager and has already arranged a room for me. Not only that, she says that the manager has agreed that the room and breakfast should be free of charge. She has put me in room 12, across the corridor from Catherine. I am at very low ebb at the moment and this brings tears to my eyes. The tragedy, the journey, the state of Catherine, this kindness of the receptionist: it is all too much. I pull myself together. There are still things to be done.

I go back up to Catherine. She is sitting on the bed in the same attitude as when I first arrived. She has however, a tiny bit more animation in her face.

"Catherine" I say, "you are not going to sleep to-night, unless you have some sort of sedative. I do not suppose for a moment that you have one with you. I suggest we go downstairs to the bar and you have just one or two, no more, stiff drinks. If nothing else, it will pass some time and I could certainly use a couple."

She does not look enthusiastic but I think she sees that it can do no harm and might just let her sleep. The bar has a nice buzz of conversation from the other guests. We get a table. I do not ask Catherine what she wants. I go to the bar and ask for two Pernods with Cranberry. I ask for them to be fifty-fifty not as a long drink of one to four or five which is more usual. I want the drink to taste strong enough to make an impression. It should help Catherine perk up just a little.

"We don't have cranberry" says the barman. "Is myrtle all right?"

"Sure" I say, "it's probably better."

"Yeah, that's what I think" says the barman, "and I agree with you fifty-fifty is good."

It occurs to me that I had found it very difficult to get to this hotel, so I ask Catherine about how people get here ordinarily. It will make her talk. Apparently the hotel runs a courtesy bus once an hour during the day to the centre of St. Jean de Sixt and back, so anyone coming in by bus from the slopes or elsewhere gets a free lift. I could certainly have used that today! There is no doubt that the Pernod does something to Catherine. She gets a lot more colour in her cheeks. Then, at last, she starts to speak about it; quite quietly with very little emotion.

"I always had this dread that something like this would happen to Jean. He was so hyped up when he came back from difficult black runs. He was so keen to go off piste. He never actually seemed to take unreasonable risks. Today" she says and her eyes clouded over, "he hired a guide. He wasn't stupid but he gets caught in a freak aval…" She stops, steadying herself, "a freak avalanche. I did have a feeling that he somehow needed that high adrenaline level from time to time. Now I think 'why couldn't it have been me?' but I know that is a ridiculous thought." She gives me a weak smile. "It is going to take me such a long, long time to get over this, Jacques. Thank you so much for coming. I needed someone and all my other friends are so far away."

"I am only glad that I could be just a little help" I say.

I go to the bar and get a repeat of the Pernod and Myrtle. Catherine and I sit in silence for a while. She is looking a little better now. Of course it takes months or years to get over this sort of tragedy but I can see that the tougher side of her nature is coming to the fore. She will cope. We sip our drinks slowly. When they have gone, Catherine says:

"You are right Jacques, I might just be able to sleep now and even if not, I am not as wound up as I was. I'm glad you've got a room and we will see each other tomorrow morning."

So we go back upstairs to bed in our rooms 11 and 12 on the first floor. Because Jean and Catherine had postponed their marriage, Jean's next of kin are his parents. It is therefore his parents that the authorities are going to contact with any of the questions that unexpected death creates. Where the body is due to be buried or cremated and so on. Catherine is free, indeed probably well advised, to leave.

The next morning we have breakfast. That is Catherine only has a coffee. I have a coffee and a couple of croissants. Catherine could stay a couple of days. It is paid for. Of course, she has decided to go back to Paris. That involves a bus to Annecy and a fairly slow train to Paris. At the moment the only TGV to Paris during the day is early in the morning. That is the one that she and Jean caught when she was showing him the sites round Annecy just after they got engaged. There is talk of a more frequent service but that is for the future. At the moment the train is fairly slow and sometimes one has to change at Lyon. I offer to go with Catherine as far as she would like me to go, even to Paris. This is a one-off situation and as far as I'm concerned, I shall do whatever she would like me to.

"No" says Catherine. "You've done your bit Jacques. Even if you come with me as far as Annecy, you'll have to come back for your scooter."

That is true. The hotel says that I can take my Vespa to St. Jean de Sixt on the courtesy bus. So Catherine and I go as far as there together. Then we part company.

I see her onto the bus to Annecy. I then drive my Vespa down the icy roads very, very carefully back to Annecy. I reach my flat and fall onto the bed. This is has been a 24 hours that I shall never forget. Then I feel so self-centred. Me? It is certainly a 24 hours that Catherine will never forget.

My loose arrangement with Guy was still working very well. I had been wondering for some time whether there might be way to make it even better. I was doing a job in Alby-sur-Chéran when I happened to overhear a conversation between a plumber and his customer about the quality of some equipment and the cost. I know little about plumbing except that household electricity and water do not go well together. It was the plumber's insistence on fitting high quality equipment that caught my attention.

Plumber: "Of course I could fit those for you but I wouldn't advise it. They'll pack up before you know it and you may well then end up blaming me. The others are only a little more in price and they will last you a lifetime."

The client is further away from me and I cannot really hear what he is saying but it sounds like a rebuttal.

Plumber: "Look mate! I'll tell you what I'll do. I'll fit you the proper equipment for the same price as you can get that poor quality, cheap stuff. I'll take the extra cost myself. I do not want to be fitting taps (I think he said but it may have been pipes) that I regard as rubbish."

I didn't hear the outcome but I managed to corner the plumber before he left.

"Hi!" I said, "I'm Jacques. I'm doing some electrical fittings next door. I'd like to buy you a drink. I've something to discuss that might interest you."

He shrugged "I'm Pierre" he replied. "I never refuse a free drink. Let's do it."

Alby-sur-Chéran is a pretty little village about halfway between Chambéry and Annecy. It has a central square which is very picturesque with shops under the arches rather like Annecy Old Town although the river is pretty much dried up in summer. We went to a bar 'Aux Petits Galets' to which neither of us had been before. It turned out to be a good choice. I had a bière blanche and Pierre had a glass of Mondeuse. We sat outside under one of the arches. The square was all hustle and bustle. As I get older I find that I am a bit more confident about this sort of thing. I mean, what is there to lose?

"Pierre" I said, "I overheard your conversation with your customer about the equipment you're fitting."

"Yes" says Pierre, "the stupid idiot is insisting on fitting some cheapo stuff just because it's a couple of quid less than high standard fittings that'll last a life time. I just do not want to do that. I said I'd be prepared to take a cut in my profit just for the sake of not being made to fit second rate equipment."

"Pierre" I say, "you are a man that I understand. That is my view as well. I recently quit a firm and went solo simply because the boss was insisting on me fitting substandard electrical equipment. I told him 'It's just not safe'. More recently I've come to this arrangement with a bricklayer and plasterer called Guy who feels the same way. We have a loose arrangement where we are not the same firm but on any reasonable occasion, we leave each other's cards or suggest each other for work that might be required. You sound to me as if you would be on the same wave length and we could all do each other a favour."

"That's very interesting" says Pierre. "I see how that could help us all."

"I'd want you to meet Guy and if we all get on over a couple of drinks perhaps we could make a threesome. As I see it a bricklayer, a plumber and an electrician almost make a complete firm yet we still keep our individual identities and independence. Later if we want we can discuss strengthening the bonds or possibly even making a single company."

"Hmmm" he says. "I'm certainly on-board for the first part. I'd like to meet Guy. I live in Chambéry. Where do you think it would be best to meet?"

"Here would probably be as good as anywhere, Pierre. I live in Annecy and Guy lives in Sévrier. Here at Alby is more or less in the middle. This is a nice picturesque little square, isn't it? Shall we make it here on: you choose a day."

"Let's make it the day after tomorrow, Thursday. If we swap cards you can give me a ring if Guy can't make it. Say 12.30 for lunch on Thursday?"

Guy was very enthusiastic. "That'll be great" he said with a grin. "This arrangement with you is letting both of us keep our heads above water. The addition of Pierre as a plumber should make it work even better. It gives us a presence in Chambéry and it'll give Pierre a presence in Annecy and round the lake. That could lead to a significant rise in orders."

On Thursday we meet for lunch in Alby. It is a lovely spring day. The sun is out. There is a bit of a chill in the air. Alby's square is buzzing. Guy and Pierre are well away telling each other little anecdotes about places they've been and jobs they've done. We all get on fine but if anything I am the odd one out. We make sure we've all got plenty of cards to give out to customers. This is an encouraging development for the future. If work increases much more I shall have to take on an assistant. That, of course, has as many obligations as it does advantages but for the moment, employment-wise things are looking very healthy.

Within days, I can put Pierre onto a job. I have been called to an old house in Sillingy. The electrics have cut out and fuse again every time they are turned on. I cannot find the fault. My test kit is telling me that the fault is in the power circuit to the kitchen and living room. I cannot find the problem. Just in case I turn off all the appliances on each circuit in turn. No Joy! I carefully search the walls of the kitchen. The water supply to the kitchen has been enclosed in chipboard which has been tiled over but on the wall alongside this, there is a small patch of damp. It is about two feet above an electric socket. The damp does not appear to reach the socket but I think water in the wall must have reached down to the socket and produced a short-circuit. I inspect the socket. The wiring is intact and in good condition but the socket is indisputably very wet. I remove the socket; insulate the wires individually then turn the circuit back on. Bingo! The problem must be a water leak in the supply to the washing machine. I show the customer what I have found; the wet socket and the patch of damp.

"The water leak is going to have to be sorted out before this socket" I tell her. I give her Pierre's card. "This is the plumber I work with. He is obsessional about doing a good job."

"It is so hard to find a reliable plumber" says she. "I shall definitely give him a try."

"OK" I say. "Let me know when the leak is fixed and I'll come and refit that socket."

I ring Pierre but his wife answers.

"Pierre Rouget's residence" she says.

"This is Jacques" I say. "I've got a potential job for Pierre."

"Pierre has left his phone behind today, I'm afraid. I'm, Nadine, his wife. Pierre was talking about you only yesterday. He was quite enthusiastic about your idea of a loose collaboration. I didn't expect it to prove itself quite so quickly."

"I suggested it, Nadine, because I was so impressed with Pierre's determination only to use high quality fitments."

Come August, I find that I am missing Diane more than I thought I would. Her easy, relaxed manner, her sense of humour, her ability to keep everything in life light-hearted and yes, I miss the feel of her body close to mine. I cannot help wondering if Henri has found another expedition to go on; preferably a year or two in Antarctica. I am trying to talk myself out of trying to trace Diane to see if Henri is away. Part of me is saying that this is like stalking someone. It is an invasion of privacy. The other half of me is saying 'Not at all, Diane indicated that she would be happy to resume the relationship if conditions were right. I am only trying to find out if conditions are right'. My two halves are having a more and more heated argument as time progresses. Then suddenly I decide that I cannot do it. Diane knows where I am. If she wants me, she can very easily contact me. I feel ridiculously proud of myself for coming to this common sense decision but I do pine after her. One evening in September, there is a ring on my doorbell. There is Diane, as I have dreamed. I am delighted to see her.

"Have you anyone with you?" she asks.

This is obviously an enquiry about the immediate present but I hope it may also be a more long-term question. Like do I have a current partner?

"Diane!" I grin from ear to ear. "No, there isn't. Come along in."

So we start another two month relationship. Diane is still relaxed, amusing, sexy. However, to me it is not the same feeling as last time. This is because I know that the affair is going to end. I even know the exact day that it is going to end. This removes the spontaneity. It does not cause any friction between us. I am glad to be seeing Diane again but when these two months are over, there is not going to be a third time. When I know the time is almost up, I take a leaf out of Diane's book. I say exactly what I am thinking. It is a form of 'Thanks for the memory'.

"I have enjoyed this immensely Diane, but I do not want to do it again."

"I know Jacques" she replies. "I agree, but it is sad isn't it?"

She is amazing; absolutely never a hard word.

In February, there is an unusual very cold snap in the weather. A lot of people especially the elderly have their heating on all day and even through the night. I receive a call from a man in Pringy just to the North of Annecy on the Geneva Road. He is a Mr. Chevallier.

"Are you Jacques? You've been recommended to me by a friend of mine" he says. "I've just received a nasty shock from one of my electric convector heaters.

I suppose that it must have developed a fault. Can you have a look at it?"

"Yes, of course" I tell him. "In the meantime turn it off if you can do so without touching it. I'll be round this evening. Would seven or eight be better?"

"I'd prefer seven" he says.

So I take his address and nip round there on my Vespa. It is no distance at all from my flat on L'Avenue de Genève. He is living in a block of twelve flats. His is a rather nice flat on the first floor overlooking a beautifully kept garden belonging to a nearby house. I comment on the garden.

"Yes, it is lovely, isn't it?" he says, "I am so lucky with that. I get all the pleasure of the flowers with none of the work. Madame Blanchet keeps it a treat. It's lovely to look at even in winter."

He shows me his radiator. As I examine it, the first thing I notice is that it has a metal casing. This he agrees is what he gave him a shock when he touched it. It is wired straight into the mains not by means of a plug and socket. I turn the circuit off at the fuse box then disconnect the heater from its wall fitting and remove the back of the casing. The radiator itself has a three point fitment for line, neutral and earth leads but the earth has not been fitted. The wire coming from the mains has only a line and neutral. The two wires that are in place have been properly fitted. I can see that further into the appliance the line wire has overheated and burnt through. It has become separated from its correct position and is touching the outer metal casing. That is what has caused Mr. Chevallier to get a shock. In itself this is a simple job to repair. It needs a fresh piece of wire to be correctly attached to the connection which is already there and meant for it. The implications of what I have found, though, go far deeper than that.

"How many of these radiators have you got here?" I ask.

"There's one in each bedroom, that's two" he says. "Then one in the lounge, one in the kitchen and this one you're looking at in the hall. So five."

"Look, Mr Chevallier" I say. "This job is very easy and cheap in itself but the implications are far bigger." I show him the burnt wire. "This is the simple part. I can repair that in say twenty minutes. But here is the real problem." I show him the three point attachment in the heater which has only got two leads where it should have three.

"This heater has a metal casing and should have an earth wire attached. The heater itself is perfectly well made but when the heater has been attached to the mains, the electrician has failed to put in an earth. The implication is that all your other heaters are incorrectly installed as well and that may even apply to all the other flats in this block."

"Yes, I can see what you mean" he replies. "I'm not knowledgeable about electrics but I know enough to see that there is a lead missing where you are pointing, inside the heater."

"The trouble here" I continue, "is that these heaters have been installed straight off the mains without an intervening socket. That is normal practice but it means that to put the whole system right, one has to go into the actual wall to access the mains. This is a bigger job which I certainly couldn't manage today even for one heater."

"You're the expert" he says. "What do you advise?" I think for a moment. The question is quite clear from an electrical point of view but from a social point of view much harder.

"Well ultimately, I have to advise that this particular heater has been faultily installed and the whole of the rest of the building needs to be looked at to see to how much of it this applies. In the short term, I can repair this heater and get it to work safely off your nearest mains socket and if you wish I would have time to wire another heater correctly and do the same for it. You would then have two safe heaters during this cold spell. Looking at another of your heaters would give an indication as to whether this faulty wiring is a one-off or whether it is likely to apply to the whole building. Then," I said, "it is up to you, but I would get your committee together and decide what to do about the whole block. Considering just today what would you like me to do?"

"I'll take your suggestion that you plug this heater into a socket temporarily and do the same for another heater, if when you look at it, there is the same faulty installation."

"OK" I say. "That will take me about an hour and I won't charge for looking at the second heater."

It takes me three quarters of an hour. The second heater in the lounge is wired exactly the same way with no earth.

"While these heaters are on" I tell him, "you can use a two way extension for your vacuum cleaner or say lights but not for any appliance that needs heat, like a tumble drier or an iron. It would also be a good idea to let the other residents know that they may have a problem."

Monsieur Chevallier is over the top with his praise for me. "Monsieur Barbier in the ground floor flat just beneath me and I are the people who keep an eye on this place and make sure it doesn't go downhill" he says. "I'll have a word with him now, this evening, and I'm sure the others will go along with whatever we suggest. Thank you Jacques, give me your card so I can recommend you to all my friends. You're a gem. It was by a recommendation from a friend in Annecy that I heard of you."

So I give him a card. This has been a job with no profit. I hope it turns out to be a loss-leader in supermarket fashion because there is probably enough work here to keep me in business for some time to come. Also because the heaters have been attached with wires that come straight out of the wall without intervening sockets, there is going to be some brick and plastering work that will keep Guy occupied as well. When I get home, I give Guy a ring and tell him to watch this space because there may well be a considerable amount of pretty straight forward work coming up in the near future. Today might just turn out to be a big break. On the other hand, it may well be that the syndicate controlling this block of flats already has a contract with a building firm including electricians and they will just hand the business to someone else. It would be very ironic if they handed it to Desplaces & Cie.

As I go to bed, a thought occurs to me. The flat owner that Mr. Chevallier was going to talk to is a Mr. Barbier. It is a common name but it is also the surname of my best friend, Georges. As I doze off, I think how interesting it would be if they were related. The next evening, my phone rings and it is Mr Chevallier in Pringy.

"Jacques" he says. "I have had a word with Daniel Barbier downstairs and we have talked to most of the other residents here. We all agreed that we would like you to do this job. However there is a bit of a hitch. We rang the secretary of the firm that manages the flats. He says they have a contract with a firm at St. Julien; the firm that installed the heaters in the first place. We pointed out that this was the very firm that had made the faulty installation. He saw the justice of that and agreed to look into the possibility of not using them in spite of the contract. In the meantime Daniel and I would like you to check the heaters in all the flats so that we can see what the extent of the problem is. We have the permission of all the proprietors to let you do this."

"OK Mr Chevallier" I say. "There are twelve flats, aren't there, with five radiators each? If I am just looking at them and not doing anything else, I can do that in a few hours and just charge a callout fee. If Thursday is all right with you, I'll do that in the morning."

So that was arranged, but still I am getting no profit out of this job. It looks as if the whole thing may be delayed by some legal problem. On Thursday, I inspect all the heaters. The owners of several of the flats were not present at the time but they had left their keys with Mr. Chevallier. The inspection does not take long. I must turn the power of the relevant circuit off at the fuse box, disconnect each heater from the wall and take the back off. It is easy to see whether there are two or three leads connected. Then I must go through the reverse process to complete the job. Every heater has been fitted with two-strand wire with no earth. All sixty of them. It takes me a little longer than I thought as each time I move to a different flat the occupant, if they are in, wants a short chat but I am finished in time for a late lunch.

After Mr Chevallier's flat, I started at the top and worked down, getting to Daniel Barbier's ground floor flat last of all. He is a friendly type. He offers me a cup of coffee when I have finished, says to take a seat and presently comes in with two cups. He sits down opposite me. I imagine that I can see some of Georges' mannerisms but I may be imagining it.

"Mr Barbier" I say. "My best friend is a Georges Barbier. We were brought up in Eymoutiers near Limoges. Barbier is quite a common name but is there any chance you might be related?"

"I don't know whether we are" he said, "but it is likely at some level. I was brought up in Limoges. In fact I lived there until twenty five years ago when I was offered promotion if I took a manager's position in St. Julien-en-Genevois. I only moved to here in Pringy when I retired and these flats were built. That's three years ago."

"Did you have any relatives around Limoges?" I ask.

"I had a younger brother, Gilbert" he replies, "but he was unmarried at the time that I left Limoges and we haven't stayed in touch. I think that it was probably my fault. I was exceptionally busy when I first moved to this area."

It occurs to me with some amazement that I do not know the first name of Georges' father. Could it be Gilbert? The name doesn't ring a bell. I know that his mother is Elisabeth as I have often heard her talking with my mother and they were naturally using first names but try as I might the name of Georges' father eludes me. Perhaps I never knew it.

"I'll ask my friend if he knows of any link. It would be interesting if you were related."

"Yes" he agrees. "Let me know if anything turns up." He gives me his phone number and I leave.

A week later I have a call from Mr. Chevallier. He informs me that the firm in St. Julien have accepted the reasoning that if it were their work that was faulty, someone else who had discovered the error was entitled to be the one who put it right. It is therefore all systems go. The way that they would like to do this is a little irritating. Apparently the firm managing the block comes regularly on a Tuesday each week. They would like the work done one flat at a time with the finished job inspected by them before work on the next flat is started. This means the work is spread, unnecessarily from my point of view, over 12 weeks. I agree, on the condition that they pay for the completed flat immediately after their inspection. This will at least ensure a weekly income for almost three months. They also agree that Guy, 'as my representative' as they put it, is the right person for any brickwork or plastering that is required. Guy is still officially with Desplaces & Cie, although he has decided that he needs to hand in his notice as he is beginning to find it difficult to cope with the work we are getting offered. We reckon that if I do a flat on Saturday, he can do whatever is required on Sunday. Their inspection is on Tuesday, when we also get paid. I hope. Apparently this sort of work on these flats is covered for the first five years by insurance that the builders in St. Julien have taken out. The residents will not have to pay. The question from our point of view is whether we get paid by the firm in St. Julien who then get reimbursed by the insurance company, or will we have to wait to get paid by the insurance company. There is a tendency for insurance firms to be absurdly slow in paying their bills, whereas most individual customers pay fairly quickly.

I ring Georges. He is surprised that I do not know the name of his father. He thinks that I must be losing my memory. He says, yes his father's name is Gilbert. I tell him that I am currently doing work for his Uncle Daniel. He is very interested in this.

"I knew I had an Uncle Daniel" he says. "My dad told me he left the area going somewhere near Geneva and was never heard of again. I was very young at the time dad told me. I remember thinking that Geneva must be a place under the spell of the wicked witch."

Georges gives a little laugh and yes, it is remarkably similar to Daniel Barbier's laugh. It is odd how a family trait like a laugh is so similar in two people that have never even met. But Georges is still talking: "It seems that they had never been very close so dad just didn't follow it up. I'd like to meet him at some time, if you can arrange that, Jacques."

"Of course, Georges" I say.

This block of flats is only three years old. Most of the owners are fairly elderly but when I get to Flat number 4, the end one on the ground floor, I am greeted by a woman in her twenties. She was not there when I completed the first inspection. I suppose she was at work. She shows me where the heaters are. Of course by now I know perfectly well where they are. I imagine she is just wanting to say a few words before I get to work. All the residents have been like that. It is very friendly. When I have done three of the five heaters she offers me a cup of coffee and I am glad to say 'yes please'. I work on the fourth and she brings me the coffee.

"Why don't you take a break" she suggests. "Take a seat in the living room."

I do that and she sits in another chair. "I'm Marianne" she says. "I teach at the Elementary School here at Pringy. I bought this flat when they were new. They were completed at just the right time for me to move in, just before the appointment started. Mr Chevallier upstairs says that he has had several reports of your work. Everybody seems to say you're so neat and tidy and never create a mess."

"I do my best" I say. "This job involves getting into the wall to replace the flex that has two wires with one that has three. It inevitably makes a bit of a mess of the wall and plaster. I work with a mason and plasterer called Guy who is going to repair any damage to the wall. These heaters are quite safe with the wiring that they have until they develop a fault. Then they may cause a shock."

I find Marianne very attractive. She has dark brown hair and eyes that sparkle as she talks. If the circumstances were different I would ask her out but to enter her flat and make any kind of advance would be a complete breach of trust. I complete the work on the fourth and fifth heaters.

"My colleague, Guy should be here tomorrow" I say as I leave.

A couple of days later, I am in the Carrefour Supermarket in north Annecy. It is on the Avenue de Brogny; no distance from my flat and only two miles from Pringy. I see Marianne looking over the fresh vegetables. I go over.

"Hello, Marianne."

"Oh! Hello Jacques. This is a surprise. Do you live near here?"

"Yes in L'Avenue de Genève just a few minutes away."

"I often come here" says Marianne. "It has a lot more in it than the supermarkets in Pringy."

I take the bull by the horns. "This" I say, "is an entirely unplanned meeting but after meeting you at your flat, I have been thinking that it was a pity that I wouldn't be seeing you again. Might we meet for a meal some time?"

I cannot say that she looks thrilled. There is a significant hesitation but she does say:

"Yes, Jacques, that would be nice."

We settle for one o'clock on Saturday, in a few days' time. I say that I will book Les Jardins de l'Auberge. Marianne knows where that is. I arrive earlier than 1 o'clock. Go inside to check that she is not there. It is highly unlikely but it would be disaster to wait outside if she had already arrived. While I'm in there I check that we've been given a window table. They are so much nicer overlooking the Thiou. I then go outside again and wait for Marianne. She arrives a few minutes late, about five past. Marianne looks terrific. I said she was attractive when I saw in her flat. Now she is eye-catching. She is wearing a striking blouse which is high neckline and a skirt which is mid-calf but they manage to show a beautiful figure without showing much of Marianne. I am glad that I have also made a bit of an effort. I am wearing pale beige trousers and a new in-vogue jacket. She looks pleased to see me which is a relief as she was obviously rather doubtful about coming. We have salad followed by Fera, the fish from the lake (The name of the fisherman is mentioned on the menu). I ask for a carafe of house white which is Apremont. Marianne does not want a sweet but we have coffee. The conversation goes well. I tell her about some of the more interesting houses I have worked in, including the story of the potential ghost, which she finds interesting. She tells me of some of the funnier moments with the younger children at school. She also told me that when she was looking for a teaching post in this area, she had looked at The Gabriel Fauré School which is in central Annecy. Fauré's Requiem had been on at the Bonlieu at the time so on a whim, she had got a ticket to it. She had thoroughly enjoyed it. Unfortunately the advertised post had not been what she was after whereas the one in Pringy suited her much better.

Although it is October, it is a sunny day with little wind and we walk to the lake and follow it along to Le Parc des Marquisats. I remember the same walk with Sylvie. This lady is a different proposition. I cannot see anything like that kiss being repeated. I think I can risk taking her hand in mine. I do this by distracting her and doing it mid-sentence.

"Aren't the little sailing boats with" (take her hand) "children cute out in the middle of the lake?"

Again she doesn't actually grab her hand away but certainly doesn't give the idea that she was thinking it might be a nice idea herself. When we get to the end of the park where Sylvie and I had our first kiss, I drop her hand as we turn to go back. It is a pleasant walk, a pleasant day but in terms of romance I do not feel that I have made any progress at all.

"Thank you Jacques, that was a lovely meal and I enjoyed the walk."

"That's good, Marianne. May I see you again? Say next Saturday?"

Again that hesitation but again agreement.

"Yes, shall we make it evening? We could take in a show."

"Great" I say. "I'll book something and give you a ring. I've already got your phone number in case I needed it for the job. Are the heaters OK?"

"Yes, Guy came and made good the wall but really you left it in very good condition. Yes, Jacques. You book something for Saturday evening and we can arrange when and where to meet when you ring me."

Just the merest little trace of enthusiasm there, I think. On the other hand, perhaps not. We part very amicably but there is no sign of the spark that I experienced with both Sylvie and Diane on the first date.

So I have the problem of what to book for next Saturday evening. I run through the usual sorts of things one might do. Then I remember her saying that she had booked a ticket for Fauré's requiem and enjoyed it. The way she had said it suggested that she was not actually a fan of classical music but had found, perhaps with surprise, that she enjoyed it. The timing suggested to me that Fauré's requiem was on at that time because it was the centenary of its first public performance and Fauré is associated with Annecy because of the summer holidays that he used to take in the region. I looked at what was playing at Bonlieu scène nationale on Saturday. It was again music. That was lucky because they do all sorts of different stuff there. Vivaldi's 'Four Seasons' was on. I grin to myself. I think anyone who enjoyed Fauré's requiem is going to love the 'Four Seasons'. If Marianne is not a classical music fan she is bound, I think, to prefer Vivaldi's light hearted cheerful work to a requiem. If she is a classical music lover she will like it anyway. The way Marianne dressed for lunch suggests to me that she would not appreciate cheap seats. The seating at this site is slightly unusual. As well as the two main aisles going from back to front and one in the middle going side to side, there are two small aisles penetrating no more than ten seats on each side. The seating is also slightly fanned with there being more seats per row at the back. This means that the aisle seats in row F that are not in the central block have leg room and a completely unobstructed vision. They are also a little way back from the stage so that the view is far more comfortable than in the front row. Ideal. So the best seats in the house are F24 and F25 with F8 and F9 a close second. 24 and 25 have gone but I am very lucky to get F8 and 9. I book them. I give Marianne a ring and tell her that I have booked Vivaldi's Four Seasons. Again there is that hesitancy. It makes me feel uncomfortable as if she is making a real effort not to say 'No'.

We arrange to meet in the café on the corner of rue du Pâquier, near the Bonlieu centre. It has an upstairs with a view to the canal, lake and mountains. The theatre bar is likely to be crowded out. She arrives right on the dot of the time arranged. Does this lady know how to dress or does she? Marianne looks stunning. She has on a purple and blue trouser suit in alpaca and cashmere bouclé. Again it shows her to perfection at the same time keeping her completely covered up. Any man would be proud to be seen escorting a woman like this. I feel very humble. No wonder she is hesitant, slumming it with her electrician. I almost feel embarrassed. Marianne has a glass of Beaumes de Venise. I have a bière blanche. I tell her how much I like the suit she is wearing. It would be an insult not to. She looks pleased with that. I chatter nervously about how good a view it is and what a shame it is that the weather is not a little warmer because the balcony would be open. After a couple of minutes, my nervousness goes and I start to enjoy being with her. We go into the theatre. There is no doubt at all that many an eye is following us and it is not me they are looking at. When we reach our seats there is a sea change in Marianne. She gets back that beautiful sparkle in her eyes as she talks that attracted me to her so much in her flat. She smiles at me. For the first time since I asked her out, my heart is responding as I expected it to.

"These are first class seats, Jacques" she says. "No-one in front and set a little back. I hate having to crane my neck throughout a show. These must be a couple of the best in the theatre."

"They must have had a cancellation, I think. I felt lucky to get them only one week before the performance."

I love Vivaldi's 'Four Seasons'. I find it a joyful piece of music. Sitting next to Marianne and seeing her loving it too, I was amazed at how much my feelings had changed in just a few minutes from being a bit ashamed and out of my depth to simple pleasure with both the music and with sitting next to Marianne. The performance was spellbinding. Neither Marianne nor I moved an inch. I noticed that there were two women sitting to one side of the musicians throughout the Vivaldi. There is a custom with musical performances which I suppose has something to do with value for money that in order to make a performance last an acceptable time another piece is added. For me this often breaks the spell and so it was with the Vivaldi. I like Offenbach but it does not compare. In this case it was a selection from Offenbach's 'Tales of Hoffmann'. This is what the women sitting down taking no part in the 'Four Seasons' are for; a soprano and contralto waiting for the famous Barcarolle 'Oh beautiful night; Oh Night of love'. Not tonight, I think. Marianne may have a dreamy expression on her face after the beautiful music but …

Marianne is elated "Jacques" she says, "what a lovely choice. That music is divine and the solo violinist was superb."

When we have left the theatre and are in the Bonlieu centre, I suggest a taxi to take her home and I shall stay in it to get back to my flat. Marianne agrees. We are sitting quite close in the back. As we reach Marianne's flat she turns to me and kisses me on the lips. It is short. It is not passionate. I get a gentle whiff of her perfume. It is light, with high-pitch tones and fragrant. I remember Diane's. It was warm, with deep tones and very sexy. Marianne's kiss may not have been long, passionate or sexy but it stays deliciously on my lips all the way back home. She is confusing me badly but I think I am hooked. Over the next months, Marianne and I go to the cinema, the theatre. We go to museums. The 'Animation' museum at Annecy is famous. I invite her back to my flat but she says no. I keep getting confusing messages. One minute she seems to be all over me and the next repelling me with some force. I am at a loss. However lovely Marianne is, I do not feel about her quite the same way as Sylvie or Diane. I think probably because of these perpetual mixed messages. You know, she will let me give her a hug one moment and then it's:

"No, No, that's enough, leave me alone now." I am perplexed. She will not come to my place and she will not invite me to her place. In short, she is frightened of being alone with me. I love being with her. I love her kisses but they are always very short.

I have been doing very well in business. Far better than I thought would happen and I now have a tidy bit saved. I want to give a party but my flat isn't big enough. I need to hire a hall. I do not feel that I can afford some grand place like L'Impérial. I am happy to have a nice venue where we can bring our own food and drink and clear up afterwards. It would nice to have some feature to make it a little special, a view of the lake say or a river or mountain view. I research this for some time. I cannot find a site that is convenient, affordable and with any special feature. Eventually I settle for a set of rooms in Le Boulevard du Fier. It is very close to my flat and easily accessible from Pringy. It can be hired from six in the evening but must be in immaculate condition by six in the morning. There is 45 sq. metres of hall in two rooms with a kitchenette and loo. There is some limited parking. It costs more to hire than I had anticipated but is affordable. There should be just under twenty people that I wanted to invite. Marianne has two couples and two single women that she would like to come. We reckon 20 to 25 including ourselves. Marianne suggests Valentine's Day for the party. It is a Friday this year so no-one will have to get back to work the next morning. I think that is a nice touch.

"That is a great idea" I tell her. "Let's do that."

A few of those invited were coming from a long way away and might not be able to make it. Jules was in Provence and had a girlfriend, Georges was in Lyon and did not. I wanted to invite Catherine. She was in Paris. I did not know quite how she had got on after the disaster of Jean's death. She had sent a couple of emails but they really only described how she was progressing at The Sorbonne, which as usual appeared to be very well indeed. I sent her an invitation saying 'bring a friend of either sex if you like'. She sent an email back almost immediately saying that she would bring her friend Jeanne who was on the same course as she was. All the rest were in the Annecy area. Guy was still seeing Eugénie. There was Pierre and his wife Nadine. It was essential that Georges and Daniel Barbier came because that was the main purpose of the party. I invited Mr Chevallier as he had been instrumental in me finding Marianne and finding Daniel Barbier. I invited Claude and Marie. Rather grudgingly I invited Dominique and his wife. I was delighted when everyone accepted the invitation. However it did mean that there were five people coming from a distance. Marianne very kindly said that Catherine and Jeanne could have her spare bedroom if they didn't mind sharing. I couldn't help thinking that she wouldn't let me into the flat at all. I could put up Georges. I asked Jules if he could make his own arrangements. I didn't know whether he and his girlfriend, her name was Barbara, were on same bedroom terms or not. He said that was fine. He'd book a hotel room but in the end they couldn't come. Marianne and I worked hard getting food and drink in and arranging the place so that it looked in party mode. Marianne looked delectable in a pale blue mid-length skirt and a loose fitting multi-coloured blouse. It gave off a really happy party feeling. I gave her a kiss and a hug being very careful not to spoil her hair. The faint smell of her perfume was enticing.

"Thanks for working so hard on getting this ready" I say to her. "I really appreciate it when you're all dressed up for the party."

"I'm looking forward to it" she says.

We had put 19.30 to midnight on the invitations. At quarter to eight, people started to arrive. The first were Guy and Eugénie.

Catherine 2001–2003

I am on the train back to Paris. I am very embarrassed at what I have put Jacques through. I certainly needed someone to be with me that first day. He was the only friend near enough to help. I had no idea what I was asking of him. Today when we left the hotel, I saw the smashed up Vespa on which Jacques had managed to reach me. He never told me that he had had an accident until I asked about the Vespa. He had managed to hide his damaged foot from me yesterday indoors but he could hardly walk this morning. After we had parted company and I was on the bus back to Annecy, I saw how the roads were snow-bound and frozen. Poor Jacques. That journey must have been an absolute nightmare. He did it willingly for me. I shall owe him for that for the rest of my life. It is strange we seem to see each other so seldom and only at the most dramatic times of our lives. I don't know how I am going to get over the death of Jean. I love him so much. He still seems a part of my life. Even now when I was thinking how kind Jacques had been, I was also thinking Jean will think that was so nice of Jacques. I can give myself a little time to mourn Jean but I must not let this ruin the rest of my life. I am surprised to see Jeanne when I get off the platform at La Gare de Lyon. I have some very kind friends.

"Hello Catherine" Jeanne says cheerfully. "I am devastated for you about Jean but I am not going to mention it again unless you do. Come and have a coffee."

We find a coffee shop and sit. Jeanne keeps a steady flow of conversation about the inconsequential things she has been doing in the last few weeks. Then we head back to my flat. There, waiting on the doorstep, so to speak, is Louise. She gives me a big hug.

"I thought I'd come uninvited and spend a week with you" she says. "I thought you'd arrive about now. I've only been waiting quarter of an hour." I introduce them.

"Jeanne and Louise, I am so glad that you have now met. You two are my very best friends."

We go inside and having two friends there is so much easier than having one. They can ignore me and talk to each other if I am in sombre mood yet I can join in if I wish. I am already realising that I am tough enough that I am not going to let this interfere with my legal studies. Jeanne and Louise seem to get on very well. They chat about University life and Louise describes a little of the plant research that she is involved with. Jeanne leaves after a while to go back to hers. Louise says that she will cook dinner. She has very thoughtfully bought food realising that there might not be much in the flat as I was not expecting to be back just yet. For the next week Louise and I re-explore much the same features of Paris that we did those years ago when I first came here. I cannot say that it was as enjoyable as last time as I got occasional spells of abject misery. Louise was brilliant at ignoring me when I wanted to be ignored and talking me out of it when I needed some of that. Time passes as it always does and Louise has gone back to Toulouse.

Several of the people at work seem to be deliberately avoiding me. I suppose that they just don't know what to say. I have not really been here at this firm long enough to be well known. There is a clerk called Anna who seems very nice and we have taken to having lunch together from time to time. This job is busy. That is a help because I seldom think of Jean during the day. When I get back to my flat in the evening, I do feel very lonely. I have my studying to do too. This part of the course is not just an apprenticeship, learning about the practicalities of the job of a notaire, there are also more frequent exams than there were on the earlier parts of the training. I am lucky that I seem to be sleeping all right, so I am not getting in to the firm in the morning already tired. Jeanne is with a firm called Lambert-Régnier in Avenue de la République. She has moved from where she was living which was quite close to me. She is now in rue Mesley, which is in the 3rd Arrondissement. I am glad that metro line 5 runs from the metro station République which is very near her new flat to close to where I am. It is early evening and I am on my way to visit her to see what her new place is like. It is on the 6th floor of a 7 storey building.

When I arrive, I find that it is one of those typical Parisian buildings with a central courtyard. Jeanne's flat faces in towards the central courtyard, so it is very quiet. Also being almost at the top of the building it is quite light. The top floor rooms only have skylights but Jeanne's has proper windows that you can see out of. All that is very nice but the rooms are minute. The kitchen area is a small part of the living room, which itself, only has room for a table and dining chairs. The bedroom has a double bed that stows into the wall.

There is just room for a sofa alongside the bed and a chair with a small coffee table at the end of the bed. You cannot sit on the sofa unless the bed has been stored. There is also a small room with a loo and a shower. The whole flat is light, airy and quiet but very small. Jeanne makes us coffee which we take into the bedroom Jeanne sits on the sofa so I take the armchair.

"I think that you've made a good choice here, Jeanne" I say. "It is lovely and quiet and looking inwards onto the courtyard, you don't get any of the traffic fumes. Being so high it is very light and you can see the sun almost to the last minute before it sets. The flats lower down in the courtyard will get dark much sooner."

"Yes, I think so too, Catherine. It is certainly very small but as you can see, as long as I stow the bed, this bedroom turns into a very nice little sitting room. Have you noticed that the windows are quite low and wide so from where you are sitting it is really quite a good view? It is expensive but all of central Paris is almost prohibitive. I am in easy walking distance of the notaires that I am with and République metro is even closer."

Jeanne makes us fish and chips for dinner. It is very nice but she does not regard herself as a cook. It is frozen fish fingers and oven fries followed by ice cream. I think of the contrast with the special meal that I cooked for mum….and Jean…..I get a bit melancholy. Jeanne puts on some Jazz. It is Sidney Bechet. It is great. I love Bechet. It may be old fashioned but for me there is no jazz better. I remember thinking about mum. Those who have a reason to be depressed can be snapped out of it. Those with medical depression, endogenous I think they call it, only get worse if someone tries to cheer them up. It just emphasises that they can't. The thought cheers me up even more. I leave to get back to my flat. Neither of us can afford to get behind with the studies. It is amazingly easy to get home. I virtually fell out of Jeanne's flat into République Metro station, took the Metro to Place d'Italie and my flat is as close to that metro as Jeanne's is to République. Both our flats are on the 6th floor. When I get home someone is repairing the lift. Oh well!

A couple of months go by and I am mending well. My birthday is coming up. 23 seems so old and I've still a lot of time before I'm a qualified notaire though I am now well on the way. I think that I shall have a little party; just a small hen party. It may turn out to be only Anna, Jeanne and me. I also invite Louise. I'm sure she won't come. Toulouse is over 500 miles away but asking her maintains our friendship. I also thought that I might invite Marie. She has that job in Rouen. Jeanne and I haven't seen her since she started the post. It would be interesting to know if she is pleased with her decision to give up the last bit of the Masters 2 course. Everyone accepts. I break down for a minute when Louise's acceptance arrives. She'll really come all that way just for my birthday. I remember that she was actually waiting outside my flat for me to arrive home after she heard of the death of Jean. She is so good to me. That leads me to a thought of Jacques. I wonder how they would get on if I introduced them. Not that there is much chance of that. They are also hundreds of miles apart.

I decide to cook a variety of Quiches. They are so much nicer home-made and they freeze well. I cannot resist making some little Vacherin cakes. They are typical for a celebration. The way I do them is three layers of meringue with vanilla ice cream between the first two layers, raspberry sorbet between layers two and three and Chantilly over the top layer of meringue. I go easy on the Chantilly and add a glacé cherry on the top, largely for the look. That's six layers or seven if you count the cherry. I have a silly thought. It would be fun to make them all different just by putting a different small fruit on each at the last moment when serving them. So I could make one with, say, a raspberry, a myrtle, a small grape, a strawberry and the glacé cherry.

It turns out to be a very relaxed party. Everyone seems to get on very well. Marie is delighted with her job in Rouen. She is also very pleased to see Jeanne and me again. She is a little hyper about her job: 'best decision of my life': 'don't know what I'd have done if I'd had been forced to stay on that course', etcetera. Jeanne and I know that she was, in fact, very doubtful about leaving. I'm glad she is so happy in the job. I see it as a sort of memorial to Jean. He helped her so much. Anna seems a bit subdued. It may be that it is only because she has not known me as long as the others. They have mostly met each other before although it is the first time that Louise and Marie have met. No, I think there is a bit more to it than that. Something is upsetting Anna. I do not think it has anything to do with any of us here. I must keep my eyes open. At about 11.30 everyone gets up to go. Louise says that she'll stay the night and leave in the morning.

At my apprenticeship, Favre et Dubois, rue Racine, I start keeping an eye on Anna. She is behaving quite normally but seems a bit down. On the Tuesday after my weekend party, we have lunch together, as we usually do on Tuesdays and Fridays. At the end of the meal, she gets up to go to the toilet. I pay the bill (we take it in turns and it is my turn) and follow her. She is putting some cream on a nasty looking bruise on her left arm. She covers it quickly and I pretend not to notice. This bruise might well be incidental but it might have something to do with Anna's rather withdrawn, moody nature these days. A few weeks go by and I think that I am imagining it. Then one day she has a limp. It is only slight and she is trying to hide it. 'Why is she hiding it?' I ask myself. How long should I wait before I ask her what is going on? I decide that I shall let it go but the next time that I think she is trying to hide an injury, I shall confront her with it. May runs into June. Anna seems happier. Then on a Monday in early July, she is once again trying to hide a limp. I say to her quite cheerfully:

"Shall we have lunch together, today Anna, I feel like a chat."

Anna is fine with that. When we are seated, I confront her with it.

"What is going on Anna? You are getting far more injuries than is reasonable and for some reason you're trying to hide it. If I twisted my ankle or something, I'd let people know. So what's going on?"

Her eyes fill with tears. "If I tell you" she says, "do you promise not to tell anyone else?"

"I'll promise not to tell anyone unless you agree to it or I think that you're in real danger." I say. She looks very sad and is fighting back the tears rather unsuccessfully.

"It's André" she says, "my partner. We used to be so close until recently. He's a motor mechanic. He lost his job in March and doesn't seem to be able to get another one. He has started hitting me when he's annoyed. He always finds some excuse; something that I've done or he thinks I have done. Then he loses his temper and hits me. It happened for example after your birthday party. He accused me of being unfaithful to him. I assured him that there weren't even any men there to be unfaithful with. He called me a lying bitch and hit me hard on my arm. It hurt me quite badly. I had a nasty bruise and found it very difficult to hide it. We're not married but we were, or seemed to be, so much in love that we have put down a deposit on a small flat. We went fifty-fifty on the deposit and it is in both our names. It makes it difficult to know what to do."

"Yes, we will have to think about that" I tell her. "For the moment, I shall give you my phone number and my address. Any time that you feel that you need to, you can come and stay with me. We need to find out what the law is exactly about your co-ownership. That ought to be easy. As you are trying to keep this secret, you will not want to use Favre et Dubois but I have good contacts that can help there. Then you need to think very clearly, with no melodrama, about what you regard as the best outcome. If he stops this atrocious behaviour, do you still love him or has he gone too far? That sort of thing. Do you want to have the deposit on the flat back or do you want to stay there with or without André? Write it all down, one lunchtime, not at home. You certainly don't want André seeing it. When you've done that, give it to me and I'll think about what is the best way to achieve whatever it is you want to result from all this. You want evidence. In the best case scenario, you won't need it but start trying to collect it.

Take a picture of any injury. If you can, buy a small recorder that you can turn on easily so that you can record for example if he is accusing you of something, like being unfaithful with my non-existent male friends. On another tack, do you know why he lost his last job or do you have any thoughts about why he cannot get another because one outcome might be that he just finds employment."

Anna is looking at me the same way that I look at Louise when she is being practical.

"You are so helpful Catherine" she says. "If nothing else, you have made me happier for the rest of the day."

When I get home, I ring Jeanne. I tell her that an unmarried client has the problem of a fifty-fifty stake in a property shared with a partner. We both know that one of two owners can force a sale but I think that in this case the person involved would like to be able to stay in the property. Does she know any relatively easy way that this could be achieved or can she tactfully ask one of her bosses? She says she'll think about it. Only half an hour later she rings back.

"Anna's boyfriend is beating her up is he?" says Jeanne. "And she wants him out of the house. There is one way that I think she could legally sort this but the trouble is that as budding notaires, it certainly must not get out that we had anything to do with it because it is a bit sharp."

I stand there with my mouth open and a silly expression on my face. I forgot that Jeanne has this unique perception, this sixth sense that seems to tell her everything the speaker is keeping hidden. Now I have betrayed Anna's trust. At least it is Jeanne. I know I can trust her.

"Anna doesn't want it known, Jeanne. Please don't tell anyone that it is her."

"Of course I won't" she says.

"Before you tell me what you think, how did you know it was Anna?"

"I noticed at your party that she had a fading bruise on one leg. I didn't think anything of it until now. She was also rather subdued, as if she had a problem. Now you come to me with a legal problem about property. It is one that involves two people falling out. You're pretty well qualified yourself and you work for notaires for heaven's sake. You'd ask them if you could. Therefore you can't. That means that it is someone in the firm. Anna is your friend and therefore likely to be the one confiding in you. So Anna it is."

"Jeanne you are a miracle. You really should have aimed for being a barrister. That talent of yours is not going to be anything like as helpful when you're a notaire. What do you think?"

"I'm serious that we should not get involved Catherine really I am. Would you like to come over for a meal tonight and we can talk over old times at Uni?"

"Sure, Jeanne, I'd be up for that. I'll see you in an hour or so."

I get it. Who knows if it's true or not but a lot of people think our mobile phones are perpetually being tapped. Jeanne, I'm sure, will tell me what her idea is but she is obviously serious that we shouldn't get involved. The scheme must be legal but a bit close to the wind. Notaires have a very high standard to keep up and have to be seen to be entirely unbiased at all times. Telling one of two owners how to pull a fast one on the other would end our careers before they started. I realise that I don't even know if that is the solution Anna wants but it is what I'd want if it were me. A man that has hit you three or four times already cannot be trusted not to do it again. I'd want him out. Also I'd want to keep somewhere to live. I take the metro to Jeanne's. It only takes a few minutes and as Place d'Italie is a terminus, I get a seat.

Jeanne is laughing at me. In a kind way I'm glad to say.

"I can just imagine you standing in your flat with the phone in your hand, your mouth wide open and a silly expression on your face." She bursts out laughing again. This girl has a vivid imagination and it is so often spot on. She pours us a glass of wine each. We do not usually drink wine at each other's or we'd be squiffy half the time but Jeanne obviously thinks the occasion deserves it. I take a gentle sip.

"So what's your idea?" Jeanne checks her phone is off and even asks me for mine, pulls down the bed, sticks them under a pillow and stows the bed again.

"OK Catherine, listen. Because here in France Joint-Ownership is said 'never to be forever', a single owner of a property with more than one owner can sell their share. The other owners have the first right to buy but do not have to. We both know that, OK? So the first question is whether Anna's boyfriend…"

"André" I interject.

"Right, whether André can afford to and would want to buy Anna out. If she is going to sell, that cannot be stopped."

"I don't know, but as he hasn't got a job I very much doubt that he could buy her out."

"Let's assume that he won't then. Anna arranges for someone she knows well to buy the flat. A maternal uncle would be ideal if that is practical; different name; low risk of people catching on; high likelihood of him playing ball. André and also Anna are kicked out. Anna's uncle sells the flat back to Anna or just lets her stay there; some flexible arrangement. This scheme does have costs. The flat is potentially sold twice. Each has a cost. Anna is now responsible for paying all the outgoings. It is quite likely that there will be capital loss as well if there are two quick sales. Anna would have to find somewhere to live while she didn't own it otherwise the underhand nature of the scheme would be so obvious that it might cause trouble. Mortgages could also be a problem, particularly if they have a joint mortgage."

"That is very clever, Jeanne, brilliant even and as you say it would not actually be illegal. I hope it doesn't come to that. Anna is going to think about it at lunch and write down clearly what is the outcome she wants. I have not met this André. It is possible that he would just let Anna buy him out if it were a slightly generous deal."

I hold my glass up for us to touch glasses. "Thank you, Jeanne, it is always nice to have a plan in the back ground."

We finish our glasses. Jeanne pours another. We sit and chat until eleven then she gives me my phone back and I take the metro back home. The next day, I go to a camping store and buy a blow-up mattress and a sleeping bag. I know that I have shared my bed with Jean and also with Louise. But you have to be a very special person to do that. I think I am going to have to put Anna up for a bit, but she can sleep on the floor.

I am with Anna for lunch. On a piece of paper, she has her best case scenario and a list of priorities within it.

"What I should really like, Catherine, is to not have to live with André any more. That is my priority. I should also like to remain living in the flat that he and I are both in at the moment. In addition, I should like André to have a job. I do not wish him any harm. André told me that he lost his job because he failed to connect a petrol feed to one of the cylinders of a six cylinder car. He said a six cylinder car doesn't run as badly as all that on five cylinders. It was a while before the owner brought it back saying something was wrong. When a colleague opened the bonnet, there was petrol spurting on to the hot cylinder-head and it might have all gone up in flames. They said that this was a really dangerous mistake and that he must take a six week refresher course at his own expense. He said that he couldn't afford to do that; he was only just managing to pay for the flat as it was. So they sacked him. I imagine that he cannot get a job because word has got around."

"Right. I get the picture. Anna, what can you afford? One way or another, this is going to cost some money. I mean can you afford to buy André's half? Can you afford the full rent? Could you afford a little bit over the top if it sweetens André and allows some of this to happen? Then are you lucky enough to have a doting relative who would be prepared to help out a little, either on a one off basis or an allowance for a limited length of time?"

"Hmmm, that is difficult to say because obviously it depends on how much. I have enough saved to buy André's half unless prices have rocketed. I am on a wage now where I could pay the total rent but only just. I think it would leave me a bit short but I'd manage. My parents couldn't help. They are not at all well off. I had been thinking of sending them a percentage of my wages but that is now certainly out. I have an Uncle Blaise who thinks the world of me and is reasonably well off. He might be prepared to give or lend me some. I don't think he'd like the idea of any long-term arrangement. I wouldn't like to ask him but I will manage to do so if that proves necessary."

"OK; let me suggest a plan and we can see what you think. First, from now until any negotiations are over, avoid any row with André. As far as possible, no matter how unpleasant he is, try not to respond. We want him neutral or even in favour of the plan, not against it just because you've had a recent row. I shall come with you but after an introduction, telling him that I am a trainee notaire and I am not allowed to take sides, I shall not say anything unless either of you asks me to comment. You tell André something along the lines: You don't bear him any animosity but him hurting you on those occasions means that you cannot trust him anymore. You would like to buy out his share at a realistic market price. He probably will not be keen because he hasn't got a job and will be unable to see how the future will unfold. If that is the case, you can tell him that you will pay him the amount of the six week course. That is where your Uncle Blaise might be handy. If he thinks you're wonderful, I imagine he will cash out a bit when he hears your story of being beaten up and having to find a way out of the situation. In case you don't know, the law is that if you want to sell your half, you can. Nobody can stop you. André has the legal right to buy it at market value if he wants, but if he does not, you can sell it. If nobody wants it, and I can't see that they would if André is going to be living there, the whole flat, legally, must be sold."

Next, I tell her Jeanne's back-up plan: that she could sell it to Uncle Blaise then buy it back from him. There would be some complications with the mortgage that might cost a bit. I point out that as far as organising plan B goes, she is on her own. Neither Jeanne nor I are going to be anywhere near to help, because the plan is a bit close to the wind and we have to be squeaky clean. She gets the scene.

"If we can get the agreement that you want, Anna, I think it would be best for you to stay with me for a bit, if you don't mind a mattress on the floor. I think you'd be vulnerable to a kiss-and-make-up session and in the long run I'm sure that would be a mistake. So pack your things tonight, just in case."

"You're a marvel, Catherine. Do thank Jeanne for Plan B for me. When will you be able to come and see André with me?"

"I could come after work tomorrow or would you like several days to practise what you are going to say?"

"No, I don't think so thanks Catherine. I think it is pretty clear in my mind. Tomorrow would be fine."

So the next evening, we leave the firm together and go to Anna's place. I do appreciate the allowance that my father gives me. My flat is so much nicer than Anna's and so much bigger than Jeanne's. This one is about the same size as mine but in a much rougher neighbourhood and somewhat run down. We enter and André is already there. Anna introduces me and says that she wants a serious word with him. He scowls at me rather ominously. I give him the spiel of a notaire having to remain unbiased: I'm just there to see fair play. He looks sceptical. I add that I shall not say a word unless he or Anna actually asks me to do so. So the serious stuff now starts. Anna says that she doesn't have any ill feelings but the romance is over and she would like to buy his share. He looks quite positive but wants details. She says full market rate. He says that the trouble is that, with nowhere to live and no job, the money is going to run out in no time. He will then be on the streets, completely broke. He looks fit to breakdown and I can see his fists clenching and unclenching. With me there he is not going to use them I hope.

Anna says that she will add the cost of his six week course if she can manage to borrow it off her uncle or at a cheap rate of interest anywhere else. André honestly seems to appreciate this gesture. Things appear to be looking up.

"That is really good of you Anna. I feel rotten now, treating you the way I did. I seemed to have to take it out on someone."

I saw Anna's face soften. Don't do it, I thought, but I had promised not to say anything. I am just a fly on the wall.

"Oh André" says Anna "I wish it had worked out." I sigh internally. Please not a reconciliation. "But I'm never going to be able to trust you again. I am so sorry."

There is a silence. Neither of them speaks for what seems an age. Then André says:

"If you can manage to pay the going rate for my part of the flat, that is the deposit and my bit of whatever we have so far paid off and for my six week refresher course which is about 50,000 francs or 7,500 of these new-fangled euro things that banks seem to be doing some business in these days, then I'll take it. It will help me get a new job. I really am sorry that I've messed things up for us, Anna. It was going so well."

Again I can see Anna's face soften and have to bite my tongue. Ultimately, after another silence, Anna says:

"Sorry André, next time you have a problem, you cannot guarantee that you won't do the same again. This is the best way."

Anna and I leave together. I feel a glow of contentment that this has gone so well. I am now however, stuck with the results of being such a soft touch. Anna is going to be staying with me for an indefinite period of, I imagine, at least two months. I realise that even Jean never did that!

The two months pass without us falling out although I am starting to wish that I hadn't made the offer for Anna to stay. This is a one bedroom flat. It is all right if you share the bed but having a blow-up mattress on the sitting room floor every morning is getting on my nerves. Anna's Uncle Blaise has come across like a good'un. He will have nothing to do with an allowance but he has paid for André's course and an additional 10,000 francs to help Anna over the transitional period. He says to take it as a gift. He does not want any repayment. André has finished his refresher course and has been short-listed for a job. The mortgage company have been happy to transfer the mortgage to Anna alone with an administration charge of 500 francs. That is the sort of thing that Uncle Blaise's extra cash is useful for. The money payment to André is due next week. It is irritating that everything takes so long when really this might be regarded as a simple arrangement among friends but as a notaire to be, I know full well that anything to do with real estate has to be done exactly according to the book. To be fair, this payment will be on the quicker side of average. It goes through correctly. André admits that he has got it. It takes him three days to find a suitable place to stay. I am relieved about that. I was afraid that he would spin it out deliberately. Given the initial situation that he had hit Anna hard on numerous occasions, it has to be said that André has behaved better than I could have hoped.

After work, I go round with Anna to what is now her flat just in case there is a problem. André is still there but he has packed.

"Well Good-bye Anna" he says. "Give me one last kiss for old times' sake." And she does. I don't believe it. Somebody punches you on multiple occasions so hard you get bruises and you give him one last kiss. Not me. I don't understand my own sex. This is a long kiss too. No quick peck on the cheek. It is a real clinch. Anna is not trying to pull away. This is mutual. At last they break it off and André goes out of the door. Anna collapses in floods of tears.

"I don't know what I shall do without him" she sobs.

Suddenly I can't take it. I think of Jean. Yes it is hard, very hard to do without someone you love. I almost join Anna in the sobbing session. My eyes get moist but I tell myself 'you're tougher than that Catherine'. Thank heavens I am.

It is a relief when Anna leaves. There is no doubt that I felt the tension, sharing the flat with her for slightly over two months. We are still good friends and that counts for a lot. Now that I think about it, I do not have many friends, and the ones I do have are scattered all over the country. I can now concentrate fully once again on the course. Nothing much happens for several months. I carry on seeing Jeanne two or three evenings a week. Sometimes just for chit-chat and sometimes to test each other as we are taking the same examinations and they come up quite frequently at this stage. Anna and I continue having lunch together about twice a week. Normal service is restored. I receive one of the rare emails that I get from Aurélie. She has finished her internship and now has a junior post in the Neurology department at Marseilles. She says that the hospital is incredibly busy but the Neurology department is a little quieter. I send one back congratulating her on the job and saying that it would be nice to get together sometime. It is unlikely as we are almost 500 miles apart.

Coming up to the festive season, Christmas and the New Year, there is the usual office party. This year it is rather different. Our chief clerk, Jean-Paul is very friendly with the chief clerk of a firm of notaires in La rue de Rennes in Montparnasse. As chief clerks it is their job to organise the office party and they have decided that this year the two firms will have a joint one. The chief clerk of the other firm, who is called Hubert, has hired a hall in the Montparnasse area of Paris. Office parties can be a bit of a drag. There is a tendency for people to form short term liaisons which they regret afterwards. I think the idea of the two firms having a joint party is a good idea. There will be people there whom one has not met. I wonder how I will cope if someone makes a pass. I am not feeling ready for that but at some point, life must move on. Anna and I arrange to go to the party together. When we get inside we are immediately joined by a couple of men from the other firm. One is Hubert who is their Chief Clerk and has arranged the venue. The other is a rather dishy thirty year old called Sasha. Sasha and Anna are getting on very well. Hubert obviously fancies me but I cannot see anything in him. He is fifty odd with a small goatee beard. After a while I manage to escape and join a group of clerks from both firms who are having a lively conversation. As the party is drawing to a close, I notice that Anna and Sasha have already left. I go to the kitchen area and start washing up some of the glasses. More time than I thought must have passed because I suddenly realise that only Hubert and I remain. I do not like that. Although I have no reason to be worried I think I shall be wise to leave after I have washed this glass. I am too late. Hubert comes over and before I can move, he has me pinned to the sink with his arms through my armpits feeling my breasts.

"Ah, Catherine, we are alone at last."

"Leave me alone" I snap. He does not. He pushes himself into me still holding my breasts. I push hard backwards and manage to turn round. He is now holding me very tight and kissing my face and lips or whatever he can reach. I shout "Stop." No-one hears of course. He is much stronger than me. He is now tearing at the back of my dress. I can see where this is leading if I don't act very fast but what can I do? I put on an encouraging voice.

"If we are going to do this" I say, "can't we make ourselves more comfortable?" He seems to think he's made a score. He slackens his grip on me just a little and moves back just a few inches. It is not much but it is enough. He is starting to say something when I bring my left knee up with every bit of force that I can muster straight into his groin. I am bang on target. He drops as if poleaxed and is writhing on the floor in agony. The last thing I hear as I leave the hall is the sound of him vomiting all over the kitchen floor. Well he can clean that up by himself!

I am shaken and flustered. I walk fast, anywhere. Every person seems a threat. If I can see that it is a woman, the threat goes. If it is a man, I turn down a side road to avoid him. After about twenty minutes I calm down. My pulse ceases to race and my breathing comes back under control. My illogical system of avoiding men by turning down side roads has led me into smaller and smaller streets. I am in some alley. It is almost midnight in December. I am freezing and I have no idea where I am. At least I can now think. I have come to a T junction with a railway line on the far side and the road I have reached is called 'rue Vercingétorix'. I remember inconsequentially that he was one of the very few people to defeat Julius Caesar in battle. Should I turn left or right? It all looks the same. I turn right. The road follows the railway line. After half a mile I reach a crossroads and to the right I can see a metro sign. It is Plaisance. It is late but the metro is still running. When I reach home, although I have locked it, I barricade the door. I do not think I slept at all that night. In the morning, after two cups of strong coffee, I am very tired but I am back to my usual self. Last night is in my memory but well under control. I throw open my living room window stand on the little ledge with the railings and soak in the December morning sun. I feel that my quick thinking saved the day.

On Monday, after the weekend, Jean-Paul, comes up to me:

"Catherine" he asks, "Is what Hubert is saying about the party true?"

"I don't know what Hubert is saying" I reply. "If he is saying that he tried to rape me and I kneed him in the balls, that's true. Anything else is probably a figment of his imagination."

Jean-Paul looks very serious. "No that is not the way Hubert described it. I believe your version. Do you want to make an official complaint?"

"No Jean-Paul. As so often with this sort of thing, it is one person's word against another's. Both the guilty and the innocent have their characters assassinated over months or even years and both often end up with mental problems."

I told Jean-Paul exactly what happened.

"But I dealt with it so quickly that it would be impossible to know for certain that he was actually intent on rape. Maybe he would have stopped short. I was certainly in a position where I imagined that it was the most likely outcome."

Jean-Paul was very sombre. "You are right, Catherine, It is almost impossible to get justice for attempted rape. Even actual rape is hard enough but as you describe it, I think you managed to deal with the situation superbly. I shall certainly not be agreeing to any more joint parties with Hubert."

I asked Anna how it had gone for her. She had a far more enjoyable experience at the party than I. She and Sasha left at about half past ten and found a coffee bar where they could give each other their undivided attention away from the hustle and bustle of the joint office party. Sasha is on the same level as Anna as a legal clerk. They swapped their experience of being at different firms. Sasha saw Anna back to her flat. She said he was very polite: would not come in for a drink but asked for her phone number so that he could ask her for a date at some unspecified time in the future. Anna said that if he did ring, she would definitely say yes. She found him charming and was very appreciative of the fact that he was not moving too fast. 'A good replacement for André' I thought. It did seem like Sasha was a gentle sort. I wished Anna luck. Then she asked me how it had gone for me. Before I had talked to Jean-Paul, I had reckoned on keeping quiet about it all. It is the sort of thing where some people think that you are making it up. Others are rather titillated by the idea and really I would rather no-one knew. But if Jean-Paul knew and had indeed had a different version of events from Hubert, it seemed that I ought to let my friends know so that at least they knew the truth. Anna was horrified. She said that I should report it but when I pointed out the downside she agreed. I am afraid that fate seems intent on making me a bit of a celebrity. First my fiancé is killed and then I am the victim of a rape attempt. I shall keep my head down and do my best to be unnoticed.

These are the last few months of my apprenticeship. Although there are a number of tests in this part of the course, one is assessed on how one does overall. There is no big final exam. So in the end Jeanne and I qualified as Notaries without any razzmatazz. All of a sudden those seven long years are over. It hits hard that actually this is not an end. It is just a beginning. The first problem is to get a job. Jeanne wants to find a job in Lyon. It is where she was brought up. It is a big city. Like Paris it is on a big river, in fact two big rivers, the Rhône and the Saône. Anna is obviously staying in Paris as she is a clerk at Favre et Dubois. She, Jeanne and Louise are my only friends. I suppose I could include Marie. I am feeling very vulnerable so I would like to be near one of them. This means that the choice seems to be to look for a job in one of four places; Paris, Lyon, Toulouse or Rouen. I think from the point of view of my career, being near Jeanne would be best. We could no doubt help each other even though we would be with different firms. We had managed that over the last two years. I didn't know though whether there would be a choice of suitable jobs available in Lyon. When I check there are over 20 jobs available. Several of these are suitable for newly qualified applicants. We are highly qualified. Both Jeanne and I have first class degrees. I decide that I shall wait until Jeanne has applied before I do. I could not face the idea that we would both be candidates for the same job. I am a very determined person, but not very competitive. I would be devastated to take a post away from Jeanne. Then again, I wouldn't like to think that she was given an appointment as being better than me either. So I wait. Jeanne gets the first post she applies for. It is with Maîtres Paillard-Montaigne in the Cours Charlemagne close to where the Rhône and Saône rivers converge. I then realise the big disadvantage to waiting. Naturally a whole year's worth of budding notaires finish their training at the same time. By the time it has been confirmed that Jeanne has been given the appointment, there are only two suitable positions left in Lyon. These of course, are likely to be ones that nobody had fancied. There is one in La rue de l'Ancienne Gare (Maîtres Bonneau Frères) and another in La rue du Dauphiné (Maître Pierre Tissot).

I decide to apply for the post with the two brothers, just on the hunch that a firm with two brothers might be more friendly. The junior clerk at reception is quite chatty. She says that the two partners made the mistake of each thinking that the other had arranged for the post to be advertised with the result that all the best applicants had been snaffled up by the time that the advert went in. She says that she overheard them talking and that they were amazed to have an applicant with first class honours from the Sorbonne and that unless I really mess up, I am pretty much sure to get the job. Then she realises that she has said far more than she should, gives a little giggle and clams up. She shows me upstairs to an office where there are three other candidates, two men and a woman. We all sit looking nervously at each other. I am last to be called. The interview goes all right, although I didn't feel that I did myself justice. I'm sure that if I had been up against Jeanne, she would have been far more impressive and got the job. Probably against very little competition, I am appointed. Both Jeanne and I now have a job in Lyon. We can share a flat. Then there is a very interesting development, Aurélie sends me an email. She has just finished her junior medical post at Marseilles, and has got a job in the neurology department of 'Hospices Civils de Lyon' in Boulevard Pinel. With three of us, we could afford a really nice flat. I email her straight back saying that both I and my friend Jeanne have appointments in Lyon. Why don't we all meet and discuss sharing a flat together? Although we have all been successful in getting a job, none of us is due to start for several weeks.

We meet on a Friday in La Brasserie de L'Ouest which is a beautifully situated café on the west bank of the Saône with a good view over the river to Le Parc de la Belle Allemande on the other side. The sun is shining. We arrive for lunch and it is idyllic. When Jeanne sees Aurélie, she bursts out laughing.

"You two are just about as identical as it is possible to be. I'd know you were related straight away."

Aurélie and I grin at each other. It takes us both back to being four or five years' old, wearing identical clothes just for the fun of being taken for sisters. It is strange to think that we haven't seen each other for over ten years. Jeanne and Aurélie get on fine together. We discuss just how much we can afford to pay for a three bedroom flat and agree that if we keep to the essentials, it is something we can do. We have all looked up flats in Lyon on the internet and between us we make a shortlist of four. All three of us had two of them on our list so we start with those. In the end, however, the one we find that is still available and suitable is one that Jeanne had on her list. It is on the 15th floor of a concrete tower block on rue Challemel-Lacour in the 8th arrondissement. It has a balcony facing West. If you look down, you see the railway lines but it is high enough to have quite a nice view over the city towards the confluence of the two rivers. It was reasonably well situated between our three places of work. Jeanne and I both needed to go about two miles but in opposite directions. It was rather further for Aurélie. The hospital was about four miles away. They want references but that isn't going to be a problem. They also want three months' rent in advance which is more of a problem and we can only just scrape it together. We can move into the flat in ten days' time. Aurélie still has two weeks of her post at Marseilles to run so Jeanne and I shall be resident before her. Luckily the three bedrooms are very much the same size so we do not have any arguments as to who should have which.

On my first day, the junior clerk who was at reception at the time of my interview introduces herself as Monique. She says how glad she is that I got the job. She says the other candidates were right toffee-nose. I suggest that we have lunch together and she can give me a run-down on the rest of the staff so that I know who is who. She readily agrees. She takes me to Le Café des Arts in Avenue Pierre Semard. They have a shaded patio area at the back. We order and Monique gives me the lowdown.

"The younger Mr Bonneau, Frédéric, is a pussy cat. He never gets cross with anyone. In fact he tends just to correct an error without even mentioning it, which I think is a mistake. I do think somebody needs to be told if they make an error. The elder Mr Bonneau, Gaston, is much tougher and can be very sarcastic. I have to admit, however, that he is always fair. You only get it in the neck if you have made a mistake. The person to look out for is the senior clerk, Hans. He was born in Switzerland and his first language is German. I think he feels that if he manages to do things correctly in French then all of us should be able to do the same. Sometimes he fails to check whether he is castigating the right person. When that happens, he never apologises."

I make a mental note to ask Hans's advice about one or two things. They need to be difficult questions because I don't want to look ignorant. Doing this will put me in his good books because everyone likes to be asked for their advice. At the same time from the advice he gives, I shall be able to assess how good he is. Monique and I fall into a pattern very similar to the one

I had with Anna. We would go to lunch together one or two times a week. Gaston Bonneau, from the start, entrusts me with some complicated stuff and I find that there are indeed a few questions where I would value Hans's advice. He seems right on top of the job which is good. He also takes a liking to me, without I am glad to say, making a pass. So over the months, I settle in well and am thoroughly enjoying the job. When the festive season approaches, however, I decide that I shall have a severe headache on the day of the office party. I do not think I could bear refreshing the memory of the last one.

In early January, an unexpected invitation to a Valentine's Day party comes from Jacques. He says 'Bring a friend of either sex'. This means either Jeanne or Aurélie. I do not have a boyfriend and I am not missing one at all. I even feel slightly nervous at the prospect. I am sure that Jacques would be happy if I came with both my friends but it turns out that Aurélie is on call at the hospital on Valentine's Day so would not be able to come. Jacques says that his girlfriend Marianne can put us up for the night so that we don't have to take the train home. Valentine's Day this year (2003) is a Friday so that fits very well. I have told Jeanne a certain amount about Jacques. How he was staying with us when his mother died; the unexpected meeting at Le Balcon au Lac when I was with Jean; how Jacques was the person I called on when Jean died; how I discovered that the journey that I had put him through was a nightmare. She is very interested to meet him.

When Jeanne and I get to the party, there are only four people there; Jacques and his girlfriend Marianne, and a couple Guy and Eugénie. Jacques makes the introductions. As more people arrive the introductions soon stop. There is a point where Jeanne and I are talking to each other when a smart man in his early to mid-twenties comes over and introduces himself.

"I'm Georges" he says. "I've been a friend of Jacques since we were in nappies."

"I'm Jeanne and this is Catherine" says Jeanne.

Georges looks at me "Are you Catherine Diacre? The girl that Jacques stayed with when his mother was ill?"

"Yes that's right" I say. It is silly to say but for the first time since Jean died, I am feeling attracted to a man. I have been nervous about it but it is a great feeling. Jeanne as ever is pretty much a mind reader.

"I'll just go over there and have a word with Marianne" she says.

Georges is looking at me as if the attraction is mutual. He says: "You know I have just met my Uncle Daniel, for the very first time. Jacques came across him while doing an electric job in Pringy just up the road. There he is over there."

I look over and there is an older version of Georges.

"That is what you are going to look like in twenty or thirty years Georges, still quite good-looking."

Georges grins, "Thank you, Catherine."

I like the way he says my name. It sends a little thrill down my spine. Georges is very amusing, telling me stories of some of the deals he has done. The first was when he was twelve.

"One of the boys at school had some poker dice and for some reason they caught on. They became the fad of the moment. Everyone wanted to play with the dice but there was only one set. That Saturday I was in Limoges with my mother when I saw advertised in the window of a toy shop, a set of poker dice at half price. My mother said, yes I could buy them. I went into the shop and mentioned the dice. I asked the proprietor why they were half price. 'They won't sell' he said. 'I've got twelve sets but they just won't sell.' 'If you take another ten percent off' I suggested, 'I'll buy the lot.' 'It's a deal' he said. I then had to persuade Mum to lend me the money and in the end she did. I sold all twelve sets at school mainly to the boys at fifty percent more than I paid for them, which was far cheaper than their original price. The thing is" he said, "that everyone was happy. The boys have the poker dice they want at a cheap price: I have a good profit and the shopkeeper has got rid of all the sets of poker dice that he could not move. That is the art of business. If you keep everybody happy, business thrives!"

We are in our own little bubble and the time seems to fly. I am really enjoying talking to Georges. Before I know it Marianne is suggesting that Jeanne and I come back to hers. She has ordered a taxi. I say good-bye to Georges. Jacques is putting him up for the night. We leave and I am very disappointed that Georges has not asked me for a date. The next morning, Jeanne and I thank Marianne for her hospitality and take a bus to the station to catch the train back to Lyon.

Jeanne says: "You know Catherine, there's something not right in the relationship between Jacques and Marianne. I can't quite put my finger on it. They seem to be all over each other at one moment and sort of reserved the next. It is a bit of a puzzle."

"Yes, I agree. You never met Sylvie did you, Jeanne?" I reply. "Jacques was absolutely besotted with her and she seemed very keen on him. I thought they were a permanent unit but his relationship with Marianne does seem very ambivalent."

Jacques 2003

The party goes very well. Guy and Eugénie are first to arrive. They have been together now for some time. Next it is Catherine and her friend Jeanne. I am delighted to see Catherine and glad to see that she is looking well. It is two years now since Jean died and although that is the sort of thing you never forget, I expect Catherine has mended. When she introduces Jeanne, I see a rather striking woman. She is quite tall, very elegant and composed. Not beautiful but quite attractive. When our eyes meet, just for a second, I get this remarkable feeling that my eyes have turned completely inwards and she can see my mind. Rather disturbingly, it is empty a bit like an empty eggshell. The feeling passes almost immediately. When Georges arrives I introduce him to his Uncle Daniel. They seem to get on very well but they have no common ground as the last time Daniel saw Georges' parents was before he and his elder brother Gérard were born. They swap addresses and telephone numbers. Georges also gives Daniel his parents' address. Daniel has said that he would like to contact them. He is uncertain what they would think of that after so long. It is funny to think that he and Georges have never met before. Quite late on in the party, I see Georges introduce himself to Catherine. There appears to be a spark between them but I think it is just my realisation that Georges, the best friend of me, a Parisel, has just met a Diacre and they appeared to have clicked. Is this going to be the continuation of the Parisel-Diacre legend?

A week or two after the party, I decide that at some point when I am with Marianne, I must bring up the question of our relationship. It has got to the point where I feel I must do something. I suppose you could say that as a platonic relationship it is OK; indeed it is very good. As a romantic relationship it has come to a complete halt. After a very nice meal at L'Auberge de Savoie in the old town, I invite Marianne back to my flat. As on several occasions before, she says:

"No, I don't think so."

"All right then" I say. "How about back to yours?"

She looks pained but doesn't answer.

"Look Marianne" I say. "I like your company. You are great to be with and I have enjoyed this meal with you very much. I also appreciate all the work that you put into making the party the success it was. However I want more out of this relationship than that and the occasional half-second kiss. You are holding back. What is the problem?"

She doesn't tell me what the problem is but she does say: "All right Jacques, let's go back to my flat."

I realise of course that with this attitude of hers, if things are going to progress, I must be very patient. I remember how I was with Diane when I was still down in the dumps after Sylvie left me. May be this is something similar. I must not push it. So we go back to Marianne's and she pours us a glass of wine each. It's Rousette Altesse and nicely cooled. We sit side by side on the sofa and chat for a bit then I say: "Marianne, give me a kiss."

She turns towards me and I think would have just given me one of those little pecks. I gently put my hands round the back of her neck and stroke it, being just firm enough that she cannot pull back, while I keep a very soft contact on her lips. Gentleness, I think might be the most powerful resource in this situation. I feel her go very tense but then slowly relax and then she seems to be enjoying it. I don't push it. We sit and chat some more and finish the glass of wine. Then I get up to leave.

"Give me another kiss just like the last before I go" I suggest. She comes close and we do the same again. This time she doesn't tense. When we part, she smiles at me. Marianne is absolutely lovely but, it would seem, entirely unobtainable. It drives me mad. I go out of the door and ride my little Vespa with the bashed out dent on the mudguard back to my flat. I think perhaps we have made a little progress.

After several months, I do manage to get her to allow me to stroke her calves and anything below knee. But patient as I am, I cannot get Marianne to go any further. Any breast or thigh contact just freaks her out. Eventually the day comes when she says:

"Jacques you have been very patient with me. We both know that it isn't working. I must tell you the problem. It is not unique. My father died when I was two. I don't think my mother was promiscuous, I can only remember her having three partners but one of those raped me when I was twelve and the memory of that prevents me from letting any man get really close. You were so patient, I thought it might work out but it hasn't. I can see that you will naturally want to move on, although I do hope we might meet from time to time just as friends."

So that is the way it is. From time to time, I give her a ring and we do something together and if she has some occasion where it seems useful for her to have a male partner, an escort, you might say, she gives me a ring and we go together. In some ways it is very relaxed. I really do enjoy her company. I would just find it so much easier if she wasn't so beautiful.

Meantime, the work load is mounting. Guy, Pierre and I are all overworked. Of course that means the money is flowing in but if we have to start turning jobs down, the concept of getting work solely by recommendation will start to fail. It seems to me that we probably need to start employing assistants. Twice as many people can do twice the work, or at least, that is the idea. It only works if you can get the right assistants. Even then you cannot expect your assistant to work as late as you probably do yourself. Anyway I suggest another meeting at Alby-sur-Chéran. I like the busy little square. I get there first and order three bottles of bière blanche. Guy and Pierre arrive a few minutes later.

"How are you making out?" I ask them both.

Pierre answers first. "I am working late almost every day" he says. "It brings in the money but I think Nadine is getting fed up with it."

"Yes, I agree" says Guy. "I think that I shall have to give up Desplaces & Cie. I am earning quite enough without that and, as you say, Pierre, Eugénie feels that I am not paying her enough attention. I don't want to lose her. We're getting on so well."

"I am also doing too much" I say. "I shall have to take on an assistant. Of course, paying an assistant will mean that initially I earn a lot less but with the potential to make a lot more. The idea that I want to bring up is that we should actually look for jobs that would involve all of us or at least two of us and that we should give those jobs priority over the jobs that only involve one of us. That would be a tightening of the knot and I don't know whether either of you two would like that." I wait for a response.

Guy says "Yes, as a team we could look for fully-fledged housing jobs and I think that we know enough about each other's jobs to be able to supervise an assistant if it were necessary. On the other hand, I'm not sure that I could afford to give up Desplaces & Cie and take on an assistant. The two together would mean a large drop in income."

Pierre says "I'm definitely in favour. I don't mind going back to getting the money I used to be earning and having an assistant. As you say, Jacques, it gives the potential for much greater earnings in the future when we might find that we have ended up as partners of a fair sized firm."

"I agree" I say. "But I think Guy has as problem. Maybe what we need to do is to form a company so that we can level out costs between us."

After a bit more discussion we decide that Pierre and I shall take on an assistant each. Guy will give up Desplaces & Cie but for the moment will not have an assistant. Pierre and I shall make sure that Guy is not losing out too much. We shall all prioritize any work that involves all three of us and see how that works out. We will think about forming an official company. Guy buys us all another bière blanche and we toast the future together.

In early May, an invitation arrives to Marianne and me for Georges and Catherine's wedding. That was expected in a way. I saw that they clicked at the party. Nevertheless, I would not have expected wedding bells quite so quickly. Of course neither of them knows that Marianne and I are no longer together in the same way that we were, although I am sure that Marianne will want to come to the wedding with me. She will regard it as a return for me acting as 'escort' for her to other events. I know that she will enjoy it. On the whole, women enjoy weddings more than men. The wedding is due to be in Toulouse as that is where Catherine's parents live. It is billed for 21st June, the summer solstice. (Oh ho! ho! I can see the jokes there. Will you get any sleep at all?) I contact Marianne and she is up for it. Neither of us has ever been to 'The Pink City'. Some of the pictures look incredible. We accept.

I think about how best to find a good assistant. The final CAP exams for the year will be coming up soon. If I can get to see the results for Haute Savoie I can get an idea of who is available but it will be difficult to discover who fits in with our concept of very high quality work. It is not any good employing the wrong person. Even very good exam results do not indicate that an individual is meticulous and conscientious. They indicate more that the person is a good learner and can regurgitate what they have learnt. I am at a bit of a loss. I then have one of those slices of luck that make all the difference in life. They say that you make your own luck. When I look at my life, however, all my good luck has had nothing to do with me. It has either been sheer chance or the generosity of someone else. To my mind, I have made most of my bad luck myself. This bit of luck is as a result of the platonic relationship that I now have with Marianne. As a teacher, she has an invitation to a garden party with other teachers; a teachers' get-together. She knows almost all of them are married and partners are invited. She would sooner go with someone than alone and that is where our unofficial arrangement comes in. She asks me if I am prepared to tag along. So I put on some smart clothes and off we go to The Priory Gardens at Sévrier.

It is a lovely day and most of us are outside in the garden. The introductions have been made and Marianne and I are chatting to this teacher and his wife, Paul and Valérie Bernard. He is a science teacher at the Gabriel Fauré School in Annecy. The one than Marianne had a look at but didn't think that it would suit her, so hadn't put in an application.

"What do you do Jacques?" Asks Valérie.

"I'm an electrician" I reply.

"That's interesting "she says. "Our son François is almost at the end of his two year CAP course. Then he'll be a qualified electrician. He has found the course is right up his street. He lives, sleeps and breathes it."

"Yes" adds Paul. "He is absolutely fascinated by everything electrical. He says the public just don't realise how dangerous it can be. He says that the amount of faulty wiring in the country is a disgrace."

"Would it be OK for you to put us in touch?" I ask. "I desperately need an assistant at the moment. He sounds like just the sort of person I need. I'm sure I can give him a good starting salary."

"Wait a second" he says. "You're Jacques. Is that *the* Jacques? You're not the Jacques that dealt with the beds in St Joseph's care home in Seynod are you?"

"Yes, that's me."

"My mother was in that care home at the time. The manager, Madame Thierry, was most impressed with you. She said you explained everything so clearly and charged a very reasonable amount. I think we'd be most happy to put François in touch with you. Wouldn't we Valérie?"

"Of course" agrees Valérie. "It would be nice for us. It would mean he can remain at home and if you need an assistant, it may well help you both."

Guy, Pierre and I form a single company so that we can apply for proper building contracts. These would have to be small. We would not be in a position to build a large block of flats but you have to start somewhere. We register the firm as Parisel, Rouget & Oudart. The reason for the order of our names was that the acronym would be PRO for 'Professionel'. That gave an efficient vibe to the company but it was rather nice that this happened to put my name first. Starting this firm PRO seemed such a simple idea but, wow, are there problems? We immediately get a contract to build a house for an individual who has bought the land. Initial thought; great, we are off to a good start. Second thought; total panic. The materials will cost a fortune that we do not have. We need a bank loan. We need somewhere to store a heap of equipment. We don't have anywhere. That is going to cost some too. Have we bitten off more than we can chew? We never discussed who is going to organise this sort of thing. We have an emergency meeting. Guy cannot do it. He is the one of the three of us in the most critical situation. So Pierre and I say we'll share it. Pierre will arrange the bank loan (he hopes) and I shall find a warehouse or suitable site to store stuff (I hope). We need another meeting to decide exactly what we do need and in how many instalments it is best to have the materials delivered. I suddenly realise that Dominique may have been out of his depth but if I am not exceedingly careful I shall drown too. We also need a decent van. A little Vespa isn't much good in these circumstances. It brings back memories of other circumstances when my lovely little bike has not been the ideal transport.

We are lucky. All the arrangements we need go well and fairly quickly. Pierre gets a large overdraft limit from Crédit Agricole. I find a yard with a small warehouse in rue des Passerelles in Cran-Gévrier on the outskirts of Annecy. We buy a second-hand white van then decide on what we need. To start with, it seems best to order about one third of the materials that we require. It is hectic but we are just about in business. We find that we have to recalculate time and again. To be honest Guy is not up to the maths so Pierre and I have to do it. It is the sort of thing that Georges does instinctively. He just seems to know, without doing lengthy calculations. Pierre and I can cope well enough. Pierre is very worried that Nadine will get genuinely and quite reasonably fed up if he is perpetually out with me, working over the figures. We solve this by doing the work at Pierre's home in Chambéry. If I bring Nadine some pains au chocolat for tomorrow's breakfast and maybe some éclairs or petits écoliers biscuits. She is very happy and it saves Pierre the travel time to elsewhere. I do not have any particular commitment to the opposite sex at the moment. I can easily get to Pierre and Nadine's in Chambéry. Nadine actually seems to start to look forward to me arriving with some goodies and us disappearing into another room to do some calculations. Pierre is at home. She has a guest to take coffee to and some pains au chocolat for breakfast. We take a quarter of an hour break with the coffee and chat to her and it is probably more company than she normally gets. It is, however, very hard administrative work but by the middle of June we are genuinely up and running! We have access to money. We have outdoor and indoor storage space. We have enough materials to complete one third of the house. We have a good-sized van. We also have a very substantial overdraft.

It is 20th June, the day before Georges and Catherine's wedding. Marianne and I have decided that the train is the only sensible way to travel. Even so the service from Annecy to Toulouse is not straightforward. It is well over 400 miles. Most of the services involve two changes and some even more than that. There is only one time which seems convenient and involves only one change. That means catching a train at Annecy at 9 o'clock in the morning. It gets to Lyon at about half past one. The wait for a connecting service is well over an hour so we should be able to get a quick snack at Lyon. Then there is a service to Toulouse at ten to three in the afternoon that will get us in just past seven in the evening. It really does take pretty much all day. We have reserved seats on both services. Marianne has brought a vacuum flask with enough coffee for two cups each. I should have thought of doing the same thing but the Lyon to Toulouse service is bound to have some sort of drinks service even if the Annecy to Lyon one doesn't. We both have a moderate sized bag with us as it needs to have what we shall wear tomorrow for the wedding as well as overnight requirements. I am wearing a Tee shirt with a pullover on top and a scruffy pair of jeans. My clothes for tomorrow are very smart and elegant but I figured that it wouldn't matter what I wore for the journey. Marianne is never of that frame of mind. She is impeccably turned out quite as beautiful as always. She could perfectly well wear what she has on for the journey to go to the reception tomorrow. It wouldn't surprise me if she were even more stunning for the big event.

At Lyon I have reserved a table at Le Vin Gourmand which is right next to the station. We reckon on only one course because we don't want to be getting jittery about running out of time and risking missing the train. Even then we think it would be best to have something that doesn't need cooking. So we order a salad each and a carafe of house wine. That with the basket of bread, makes a very nice lunch. Then it is back to the station for the second and longer leg of the journey. In general terms the railway follows the Rhône down to Avignon and cuts across to Montpelier. Then it follows the coast to Narbonne with a stretch where it runs on the slither of land between the Mediterranean and 'Le Bassin de Thau'. After Narbonne it follows roughly the route of the Canal du Midi to Toulouse. You would expect, having said this, that there would be some beautiful water views of one sort or another almost all the way. Marianne and I had reserved seats facing forward on the left-hand side of the train with a very good view out of the window. Although there were some beautiful views on the way, I was surprised how seldom we could see the river, sea or canal. It was a comfortable journey and Marianne and I are very relaxed with each other now after the months of almost unbearable angst.

As we get off the train at Toulouse, there are two young women going out of the exit. From the back, they look to me like Catherine and her friend Jeanne who was at the party; the tall one with the penetrating eyes. I must be mistaken because Catherine, as the bride, would surely be at her parents' house already. She wouldn't leave it until the evening before her wedding to arrive in Toulouse. I am surprised it isn't them because Jeanne is quite tall and thin with a distinctive, rather elegant figure. By the time we get to the Way Out, they have disappeared. I have booked us a room each at 'Le Castel', a hotel in the centre of the city. It is close to the station as I think that we will not want to travel any distance to our hotel after a seven hour rail journey. I have booked us in for two nights. There does not seem to be any possibility of staying only one night when the door to door journey time is almost eight hours each way. It is part of a quite elegant 19th century building; very modern inside, with some rather peculiar modern art in the reception area. The food is basic, but it is all we need. Tomorrow we shall need a taxi to take us to the reception which is in a château, Le Château de Tongras, a little way outside Toulouse itself. The hotel receptionist tells us that a taxi is likely to take about 20 to 25 minutes to make the trip. The invitation said 3 o'clock. Marianne suggests that three would be a good time to have the taxi arrive at the hotel. It would mean that we reached the reception by half past.

Today we are both in our smart clothes for the reception. Marianne says how smart I look, which is a nice compliment coming from her. I return the compliment but I cannot do her justice. She is wearing a pale grey ankle length trouser suit. The trousers have a barely discernible blue and green lattice pattern creating the hint of a heather mixture effect. The tailored jacket almost matches. It has the same faint lattice pattern but slightly more pronounced than the trousers. Under the jacket she is wearing a high-neck fitted blouse in a soft pale blue that blends perfectly with the faint blue/green of the suit. Her earrings are aquamarines only slightly bigger than studs. A small brooch matching the earrings rests on the lapel of her jacket. She should have been a model. From the start, I have said that she knows how to dress for an occasion. She certainly does.

The taxi arrives on time. The driver is the chatty type.

"You two going somewhere special then? Certainly got the glad-rags on haven't we?"

"It's a wedding reception" I reply.

"Yes, they have a lot of them at the château" he says. "You'll like it. It's not in the Grand Style – No Versailles – but it does have charm. In some ways it's more of a posh farmhouse with a tower on top than most people's idea of a château."

He keeps up a perpetual one-sided conversation for the full length of the journey. I pay him and we go in. Quite a few people have already arrived. My brother Jules has obviously just arrived. He is talking to Georges and Catherine. He knows Georges well and he knows of Catherine from holiday snaps but has never met her. We go over and join them: congratulate Georges and Catherine; 'May all your troubles be little ones' and so on. Then as others arrive we move off and chat to Jules for a while. Then I see Jeanne with this girl who is a perfect look-alike of Catherine. Yet she is so different. My heart plays funny tunes. It seems to be completely irregular and I feel a bit ill. This look-alike of Catherine's is for me completely different in that she has real oomph, the full shebang. I don't understand how it happens but I have fallen in love at first sight. I know Catherine has no sisters so this must be a cousin. I leave Marianne with Jules and go over to Jeanne.

"Hello Jeanne. I thought I saw you and Catherine on Toulouse Station but it must it must have been." I turn to this Catherine with sex appeal "…You!"

Jeanne does the introductions. "Aurélie, this is Jacques."

"Hello Jacques" says my new heart-throb. "I'm Catherine's cousin. She has told me a bit about you." Her voice is music to my ears.

"Aurélie" I say. "That is a lovely name. You and Catherine are so alike."

She laughs. It is a subtle variation of Catherine's laugh.

"Yes. Everyone says that. We used to have a lot of fun pretending to be sisters when we were little."

Jeanne who definitely seems to be able to see into the empty egg-shell of my mind, chips in. She can presumable read in my mind that am completely overwhelmed by Aurélie and she intends to bring me back to my responsibilities. She doesn't know that the relationship between me and Marianne is now on a completely different footing.

"Is Marianne here?" she asks sweetly. Implication: stop chatting up Aurélie and get back to the girlfriend that you came here with.

"Oh yes, she is here; just over there talking to my brother Jules" I say.

But yes. Jeanne has indeed high-lighted a problem. I am truly completely free from romantic involvement with Marianne but Jeanne and Catherine don't know that. They have probably given an account of the party to

Aurélie including the fact that I have a rather beautiful girl-friend called Marianne. I shall have to be very careful or my new love Aurélie is going to take me for some kind of Lothario. So for the moment I take Jeanne's hint and return to chat with Marianne and Jules. When I return Jules is looking smitten with the love-bug. Well, Marianne is lovely and to-day she looks dressed to kill. Any man would fancy her. Isn't life so complicated? I remember how Diane always managed to speak her mind without being unkind. For the moment I cannot see any way to warn Jules that romantic ideas about Marianne are doomed to failure. Nor can I see how to extricate myself so that I can pursue what has suddenly become the most important thing in my life; somehow to earn the love of Aurélie. Marianne has to be the key to both solutions but I am sure that she would not want me to mention her problem to either Jules or Jeanne. As for Aurélie, I would be presumptuous in the extreme to say 'Look you can love me because Marianne is no longer a romantic attachment of mine' when she has only just met me today. It is cleft stick.

When Marianne goes off to take a loo break, Jules is immediately over the top.

"Jacques" he says. "How on earth did you manage to make a hit with a stunning beauty like Marianne? I mean just look at her, she is superb. She is beyond beautiful. She is heavenly and dressed absolutely impeccably. She is quite unbelievable. What on earth is it she would see in you, little brother?"

At least it is not 'Jennifer'. But how do I deal with it? I cannot for Marianne's sake tell him the truth. If I deny that I have a romantic interest, I lead him on right into the problem that I had to face. I decide it is best just to be a little non-committal. I do not feel that I am being fair but it seems the best of the available evils.

"Yes, she is quite nice, isn't she Jules?"

Jules is obviously hugely envious. He cannot understand my apparent lack of enthusiasm. He looks flabbergasted.

"Quite nice?" He splutters. "Quite nice?" Luckily before he can expand on the question, Marianne returns.

Catherine 2003

Jeanne and I are taking the train home to Lyon after Jacques' party. We have got reserved seats but the ones facing us are empty at the moment. They are probably reserved for passengers getting on at Lyon to go to Paris. There is a man coming down the aisle of the carriage. Good heavens, it's Georges. Has he really got on this train specially to see me? My heart does a flip.

"Georges!" I call.

"Wow!" he says "Catherine and Jeanne. I didn't expect to see you two here. Are you going to Paris?"

"No" answers Jeanne. "We used to live in Paris but we are both living in Lyon now."

"Well that is a co-incidence. So do I."

He settles himself down in the seat opposite us. I am disappointed that he hasn't caught the train specially to see me but really that would only be second prize. The fact that he lives in Lyon means that we can easily see each other almost whenever we want. First however, he has to ask me out; or then again I could ask him. After a while, Jeanne mind-reader as ever surprisingly finds that she needs the loo. Georges immediately seizes the opportunity.

"Catherine, I enjoyed talking to you immensely at Jacques' party last night. I felt we might have something going. The party seemed to end so suddenly. I didn't get round to making sure that I didn't lose contact with you. I have been cursing myself all day. I calmed down just now when I realised that Jacques could give me your phone number. I hope I'm not being presumptuous. It is a real stroke of luck being on the same train as you. Can I have your phone number? I'd like to ask you out sometime."

"I'm glad you said that Georges, I was sad that we hadn't made any arrangement last night. If we are both living in Lyon of course we must get together. Please do give me a ring. I shall be disappointed if you don't."

We swap phone numbers and with perfect timing Jeanne reappears. Georges gives me a ring the very next evening. He has tickets for the Saturday. He has booked for La Maison de Guignol which is a puppet theatre. That's a bit different. I love the idea. We enjoy the show immensely. They do it so well. It is hilarious. We go for an inexpensive meal afterwards.

For the next month, Georges and I see each other on Saturday and Sunday. We go to either the cinema or theatre on Saturday and have an evening meal on Sunday. Every time I fall in love more and more with Georges. He sees me back to the flat that I am sharing with Jeanne and Aurélie. We have a cup of coffee or a glass of wine with whoever is back in the flat. Sometimes Aurélie is on call for the hospital. Then Georges leaves to go back home. With the memory of my botched seduction attempt with Jean, I am determined to let Georges take his own time. He is fun to be with. Eight dates have already gone. I am hoping for some development. The next week, Georges asks me back to his place. He has a lovely ground floor flat in rue Robert et Reynier with a small garden. He pours us a glass of

Vacqueyras each. We both sit on the sofa and take a sip of the wine. Then Georges actually asks if he can kiss me. It's the modern media that encourages this sort of thing. I really don't want to be asked but I suppose some women do. I give a sort of half laugh.

"Yes please, Georges, I am looking forward to it."

The kiss is very soft and gentle. It grows on me with time. I have been eagerly awaiting his kiss for weeks. We break off and then come back for more. I am really happy for the first time since Jean died. This second kiss with Georges does for me the same as my first with Jean. I see all my strange colours and shapes. I am sort of absent for a minute or so. Remembering that I omitted to tell Jean of this strange affliction of mine until he actually proposed, I think I shall tell Georges now. He agrees that it is an odd effect which he has never heard of. He is delighted that his kiss caused me so much happiness. I remember that Jean's reaction was very similar. Georges comes back for more. It is extreme happiness that produces the effect, not arousal so this third kiss does not cause the same result but a rather different one. I am feeling like more than just kissing but Georges obviously reckons that that is as far as we go this evening. I manage to stick to my plan of letting him take his time but it is hard. He runs me back to my flat in his Renault Estate. It reminds me of my father's swanky Peugeot.

By the middle of April, I have been seeing Georges regularly at weekends for two months. The clocks have changed for summertime and the evenings are getting lighter. Georges says he wants to take me to a restaurant in the Perrache area, arrondissement 2. He says that the restaurant is near the railway station and the area is not all that brilliant but the restaurant is called Brasserie Georges so he feels that he belongs. It is the oldest restaurant in Lyon and is famous for having produced the largest Sauerkraut in the world in 1986. It weighed in at a ton and a half.

"But don't worry" he says. "You don't have to have Sauerkraut. They serve a lot of international specialities but I recommend their sea food. It is excellent. We can walk along the Rhône after the meal if the weather is suitable."

I have the Sea Bass and it is very good. In spite of having recommended their sea food, Georges has a vegetarian artichoke dish. We have a bottle of Chablis with it. It is a warm evening so we have a walk, hand in hand, along the Rhône to the North.

"Come back to mine for a coffee?" asks Georges and I agree.

When he has poured the coffee, he gets serious: "Catherine" he says "I think I would like to marry you."

Think? I remember Jean's ridiculous beatific face, mimicking the statue of the boy in the church. What a contrast in proposals. But by now I am sure that I love Georges. I can see that he is a little uncomfortable and is feeling his way. All the same, hardly a good start from his point of view. He is starting to sweat a bit. Poor Georges: but it does make me love him even more. Mentally I have already said 'Yes' but for the moment I say nothing.

"I mean" he continues, "I know that I want to marry you. What I mean is I would like to make love to you before that. Sort of to check that we actually sort of click in bed if you sort of know what I mean. I... Oh dear!" He wipes his brow and looks embarrassed.

"I'm not doing this at all well, am I? I don't know what you think about that as an idea, Catherine. All I am really saying is 'I love you to distraction'."

"Georges, I'm not a virgin. Jean and I were engaged and had to postpone the wedding when my mother was ill." I keep the detail from him. He might not appreciate it. "I agree that it is a good idea to see if we are compatible in bed. I have been waiting for you to suggest this for a long time. I'm sure that it will work out fine. How about tonight, there's no time like the present and yes, I will certainly marry you. Put on some soft music and let's get in the mood first."

Georges looks so relieved it is almost funny. I sit down beside him and slowly undo his shirt buttons and give him a brief kiss on the lips. They are a mere taster of what is to come.

"You've got some bottles of Vacqueyras. Shall we have a glass of that? It will help us to relax." I suggest. He gets us a glass each and puts on some Frank Sinatra. It is old fashioned but it will do the trick. I need to put Georges at his ease. He is still feeling that he made a complete mess of his proposal. In years to come I think we shall be able to laugh about it but at the moment he is vulnerable. He is sitting in the middle of the sofa.

"I've really been looking forward to this." I say as I sit astride him and give him the full works of a kiss. I can feel him respond and he holds me tight. I stay still; just enjoying the moment; his closeness; the anticipation of more to come. Then I go back to sitting beside him and take another sip of the wine. We kiss gently from time to time until Sinatra has finished. Then I say: "Georges, I think that I'd be more comfortable lying down. Wouldn't you?"

We go into his bedroom. Georges manages to get all his clothes off with remarkable speed but I deliberately keep him waiting a little bit. I pretend that my bra won't undo and get him to help. This really gets him going. It is all action from then on. I really did need that. It releases all my months of pent up emotion since I met Georges. It must be the same for Georges. He is exhausted. After it is all over, he doesn't let go of me. He is holding me so tight that I cannot breathe.

"Please, Georges," I plead. "Let me take a breath or we will never have a repeat performance." I sleep like a new-born baby and am completely refreshed in the morning. Georges is already up and has made coffee. So now I am engaged for the second time. I hope it works out better that the first. Then a thought strikes me. I am going to marry Jacques' best friend. For the fifth recorded generation a Diacre or Parisel will marry the best friend of one of the other family. Perhaps the legend my father told me is true.

I do not want to delay with this wedding. I know it is a silly thought because Jean would still have had the skiing holiday if we had been married and there is no reason to think that if we had been married when we had originally intended it would have altered anything. I just feel that this time I want it to happen as soon as possible. I suggest Saturday 21st June: the summer solstice.

"But it is the shortest night of the year!" Jokes Georges.

"Well it didn't take you long last night" I reply. So he agrees and we start to make arrangements to be married at Toulouse on 21st June.

My parents want to make a big deal out of it. They suggest that we have the civil ceremony in the

Town Hall with only immediate family. By that they mean themselves with Gilbert and Elisabeth who are Georges' parents and Georges' brother, Gérard. I imagine they would also include Gérard's current girl-friend, Léna. The ceremony will be in La Salle des Illustres which is part of the town hall building. I think the whole thing sounds a bit overpowering. However, the whole reason for getting married in Toulouse is really for my mother who would be very upset if we just got married in some local register office in Lyon. If that is what she would like then I shall go along with it. Also dad is paying for the whole reception and that must give him some say in the matter. Their idea is to have the reception at Le Château de Tongras to the East of Toulouse. This is not a château on the grand scale like those of the Loire but has a great deal of rustic charm.

Georges has suggested that we have a week or two of Honeymoon in Martinique. He says it has the best cuisine in the world because of the mix of classical French food and Creole adaptations. That sounds great to me. Also the warmth and the water appeal to me more than Jean's addiction to skiing. The flights are booked from Paris Charles de Gaulle for the day after our wedding. I take some time off work to go down to Toulouse and see Mum and Dad before the big day. I do not want to be weary from travel. They have not met Georges and it happens that it is not a very convenient time from the point of view of his work. He has had to take some of his holiday allowance, obviously, but there are a lot of meetings, which he thinks are important, coming up and he is unwilling to miss them all. He comes down with me, just to meet my parents then after one night, he goes back to Lyon and returns in time for the wedding. I find the situation regarding where he is going to sleep, bizarre in the extreme. When he comes down to meet mum and dad he will sleep in the house and they have given us one room together. I contrast it with when Jean and I arrived we were given a room each. Somehow it shows how the world has changed in just a few years. But then, when he returns, the night before the wedding, because of some long standing tradition of not seeing the bride on the wedding day, poor Georges is expected to sleep on his own in some depersonalised hotel and not see me until the actual ceremony. I mean, just how idiotic is that? It is marvellous to see that mum and dad seem to be back together since I gave dad that talking to. I still find it hard to believe that I managed to do that. They are very much closer than they were after mum's bout of flu that put off, indeed effectively cancelled, my marriage to Jean.

The day is approaching and the first hitch occurs. Luckily it is really unimportant except for Gérard, Georges' brother. Léna has thrown him over rather unceremoniously and has gone off with some, what these days are called, 'Travellers'. That reduces the number of people due to be at the actual wedding to Georges, me and five others. No doubt this will be in a huge echoing hall intended for hundreds. I tell myself this is just pre-wedding nerves. La Salle des Illustres is certainly impressive and rather overwhelming. The Official State ceremony goes off according to the book. Georges and I are married. I am Madame Catherine Barbier. I am not surprised when I have one of my hallucinations with the indescribable colours and shapes. It is the longest one that I have ever had. I need to sit down. I think this one is brought on by relief as much as happiness. It is rather embarrassing; what a start to being married. We take wedding cars through the streets of Toulouse out to the reception at Le Château de Tongras. In a lot of respects the wedding reception is rather a bore. So many of the guests are friends of my parents or Georges' parents whom neither of us may have even met. We are very much on display. Everybody comes wishing us well and telling me how beautiful I look in my 'going-away outfit'. It is lovely to see Louise again after all this time but it seems impossible to have a chat and catch up on events with her. Someone is always cutting in. What I do take in is that it looks as if a huge partner swap is taking place. I can only get an overall view but it looks as if Jacques has ditched Marianne and is making a play for Aurélie. Jules, Jacques' brother seems to be eyeing up Marianne, while Gérard, being free after Léna deserted him, seems only to have eyes for Jeanne. It looks as if my world might be very different when we get back from Martinique. We are flying from Bordeaux to Charles de Gaulle but on the way back will take the train from Paris to Lyon. The time comes when we must leave for Bordeaux where we spend to-night before catching the flight tomorrow morning. The first morning that I shall wake up as Georges' wife, we shall be in Bordeaux. That seems strange. I've never been to Bordeaux.

Jacques 2003–2004

Here we are for the reception at Le Château de Tongras. Catherine looks very smart in her 'Going Away Outfit'. Georges and she are having a fortnight in Martinique as a honeymoon. It occurs to me that I have not had a holiday since my mother died nine years ago. May be the time will come. I manage to spend some of the time talking to Aurélie but I am bearing in mind that she thinks I am with Marianne so I have to watch what I say and how I say it. I think I am managing to make a good impression but I have to leave it at that. For the moment, I have this dual problem. How do I warn Jules against falling for Marianne and how do I manage to connect meaningfully with Aurélie. The key has to be Marianne. She does hold me in high regard because I was so gentle and patient with her and because we now have what is a very good but unromantic relationship; one indeed that I would be extremely sorry to lose. So if I can talk to her alone, I can probably get her to agree to tell Jeanne that I am not a romantic interest for her. Jeanne seems to be the moulder of opinions where Catherine and Aurélie are concerned. This is understandable because any useful fact seems to occur to her ages before anyone else. Her ability to put two and two together correctly is far in advance of most people. However even then, I can hardly ask Marianne to spare my brother the pain of falling in love with her.

So mentally I leave my brother, poor Jules, to fend for himself. On the other hand, I think that I can reasonably ask Marianne to clear things with Jeanne, although it would need the right sort of opportunity. If I am very lucky, this might just happen tomorrow if we all take the same train back together; Jeanne and Aurélie to Lyon and Marianne and I to Annecy.

Back at the hotel after the reception (the taxi driver on the way back was the taciturn type and didn't say a word) I have a word with Marianne. We are in the bar for a final drink. It is a bit of a come down from the château but the drinks are correspondingly cheaper.

"Marianne" I start, "I find that am very attracted to Aurélie."

"No need to tell me" she replies. "I've never seen anything so obvious in all my life. You were just like a little puppy with its tongue hanging out. How is it you think I can help?"

Oh God, everyone is so kind to me. Isn't that a lovely response when you look at her circumstances?

"If we are all on the same train tomorrow, I wonder if you could somehow work it into the conversation that we are not romantically involved. At the moment, if I come on at all strong to Aurélie, she will think that I am in the process of ditching you. Some women might relish the thought and actually enjoy that idea but somehow I imagine Aurélie will just think I'm being a right bastard."

"All right Jacques" she replies. "I get the picture. It all depends on the circumstances, because done wrong it could all backfire. I shall try, if the opportunity occurs. Let's see how it goes. You can see that it is not easy."

"Marianne you are a true friend and I hope we shall always remain so."

We are all on the same train back to Lyon first and on to Annecy for Marianne and me. Our reserved seats are nowhere near together but there are vacant seats opposite Jeanne and Aurélie. Marianne and I take those. Marianne takes no time at all in doing what I had asked her. She makes it quite clear that we are not romantically involved in two short sentences. She turns to me and says:

"Wow Jacques, your brother Jules is certainly dishy! We swapped phone numbers and I do hope he contacts me."

I can see Jeanne absorb this point. More interestingly Aurélie immediately gives me a lovely smile. It is not quite the 'come on' that Sylvie gave me years ago but to me it means everything. I relax. I think she will give me her phone number and then who knows what may happen. So we all chat for several hours on the train. I can aim more of the conversation specifically towards Aurélie than I could before. It seems to be having an effect. Perhaps I am just being overoptimistic. When Jeanne gets up to go to the loo, Marianne waits a little and then follows. I immediately ask Aurélie for her number. She looks hesitant but she gives it to me. It looks as if she feels that she can always refuse a date if asked on the phone. I get the idea that what she is thinking is 'This journey has not finished yet and I haven't made my mind up.' Jeanne and Aurélie leave at Lyon. Marianne and I have to change trains and continue to Annecy. I thank Marianne profusely for what she has done. I ask her if she and Jules really swapped phone numbers.

"Yes" she says. "If there's a teachers' convention down near him in Provence I might well go down. I enjoyed talking to him. He is very like you Jacques!"

As Aurélie lives in Lyon, I need a car. Two hours on a motorway in a Vespa is not my idea of fun. At least my 90 cc model is allowed on them. I decide that it is more use to buy an old large car than a newer small one for the same price. After a good deal of searching, I manage to find a 1990 Renault 25 Estate. It is old enough to be quite cheap and big enough to be a useful car for work. I can fit it and my Vespa in my Parking space. Indeed the Vespa will just fit inside the car, giving the possibility of finding free parking at a distance from wherever I am going and finishing the trip on the Vespa.

At the end of June, Valérie rings me. She says François has finished his CAP. He has passed with merit. It takes me back. I got a merit. Was it really six years ago? She gives me François's phone number and wishes me well.

"I hope you two get on together, Jacques" she says. "François is very bright but he is quite reserved."

"I understand, Valérie" I reply. "So am I. When you are dealing with something like electricity it is best not to be a 'happy-go-lucky' type of person. You are likely to end up neither happy nor lucky."

Valérie laughs.

"If we agree terms" I add, "don't worry, I'll look after him. I've been there."

"Thank you, Jacques" she says.

I ring François and arrange to meet in the evening at Le Bistro du Thiou. I get there a bit early. Sylvie is there with her friends.

"Hello Jacques," she says. "It's been a while. How are you?"

"I'm OK Sylvie" I say. "You gave me some good advice and I've tried to take it. What about you?"

"Oh! So-so. Win some, lose some, you know."

A young man comes in. I assume it is François. "Sorry Sylvie. I've got to go; business."

"You François?" I ask. He nods.

"I'm Jacques" I say. "Congratulations on the merit."

"Oh! You know do you?" He says. "That'll be mum. Dad wouldn't have mentioned it. Mum thinks it's a big deal."

I order us a coffee each.

"What do you want out of your first job, François?" I ask.

"I want to have a fair wage" he says. "I want to be sure that no-one in the firm is trying to cut corners and I want to be able to progress."

"Look" I reply. "Six years ago, I was exactly in your position. I had passed with merit. I didn't have a job and a man called Claude Desplaces gave me a job very similar to what I am offering you. To be fair, his company was bigger than the one I am part of but on the whole pretty similar. We insist on using the best materials and are getting recommendations by word of mouth. It is small so everyone knows everyone else. I can offer you the same wage as I had. That is allowing for inflation, but I'll add 5%. He gave me a guaranteed three months. I'll give you five. I had to do it myself from scratch with no real help because his usual electrician was in hospital following a car smash, whereas I'll be around if you need me. That is the best I can do."

I give him a piece of paper with my name, phone number and the terms that I have just offered, set out on it.

"I'll go and look at this more carefully and see what else is available" he says. "On the face of it, this looks pretty good. I'll be in touch."

He leaves. I go back over to Sylvie's table.

"Can I buy you all a drink?" I ask the table in general. They all say a glass of white. So I buy a bottle for the table and join them. It is very relaxing. Being with an ex of several years ago when there have been no hard feelings is not a problem. I owe that to Sylvie. She is still the beauty she was. I have regrets but know better than to let them get out of hand. The four of us spend a very pleasant hour before I go home.

Three days later François rings.

"Jacques" he says. "I should like to take you up on your offer. The money is slightly better than most but the real point is that I like the sound of the firm."

"You can start 1st August, François. Sometime before that I would like you to meet Guy who does the masonry and plastering and Pierre who is a plumber."

"Sounds good" he says.

Pierre has found a newly qualified plumber called Roch. He thinks that Roch would make a useful addition to the team. The five of us meet in the square at Alby. They are getting to know us there now. Everybody gets on fine but the big bonus is that Roch and François were at school together. They know each other and although not bosom buddies, are already friends. This produces a 'Happy Family' feeling to the meeting which gets everything off to a good start. Our first contract is to build a house for Monsieur Gallet. He has bought some land in Le Chemin de la Tuilerie in St. Jorioz on the west side of the lake. He has had the plans of an architect-designed house passed by the local planning committee. We are all ready to go. One of the first things that we need to arrange is to have a supply of electricity from the local mains. Without that, many of our power tools are going to be useless. I have to arrange this with EDF. As with many dealings with large corporations this takes a lot longer than seems necessary. We have hired a digger and the foundations have been started. Now that I have arranged for the electricity supply, there is nothing electrical to do for quite a while but with a firm this size everybody needs to muck in so we are all doing whatever labouring jobs are required. The main structure of the house is Guy's province. It is obvious that he needs more hands so we employ a couple of casual labourers. I can now understand how difficult it is to keep to the highest standards as a firm gets larger. Until now everyone has been hand–picked. Once one starts employing casual labour, the word 'casual' says it all. Carrying out this work is taking longer and costing quite a bit more than we had calculated meaning the profit margin is diminishing. I sympathise with Dominque Desplaces and have all the more admiration for Claude.

I wait a fortnight from when I got back from Toulouse. It takes almost that to find the car. Then I ring Aurélie at about 9 in the evening. I am trying to choose a time when she will be back from the hospital but not eating. I fail. I can hear munching. Not from Aurélie, I imagine it is Jeanne. I don't know if they have found a new flat-mate for Catherine yet. Catherine and Georges should be back from Martinique tomorrow. Aurélie answers the phone with "Dis-moi."

"It's Jacques."

"Oh Hello Jacques!" I could say her tone is totally non-committal; more accurately it comes over as bored stiff, certainly there is no encouragement there.

"I wondered if we could go for a meal next Saturday, Aurélie." There is a pause. She must know that I was going to ask her out. She is acting as if this call was totally unexpected. Eventually she says:

"I can't make Saturday, I'm on call for the hospital." Oh dear. This is not good.

"Could you manage the next Saturday?" Again a longer pause than I would like, then:

"Yes, all right. Come to the flat at about 7.30. You don't need to book anywhere. There are plenty of places quite close."

"Good. I'll look forward to it"

"Right, Jacques, see you then." Well at least she didn't say 'no', but enthusiasm? No way!

The days pass at an absolute crawl but at last the day of my date with Aurélie has arrived. Although it is Saturday, I work until four then go home, clean myself up and put on some smart clothes. I get into my 'new' 13 year old Renault and drive along the motorway to Lyon. I find rue Challemel-Lacour in the 8th arrondissement. I hadn't thought to ask but the block of flats has visitors' parking. I take the lift to the 15th floor. Reaching the flat, I ring the bell. Aurélie answers and invites me in.

"Hi Aurélie" I say. She returns the "Hi!" and we go through to the living room. Aurélie is looking very serious; even perhaps a little annoyed. This does not seem a very good start.

"Jacques, even before we start this date, there is something that needs sorting out. You know Jeanne is almost a mind reader in some respects. She has this innate ability to notice the little things that tell when somebody is telling the truth, the subconscious gestures that show what a person is really feeling. Jeanne says that there is no doubt in her mind that you and Marianne had a relationship. She noticed at your party that there was a problem with it; that you were blowing hot and cold towards each other. When we were on the train and Marianne said that she had swapped telephone numbers with Jules, Jeanne says that she was trying to mislead. It was not necessarily untrue but that Marianne knew that it would be taken in a particular way. Seeing Marianne with Jules at the reception, she was certainly enjoying talking to Jules but Jeanne is sure that 'dishy' was made up for the occasion on the train. In fact she says that for some reason Marianne was helping you to chat me up. When I told Jeanne that you had asked for this date, to quote her very words, she said 'Aurélie, if you take up with Jacques watch out because something fishy is going on there'. So tell me all. Let's clear the air before we start."

Oh dear. Marianne really would not want me to do this. On the other hand I am not going to throw away my chances with Aurélie having got this far. I am going to have to say something. The silence extends to the point where Aurélie loses patience with me. She is just about to throw me out of the flat and right out of her life, when I say:

"All right Aurélie but you must promise to tell no-one."

"Jacques, you know that it is impossible to give that sort of blanket assurance. I will promise to tell no-one unless either you agree or I think that it is of paramount importance."

"That is good enough for me. The underlying point is that Marianne was raped as a twelve year old. I started dating her and she thought she could overcome her problems but in spite of the fact that I was very gentle and patient with her over a considerable length of time, she couldn't get over her fear or memories or whatever the block was that stopped her acting as a woman normally would. As for Jules and the telephone numbers, I asked Marianne about that because I was surprised. She said that they did swap telephone numbers, but not for dating purposes. They are both teachers and she said that they might attend conferences together. My current relationship with Marianne is friendly but genuinely unromantic. Platonic it's called isn't it? I act as an escort for her if she goes to an event where she feels it would be helpful to go with a man. We were both at Georges and Catherine's wedding simply because we were both invited."

Aurélie looks at me with relief and some surprise.

"Jacques it really is possible that you have just done Marianne the greatest service that you could possibly imagine. My Professor here at Lyon, I think is probably unique. He is a neurologist not a psychiatrist but he is also a hypnotist and one of the things that he has experience in is removing the problems that victims of horrific events, including rape victims, have following their ordeal. It would, unfortunately mean that you have to admit to Marianne that you have told me about her problem. Jean-Pierre Baudouin, that's my Professor, his success rate is very high. Probably because he is a neurologist, he has a unique way of looking at the problem. Look, let's forget going out for an evening meal. I can get us something here. Let me explain Jean-Pierre's views on this."

"Certainly" I say. Isn't it strange how fate works? There was I thinking that I was betraying a trust and it may be one of the best things that I have ever done. I relax on the sofa and Aurélie sits quite close. I am nicely surprised. I thought she'd take the chair. I can just smell her perfume but I need to concentrate on what she is saying.

"Jean-Pierre is not a fan of psychotherapists who make patients relive horrific events. He says that it is easy to see that the basic thing that you will do is to reinforce the nervous pathways that support the unwanted memories, which is precisely the reverse of what is required. The more often the patient relives the memory, the stronger those nervous pathways will become, exactly as they would if they really did have to relive the experience. He concedes that one reliving of the event might just help, if you can somehow modify the patient's response as the sequence progresses but a second attempt is doomed to failure and likely to make things worse. He says that under hypnosis he does not make the patient relive the original event but feelings of fear, powerlessness and anxiety can be removed or considerably reduced by specific messages instilled during the session. He also uses metaphors, sort of parallel situations, of the horrific event giving them better outcomes so that the pathways in the brain are modified to include alternative results. This means the patient sees alternative endings to an upcoming event. This is what we all have. Is this date going to go well or be a disaster? It is what we are both wondering now. Isn't it Jacques?"

"I certainly was, but you have already made it a success, Aurélie" I say. "I shall just have to steel myself to broach the subject with Marianne as it means that I shall have to tell her that I've told you. With a bit of luck I can persuade her to see your Professor Baudouin."

"I almost forced you to tell me, didn't I Jacques? I was a bit aggressive wasn't I? Perhaps more than was needed."

She says that very tenderly and my heart leaps. My explanation and the fact that she thinks she can help has softened Aurélie. She has lost her stern look. My heart is singing as I look at her.

"We've still got time to go to a restaurant" I point out.

"No, I can make us a quick snack."

She disappears into the kitchen. She prepares Quiche Lorraine with green beans. The kitchen is big enough to have a table. We have the food there and Aurélie also gets us a small beer each. After, I suggest I wash up but she says 'no' she will. At the sink, she looks so attractive I put my arms around her. She turns round.

"Listen Jacques" she says. "Let me finish this. Then I shall give you the kiss you are hoping for. But there will be nothing further than kissing. Got it?"

"Got it" I say. I pick up the tea towel and do the drying. That should speed things up a bit. After what seems an age, Aurélie finishes the two plates, two glasses, two knives and two forks. I think she must be on a deliberate go-slow. Then she finds a baking tray and a saucepan. She is playing with me, making me wait and she knows it. The anticipation is delicious. Eventually she turns towards me and I take her in my arms. This kiss is exactly what I need. It's exactly how I imagined kissing Aurélie would make me feel. After a while Aurélie pulls back a bit and we look deep into the other's eyes for a moment.

"That was delicious; spot on for me; straight to the top of the charts." I tell her.

"I enjoyed it too" she says. "As you mentioned 'The Charts' let's go in the other room and put on a bit of music."

Aurélie puts on some Sylvain Luc, modern jazz. She puts it on low. As she sits down she kisses me again on the lips. Each time a track ends she gives me another kiss. The waiting is hell; the kiss, heaven. It is very, very sexy done like this but also relaxed because she has already set out the ground rules; 'nothing further than kissing. Got it?' About ten o'clock Jeanne comes in. She looks a little enigmatic when she sees me. She doesn't say 'Hello', just gives me a nod. Then she tells Aurélie that she may have found a flat mate to replace Catherine. One of the clerks at her firm, Zoë, has just been told that her rent is going up by quite a bit. Zoë is in a flat by herself and says that she feels rather lonely on her own. She would rather be sharing with others. Aurélie looks pleased about this. She and Jeanne talk about when they should all meet to discuss it. Jeanne must have accepted my presence because she makes us all a coffee. Then I drive back to Annecy, singing to myself with sheer delight.

Then I sober up. I remember that I am going to have to deal with a very sensitive issue with Marianne. I have broken a confidence. Admittedly she did not swear me to secrecy or anything like that but I know perfectly well that she would not have wanted her problems divulged. I do not even know if she will want to see Professor Baudouin at Lyon. If she does not, then she will be really miffed with me. I give her a ring and ask her to dinner. I say I need to talk to her about something important. I tell her that I shall book Le Clos des Sens at Annecy-le-Vieux. It is expensive enough to make her realize that this is going to be a very serious discussion. I make sure that I arrive first which means hanging around for about quarter of an hour then going in ten minutes early. Marianne arrives looking her usual beautiful self. Everybody in the restaurant is watching her as she is shown to where I am sitting. I get up old-fashioned-wise. This is mainly for the audience, Marianne wouldn't mind if I remained seated. The whole restaurant is thinking 'what on earth does she see in him?' I am afraid that in a moment or two the answer will be 'he's nothing but a creep'.

I let her get settled and we order. We decide on a salad to start. They have Omble Chevalier as an option for main, served by the weight. It is a lovely fish, but expensive. I encourage Marianne and we both order the Omble. I add a bottle of Chignin Bergeron. This is going to be a beautiful meal but if the conversation does not go right, it will turn to ashes in my mouth. Marianne can see that I am nervous as hell. She gives me an encouraging smile. I decide not to try any excuses. I'll make it sound worse than it is and if all goes right, the outcome will seem all the better. I start in.

"Marianne, I feel that I have let you down badly. I have told Aurélie about what happened when you were twelve."

She looks very surprised but doesn't say anything.

"Jeanne picked up on a lot of vibes on the train and didn't believe you. She said something didn't ring true. She picked up very accurately that you were trying to help me chat up Aurélie."

"I thought it might all go wrong."

"Aurélie was going to have nothing to do with me unless she got an explanation. So I told her."

"It really is not that important Jacques. You are quite right that I do not want it generally known but please, don't feel too bad about it."

"It has a possible upside" I continue. "You know Aurélie is a doctor at the hospital in Lyon. She is part of the neurology team. She says that her Professor, Professor Baudouin, is not only a Professor of Neurology but is also a hypnotist who deals with people who have had horrific experiences, like rape. She says he doesn't agree with making the victims relive their experience but links parallel situations with more favourable outcomes. He has a very high success rate. She offered to arrange something if you are in favour of it."

"Thanks Jacques." Marianne is looking serious. "I do know that hypnosis is used for cases like mine. I know it can sometimes be a case of making the victim relive the experience and a psychiatrist then recording the event as evidence for prosecution. Anyone can see the holes in that. It is obviously not reliable evidence and it sometimes leaves the victim feeling much worse rather than better. But Professor Baudouin does sound like someone with a different approach. I am sceptical, but it would be a good idea for me to talk to Aurélie about it. As a female doctor and someone who knows both me and the professor, her opinion is very clearly one worth having. I should be grateful if you would arrange that Jacques. As you know, I'm available almost all the time outside school hours. I'm not hopeful but who knows."

By now we have finished the salad. What it tasted like, I have no idea. Now the difficult bit of the evening is over, I hope that I, and indeed Marianne, will be able to appreciate the Omble Chevalier and the remains of the Chignin Bergeron. Marianne has a faraway look in her eye. Presently she says: "You know, Jacques, you and I have a very good relationship now without the romance and sex getting in the way. I hope we can maintain it."

"Yes I agree" I say. It is true.

I drive Marianne to have a chat with Aurélie at the flat. They are closeted in a separate room for an hour and a half. When they emerge, they both look exhausted.

Marianne says: "Aurélie has removed most but not all of my hesitation. She says she'll talk to the professor and arrange a meeting."

"Yes" says Aurélie. "I get on pretty well with Professor Baudouin and I feel sure that he will want to help."

In the car on the way back to Annecy, Marianne is still very nervous about the whole idea.

"So many things go wrong. The idea of having one's mind manipulated even for one's own sake is a thing that scares me. It is only the idea that this is a professor of neurology, one who understands the brain as a machine, if you like, as well as a thought producer that makes me feel that his combined approach may work better than either on their own."

I am now on my way to see Aurélie again. There is no doubt that our joint effort to help Marianne is drawing us together. Her eyes when she looks at me are soft and kind. I would like them to be longing and hopeful but not so far. When I arrive she gives me an immediate kiss. This is more than I expected.

"I've had a word with Jean-Pierre" she says. "He is very willing to help. He says he is prepared to see

Marianne here with me as a chaperone. He always has a chaperone for both male and female patients. He says that it is best when the chaperone is acquainted with both him and the patient. He also says" and at this point Aurélie looks a bit embarrassed and blushes slightly, "that because I'm his favourite assistant, there'll be no charge."

"OK" I say. "I'll run her here whenever you have it arranged and make myself scarce for: how long is a session?"

"Usually about 45 minutes."

"Right, is there a time yet?"

"Jean-Pierre said definitely weekend, preferably Sunday, any time between 10 and 4. He suggested 2 o'clock next Sunday. He says 'four sessions, one a week for four weeks, then leave it for at least three months and see what happens'."

"I'll put it to Marianne" I say. "But I'm sure that she'll go along with that."

The next four Sundays, I drive Marianne to Lyon. She has a session with Professor Baudouin. I leave her at the bottom of the block of flats. So I never actually see the professor, let alone meet him. I then go and have a coffee in a bar with a television screen and watch some inane programme for three quarters of an hour. Just one time, the third week, there was a huge coincidence. They were showing excerpts from the best France v England Rugby matches. There was a section covering the game that Claude and I watched, just after I passed my CAP. That French try looked just as impressive in replay so many years on. Nevertheless, it made me think, where would I be if it were not for that match? I remember that it was because I reflexly stood up in response to that try, that Claude talked to me. It is possible that it is that try that has shaped my whole life. After the session I collect Marianne, give Aurélie a quick kiss (the highlight of my week) and run Marianne back to Annecy. The four sessions are over, but there is nothing to test the result against. Marianne says that she does feel different in some situations where previously she felt rather threatened but cannot say how things will work out if really put to the test.

The house we are building is progressing in leaps and bounds. It is amazing with modern forms of mass production that whole sections of wall with spaces for doors or windows can be purchased ready-made and once on site, can be put in place in minutes. Although they have the 'holes' for doors or windows, they do not come with already defined positions for electric sockets, heaters and so on. Our agreement with the customer was that our bill would be settled at each quarter of completion. We have received the first payment and the second is now due. As a new firm with no money in the bank, indeed a large overdraft, we are very dependent on the customer cashing out on the nail and he does. This enables us to buy the next set of materials. This is the first time that we can actually be sure that we can complete the building without exceeding our overdraft limit. It is worth a little celebration. So Guy, Pierre, François, Roch and I meet for a meal in the square at Alby-sur-Chéran. There is nothing posh there but we are quite happy with our usual café. I detect that Pierre and Guy have some reservations about our position but I am glad to see that both François and Roch seem to be enjoying their first proper job and are not feeling put-upon in any way. We are not out of the woods yet but as long as the rest of this building goes according to plan, we will have made a tidy profit. This will mean that we are in a much more secure financial position for the next contract.

In early November Marianne gives me a ring. She is going to a 3 day Teachers' Conference in Nice. She is quite excited about it. I ask her if she wants me to come with her as we have done from time to time. She says:

"No. Thank you Jacques. I have given Jules a ring and we are going to meet there."

I think I can see the sub-text here. It must have been obvious to Marianne at Georges and Catherine's wedding that Jules really fancied her. He couldn't keep his eyes off her. Perhaps she is using Jules as a test case to try out the results of the hypnosis sessions. I keep my thoughts to myself but say that I hope she enjoys the conference. When she gets back she is very pleased with how it has gone. She and Jules were in the same hotel. He was delighted to see her and they got on very well. She said Jules wanted to kiss her goodnight on the last evening. She had agreed.

"It was so different this time, Jacques. I wasn't in the position of having to make myself do it. It was so enjoyable being kissed and held tight. Jules and I are going to see each other from time to time and things may develop. It was only a kiss but the difference in how I felt was huge."

I pass this good news on to Aurélie. She is delighted and says she will let Professor Baudouin know. I am seeing her only once a week most of the time. With us both working and over two hours by motorway apart, it is difficult to see her more often. I am completely and utterly in love with Aurélie. I do not understand how 'Love at first sight' occurs; I only know that it happened to me. Aurélie is calling all the shots. I remember 'nothing further than kissing. Got it?' She has dictated every move. When I look back I can see that in every relationship that I have had, the woman has controlled the rate of progress. Does this make me weak? Am I imagining that and they also think that I've controlled things just as I think they have? Surely not. The only time that I can see that I may have been a little pushy, was when getting a telephone number and first date off Aurélie. She was very reluctant. Since then she has controlled every advance and every stand-still. She is now letting me caress her in some intimate places and appears to be enjoying it as much as I do. I want to be with her for all time but I am a cautious type. I do not want to lose what I've got. Soon I shall propose marriage and hope she doesn't just laugh. She gives me a ring on a Monday evening.

"Jean-Pierre says he is delighted with Marianne's progress. He says no more sessions unless she encounters a block that worries her. He says it is best to have the minimum number of sessions that work. But" her voice rises in excitement, "Jean-Pierre has also been giving me some career advice. He wanted to see me in his office. I was a bit concerned in case I had made some mistake or other. I didn't think it would be that because, quite frankly, I do not make mistakes. If I do not know what to do, I ask him. He wanted to talk about my career. He says there is a position coming up at Annecy which he advises me to apply for. He says that I am ready for a permanent position. As I expect you know, because it is very near to Marianne's flat, they are building a new hospital for Annecy at Pringy. The old one in Annecy will stay open until that is completed. Apparently in the pipe-line and few people know about it there is a plan to combine the new hospital with the one at St. Julien-en-Genevois. That will make it the fourth biggest take-area in France and correspondingly important. Jean-Pierre says if I get in now and the plan goes ahead, I shall have one of the most prestigious jobs in the whole of France. He will give me a good reference and he says he knows some of the people who are likely to be on the interview panel."

She is talking nineteen to the dozen. I take in her excitement and that she is going to apply for a post at Annecy. The detail goes over my head. I also think that maybe I should worry about Professor Jean-Pierre Baudouin. It is Jean-Pierre this and Jean-Pierre that. I also remember her blush when she said Jean-Pierre called her his 'favourite assistant'. However, if he is encouraging her to move to Annecy, I am probably being unreasonable.

It is the festive season once again. I wonder how much I shall be able to see Aurélie. Then to my surprise Aurélie actually almost tells me that she is going to spend the weekend with me. I do not understand the detail but it appears that Jeanne, the one with the penetrating eyes that can see straight into my empty head, wants the flat for the weekend to have a tryst with Georges' brother, Gérard. Well that suits me. We have kissed and petted but Aurélie has never suggested that I might stay at hers or she at mine. Now without any effort on my part she is going to stay the weekend. When the Friday night arrives, I collect Aurélie from the hospital. She says she is not sure when Gérard is due to arrive at the flat, so we drive straight back to mine. As soon as we are comfortably sitting down, Aurélie becomes serious. Since the first time this happened, I have always liked her becoming serious because each time my life seems to get even better. This turns out to be the case once again, although it has been a huge stress for poor Aurélie.

Looking very serious Aurélie says: "I love you Jacques. I'll tell you how I know. I can't give you the full details because of patient confidentiality. A few days ago, I had to put up with a torrent of abuse from the husband of a patient that I have been caring for. Her disease has taken a turn for the worse and he was calling me all sorts of things, some of which I had never even heard before. It is incredibly upsetting when you have been doing your level best to help someone. The thing that has changed my perspective, changed my whole life, is that as I was being sworn at, cursed at, shouted at and threatened, what I thought was 'I need Jacques. Where is Jacques? Please Jacques where are you?' So you see, I must love you! So hold me close, Jacques, will you. I want to feel you close to me."

I hold her close. I just hold her for a long time and when I release her. She seems to be in dreamland. She is sort of not quite there. Then that effect is gone and she is back to her normal efficient self. But her eyes are still soft. I feel that this is some kind of watershed. I do not understand what has happened but I feel as if I have been finally accepted as a true partner.

Next comes an ultimatum.

"Now there is no going back. I now know that I need you. It is up to you, we part now or we stay together for ever."

This is nothing like the way that I imagined getting engaged but it appears that the surprises are not yet over.

"Before you tell me what you think" says my lovely Aurélie. "I need to tell you something which may make you stop and consider. When I asked you to hold me close just then, and you did, you may have noticed that I was in some kind of partial consciousness for a bit?"

"You did seem to be in dreamland for a moment. Yes. I loved it as a reaction to me holding you."

"It is not quite like that Jacques. When I am very happy, I hear soft, dreamy music in my head. I can tell that it is not from the real world. It is slightly different every time this happens and it is not music that I have ever heard before. At the same time, I am out of action for a minute or so. I think that if an emergency occurred, I could still act but that has never yet happened, so I am not sure. It is a form of synaesthesia. We were taught about it in medical school. If you include all the different types and degrees, about one person in twenty five has it but most go unnoticed as unimportant. Most commonly it is a colour being associated with a specific number or sound. It runs in families and it is said that no two cases are exactly alike. That is something that it is impossible to prove. What the experts mean is that even identical twins have slightly different experiences. Mine has this slightly worrying element that I am adrift for a minute or so."

I tell Aurélie that I have been in love with her since I first saw her at Catherine and Georges' marriage. Being with her for all time is just what I have in mind.

"Sit down and relax. Put on some music. I shall get us a snack" I say.

She finds some modern jazz. I recently bought Guillermo Gregorio, Ellipsis.

She says: "Don't bother with the snack, Jacques, come and sit down with me."

Then exactly as she had with the Sylvain Luc, as the first track ends she gives me a kiss; and again when the second and third track end. Her kisses become more and more demanding with each track. This time there is no 'Nothing further than kissing. Got it?' After the kiss following 'Orion's belt', the last track, we move to my bedroom.

Marianne says that she has had Jules to stay for the weekend. She says that they kissed a lot and went further than that. She thoroughly enjoyed the whole experience. She would like Aurélie and me to come to dinner next Saturday. It is a great occasion. She is so grateful to Aurélie and of course Professor Baudouin. She and Jules are seeing each other very regularly. It looks as if Marianne may end up being my sister-in-law!

The house in St. Jorioz looks almost complete from the outside. Pierre and I have some plumbing and electrics to do but all is going well. Pierre and I have decided that, as part of 'going the extra mile' we will make a plan of all the pipes and wires in the house, whether in walls, under floors or over ceilings. We can give the plan to the owner. It means that when someone needs to drill into a wall or ceiling, they will know where the pipes and wires are and can therefore easily avoid them. There are so many stories of someone wanting to put a picture up and drilling through a water pipe. Making a plan of them is the sort of thing that takes very little time, costs virtually nothing and may make a big impression on the customer. By February, the house is finished and the customer has paid. PRO's bank account is in profit for the first time. Admittedly as soon as we need to cash out for more materials it will be in the red again but by far less than last time. Another order has come in so we have enough business to survive. The post at Annecy has been advertised and Aurélie has applied for it. We are back to seeing each other once or sometimes twice a week. It is difficult to get together more often as she works in Lyon and I am working around Lake Annecy. Sometimes, but not often, I collect her from her flat on Saturday morning, we drive to Annecy and spend the weekend before I drive her back to Lyon on Sunday evening. When that happens we can spend the night together in my flat. One Saturday afternoon late in March, I drive her to Le Roc de Chère and we walk on the woodland path to Le Balcon au Lac. I tell her about my mother's death, the meeting with Catherine and Jean and about the day Jean was killed.

"I think because I spent a whole month with Catherine when we were 13, she became like a sister to me. I have loved Catherine as I would a sister since that holiday but I have never had any romantic thoughts about her. You are so similar in many ways yet I love you in a completely different way."

"This is a beautiful place" says Aurélie; "romantic even." She gives me a gentle kiss. We stand hand in hand for several minutes just admiring the view.

The interview for the Annecy post for which she is applying, is in April. It is on a Tuesday. The weekend before, Aurélie is as nervous as a kitten. She is very quiet, rather depressed and does not want to go anywhere or do anything. She sits on my sofa and if I didn't know the reason I would think she was having one long sulk. She comes and spends Monday night with me to make the journey to the interview much easier. She is much more relaxed. We have a quiet evening with no hanky-panky. I run her to the hospital for the interview and stay in the car for what seems hours. When she comes out, she is all smiles and very relaxed. She says the interview went very well. She doesn't feel it could have gone any better but they are going to let the candidates know the result on Thursday. I spend all Thursday looking at my phone, waiting for it to ring. I hardly get any work done. At 4 o'clock it does.

"Hello Jacques" she says, "how's the house coming along?"

I know straightaway that she has the job, I can tell from her voice. She thinks that she is delaying telling me for the fun of making me wait, but I know.

"Tremendous!" I say, "you got it. Well done Aurélie."

She laughs. I love her laugh. "You could tell. Yes Jacques I got it. I start in July."

"We must have a big celebration on Saturday, I shall book somewhere for dinner."

"Yes...Jacques?"

"What, my darling?"

"I love you." The phone goes dead.

I book Les Jardins de L'Auberge for the celebration. I check that they will give us a window table overlooking the Thiou. I am going to suggest that we have the Pierrade de Boeuf. I shall feed Aurélie from the hotplate. That goes down very well. We are laughing and giggling as we feed one another, just like couple of kids. After, we walk arm in arm back to the car and home to bed.

By June PRO has built another house. It is on La route de la Chapelle in the Ramponnet area of Menthon St.Bernard. With the prefabricated parts, it is amazing how quickly they go up. This time we will be almost out of debt even after ordering the stuff for our next house. Things are going well. Then disaster. The customer has died and the benefactors of his will are not going to pay. Theoretically we could take them to court but we don't have the resources and it would take years. We have an emergency meeting but none of us can come up with a solution. It is unlikely that the bank will increase our overdraft limit. This looks like the end of PRO. It all seemed to be working out so well. Then I think of a madcap scheme. Remembering Sylvie's advice and it was good advice, I must talk to Aurélie about it.

I sit Aurélie in the armchair with a glass of Beaumes-de-Venise. She knows something is afoot. I am looking serious. I hope this will work out as well for us as it seems to when she looks serious.

"Aurélie" I say. "I have what may be a crazy idea. I want your opinion."

I tell her about the house in Ramponnet and how the customers have defaulted. How it probably means the end of PRO.

"What is your crazy idea Jacques?" she asks.

"Listen" I say. "I can always get a job as an electrician with a firm. So if PRO folds I shall not be out of work. The firm will not be greatly in debt and it should be possible to pay it off."

Aurélie gets out of the chair and gives me a hug. "Jacques" she says. "Do get on with it. What is the crazy idea?"

"With our combined incomes we could get a mortgage on the house I'm talking about, sell this flat and retrieve my deposit and however much has been paid off and have what is a very nice house in Menthon St. Bernard. The firm would get paid. It would save the firm and give us a house."

Aurélie is quite taken with the idea. "It needs very careful attention to the detail, Jacques. What the mortgage rate is. How much we would get from this flat. Perhaps more doubtful still is how much a mortgage company would assess your possible income at in view of the firm's financial position. But" she continues, "I do like the concept. Another thing that I obviously want to do, as with any house purchase is to see it first."

I take Aurélie to look at the house and she immediately falls in love with it. It has three bedrooms. The master bedroom has a balcony facing west. It is looking towards the lake. In the distance over Menthon St. Bernard you can just see a postage stamp's worth of the actual lake. The château at Annecy is visible in the far distance. Downstairs the main room is a good size with double doors opening onto a terrace facing South which will get the sun for most of the day. The terrace has a view of Les Dents de Lanfon, the most iconic of the mountains round the lake. There is a nice large kitchen and slightly under ¼ acre of grounds which at the moment is rough grassland with a couple of small trees.

"Oh Jacques" she sighs. "Do you think we could really live here? It is beautiful and to live in one of the very first houses built by a firm that you founded! That would something I remembered every time I came home. Let's see if we can really do it."

When Aurélie starts her post at Annecy Hospital, she moves in with me. This is the big test of a relationship. I love it. Sometimes I am home before Aurélie and sometimes she is home first. I don't mind which. Waiting for her to arrive is heaven and seeing her in the flat when I arrive is what I have dreamed of since the day I first saw her down in Toulouse. I was going to propose to her but in the event, she got there first. It was not actually a proposal of marriage more of life-time commitment. I laugh when I think how she presented it more or less as an ultimatum. I should like to be actually married to her although I do not really see why: at least not until we are trying to have children. Aurélie starts her new post in July. For the whole of the first week, she isn't home until late. She says that this is not going to continue. Neurology is not a speciality that has a high level of emergency or work out of normal hours. She says starting a new job, if you are going to do it well you must be meticulous about learning all the facets early on. That is something that I understand and agree with. So I even encourage her to be as late as she wants, if it will make the job easier later on.

When the hectic first two weeks are over, I decide that I shall suggest that we get married.

I buy some of those beautiful cold dishes that you can get at Pauvert in rue Grenette, some easy to cook fresh fish from the fishmonger in rue Jean Jacques Rousseau; some fresh raspberries and vegetables from Aux Quatre Saisons in rue de la Filaterie. To go with it I buy a bottle of Chignin Bergeron and some Badoit from the Monoprix opposite L'Église Notre Dame de Liesse. I am no cook but this should not test my culinary powers. The first course and sweet do not need cooking at all. I cook the fish as a parcel because that way it is not very time dependent. It will not dry out if overcooked. When Aurélie arrives I have the first course, Lobster cocktail, beautifully presented in its own glass just as it was in Pauvert, already on the table with a glass of the Chignon Bergeron ready poured. The fish in its parcel is cooking in the oven and I have very gently rinsed the raspberries and have them ready to serve.

Aurélie laughs: "What's the occasion, Jacques?"

"The occasion is just that I love you even more than yesterday."

She looks puzzled and continues to do so throughout the meal, even while she chats happily about her day.

When we have eaten the last raspberry, I say: "Aurélie, will you marry me?"

She laughs again. I love that laugh.

"Oh! That's what it is all about. Of course" she says. "But why?"

"I'd just like to make it all legal" I say. "I know that there is no real reason to, at least at the moment. It does crystalize my commitment to you."

"Yes, of course I will" she says again. "Where and when do you think?"

"That is usually the choice of the bride I believe, but if you are uncertain, we can talk about it."

"I think here rather than at my parents' in Provence." she says. So we settle on Annecy with a reception at L'Hôtel Impérial on Saturday 14th August. It is not that long to go so we send out the invitations almost at once.

Catherine 2003–2004

To have an immediate honeymoon after getting married is traditional. Georges and I decided to go to Martinique. Neither of us had left Europe before. I found it rather strange that Martinique is regarded as part of France and it seemed particularly peculiar to be using euros for currency when on the other side of the Atlantic. An immediate honeymoon does have its downside. Our first night married was in an airport hotel in Bordeaux and we had to be up early in the morning to catch a flight to Charles de Gaulle Airport. The main leg of the trip left Charles de Gaulle at about 3 p.m. With the time difference we should arrive in time to have an evening meal. We had decided on economy seats for the first leg to Paris and premium economy for the long flight to the Caribbean. This proved difficult on-line. The site insisted on booking the whole journey either as economy or premium. Eventually we had to book the trip as two different items. There were no problems with the flights. Everything was on schedule but we arrived at Fort de France in Martinique completely shattered. We skipped the evening meal that we had intended and were in bed by 9 o'clock. I was asleep immediately and slept a full twelve hours, waking at nine in the morning. When looking at the possibilities of where to stay on the island, we had fancied Plage de Madiana slightly to the west of Fort de France. It had a beautiful beach but we saw that there was a military area very close and were uncertain what effect that might have. We didn't want some kind of army manoeuvres with gunfire interrupting our holiday. In the end we chose Hôtel Bakoua on the beach at Les Trois Îlets. We hired a car for the second week so that we could explore the rest of the island.

It was a beautifully relaxing holiday. I remember the things that particularly surprised me. Both Georges and I had learnt to swim at a young age; he at Lac de Vassivière; I at Lac d'Annecy. These are fresh water lakes. Neither of us had ever swum in salt water. Perhaps my most striking memory of Martinique was the buoyancy of the sea. I felt that you could almost sit in it without sinking. The sea water stung my eyes far more than the lake water had. The next surprise, even though Georges had mentioned the cuisine to me before we left, was the food. We went to a number of restaurants around the island, particularly in the second week when we had the car. The standard of the food was superb. The restaurants had an impressive blend of French cuisine modified, improved is perhaps a better word, by the Creole influence. I took down a couple of recipes to take home. I particularly like Écrevisses Étouffées and their version of Fricassée de Crabes. There was a dish they called Ti-nain morue mainly dried cod with banana which seemed to put one on a high for a couple of hours a bit like magic mushrooms. On the other hand sometimes I felt the spice was overdone. Avocat féroce was too much for me. I suppose the warning is in the name.

The third surprise was the temperature. The day was no hotter than Toulouse in summer but it seemed to stay stiflingly hot at night. It was almost as if the night was hotter than the day. The other temperature surprise was the Prèsqu'île de la Caravelle to the East projecting into the Atlantic. We took the car there for a day in our second week. The temperature there was quite cold; very cold compared to elsewhere. Perhaps we had a freak day. The whole holiday was a great experience. Then the return flight to Paris followed by the train to Lyon, with the resultant jet-lag, spoils all the benefit of the relaxing time that we have just had. We are back in Lyon, just as shattered as when we arrived in Martinique. I have naturally moved in with Georges now we are married and we are both are back at work.

As is usually the case the first day back at work after a holiday, there is a lot of catching up to do. I am far too busy for lunch but by the next day, I have caught up with the backlog. Monique and I go to our usual café, Le Café des Arts in Avenue Pierre Semard. There is a little notice on the door saying that it is closed for their annual holiday and will reopen on Monday, 2nd August. Leaving the railway line behind us, we find another café in L'Impasse de l'Asphalte. The name gives you an idea of the area we are working in. Now that I am completely over the attempted rape scene, I sometimes regret coming to Lyon so that I would be with Jeanne. The people at Maîtres Bonneau Frères are very pleasant but the firm is not in the best neighbourhood. We usually have a salad for lunch and I order one today. Monique has vegetable soup. It is a hot day. Not as hot as Martinique but hot for all that.

"Monique" I say. "You always have a salad. Why the vegetable soup?"

"This place has egg in the salad, Le Café des Arts never does" she replies.

I raise my eyebrows just a touch.

"I didn't know you were allergic to eggs, Monique."

She looks slightly embarrassed.

"I'm not allergic" she replies. "Several months ago my brother and both my sisters went vegan and they persuaded me to do the same. The salad at Le Café des Arts is always vegan."

"Well OK" I say. "Don't you find it a bit difficult? Not everywhere does vegan food."

"I'm not extreme. If there isn't anything vegan on the menu, I order something close to vegan and just leave the non-vegan element of the dish. I don't make a fuss about it. It seems to work all right."

Now that we know that Le Café des Arts is closed for the rest of the month we take the trouble to find somewhere a bit better than L'Impasse de l'Asphalte. It is an Italian, 'Cucine-Apéro' in Avenue Jean Jaurès. It is very nice and although it is a little further to walk, it might just replace Le Café des Arts for lunch on a more permanent basis.

Aurélie already has agreed a date with Jacques. I detected that as an upcoming event at the reception. It looked as if Jacques was ditching Marianne then. I wonder how Marianne felt about it. I'd have thought that Aurélie would have been put off by seeing that. She must be very keen on Jacques. However, when I invite Jeanne to dinner, she puts me straight. Although she doesn't seem to know the details of why, she says that Marianne was actually helping Jacques make a good impression with Aurélie. That is curious. Jeanne also tells me that that one of the clerks at her firm may be going to fill the gap that I have left at the flat. It is not yet certain. She is called Zoë, is living on her own and would rather have some company. That is helpful. I would naturally pay for my third of the flat until they find someone to replace me but it would be nice to have that happen sooner rather than later.

I think that I shall have a proper dinner party in a month or so. I want to try out those recipes from Martinique on my friends. Perhaps I need to practice on Georges and me first in case there are any unforeseen difficulties. I try the Ti-nain morue recipe first. Georges is disappointed. It tastes all right but there is no doubt that it does not produce the effect that it did in Martinique. There, both Georges and I experienced a definite high, a sense of elation, for several hours after eating it. This did not happen with my version. I think it may be something to do with the way the cod is dried. There is a fish, which I know as Saupe but is also called the 'dream fish' which if it is prepared in a certain way produces hallucinations. If it is gutted immediately and cooked early, this doesn't happen. Perhaps it is the same with the Ti-nain morue.

It is now early August. Monique and I are back in Le Café des Arts. She is worried.

"Catherine," she starts. "I am getting some curious things happening to me. I cannot quite put my finger on it, but my sight is changing. It isn't much but quite definite. I have two pairs of almost identical kitchen scissors. The only difference is that they are a very slightly different shade of red. Now I cannot tell them apart. They look just the same colour. I also think, although I can't be sure, that I don't see as much out of the corner of my eyes as I did. I have seen a doctor but he didn't seem to make anything of it. I'm also getting a tingle in my hands from time to time."

I am as sympathetic as I can be. It is hard to know what to say. If she has seen a doctor, what is next? A month later she mentions it again.

"I know that something is up. I'm definitely getting tingling in my hands and it seems to be starting in my feet."

I am still at a loss as to what I can do. I mumble reassurances. Then it occurs to me that Aurélie is a doctor and a neurologist. If the doctor that Monique is seeing can't help her, perhaps Aurélie would be prepared to talk to her.

"I've got a cousin, Aurélie, who is a neurologist at the Hospices Civils in Boulevard Pinel." I tell her. "I'll mention it to her and perhaps she'll see if she can help."

"Oh! Thank you, Catherine. That would be so reassuring. I don't suppose that it is anything serious but it does seem to be getting worse."

I give Aurélie a ring. She will happily see Monique at the flat on Saturday. Why don't we both come for lunch? When we arrive Jeanne is there as well. We have cold peppered mackerel with a salad. Monique leaves the mackerel but eats the salad. Then she and Aurélie disappear for almost an hour.

Jeanne is trying to play it down but I can see that really she is quite excited.

"Gérard, Georges' brother!" she laughs, "is coming to Lyon in a couple of weeks and has suggested that we have dinner together."

"Are you going to accept?" I ask innocently, pretending that I don't already know the answer.

"I'm not sure" she lies (she's not the only one who can see a deception, although for me it has to hit me in the face). "We talked a lot at your wedding but I'm not sure he's my type."

I egg her on "Oh go on Jeanne, give the guy a break. It would be fun if you were seeing my brother-in-law."

"Yes all right, perhaps I will. He was quite sweet." And indeed, it would be fun if one of my very best friends and my brother-in-law hit it off.

When Aurélie and Monique return, Monique says: "Aurélie thinks she might know the answer. She doesn't want to say because it's confidential and she is not sure. I said that I wanted you to know what she thought and she could explain it better than I. Go on Aurélie, it is interesting."

"Well, I'm really not sure. It needs several tests to confirm. We can do those at the hospital. I can arrange that. It shouldn't be too far in the future. I think what Monique has is Vitamin B_{12} deficiency. She is getting pins and needles, has reduced optic acuity and a slight, rather unusual degree of colour blindness. She tells me that she has been on a vegan diet for almost six months without taking any supplements. No plants produce vitamin B_{12}: actually no animals do either. It is all produced by micro-organisms but animals do store it, plants don't. The only way to get vitamin B_{12} if you are vegan is by taking a B_{12} enriched food. As I said, this needs confirmation because it is rare to get signs of a deficiency this quickly and the eye symptoms are very rare anyway. So I may be wrong. Monique, I do not want to stop your vegan experience when there is so much doubt. Today and until I can arrange the tests, have at least a pint of oat or almond milk that says it has been B_{12} enriched, because the eye problems you are getting very quickly become irreversible. We certainly don't want that. If this does turn out to be vitamin deficiency, unless you are a committed vegan, I suggest that you at least scale it down to vegetarian and have milk and eggs. You would need up to two glasses of milk and an egg a day for maintenance. If you had what I shall call a normal diet, you wouldn't need so many eggs which can be a problem in themselves. You have shown a high tendency to get the problem so you would be well advised to have more than the minimum recommendation. Let's wait for the tests."

"Wow!" I think. "Good for Aurélie. If she is right, she has probably saved Monique's eye-sight from being bad for the rest of her life."

Looking at Jeanne who picks up those almost imperceptible vibes, I can see that she knows that in spite of the disclaimers, Aurélie is close to certain that she is right. The tests are carried out within two weeks. I think Aurélie must have pulled a few strings. They confirm the B_{12} deficiency and the electromyogram (EMG) is compatible with her pins and needles being part of it. Aurélie says the medical world is divided as to whether there are any EMG signs specific to B_{12} deficiency. Monique is full of praise and says that she is giving up any thought of veganism and is advising her brother and sisters to do the same. The next time we have lunch, she has salami. I think she is trying to make a point.

Georges' brother Gérard is a Graphic designer with a firm in Limoges. Most of the time, his work does not require him to be at the office. In fact he gets most of his income from freelance work which he is usually able to do from anywhere that has a computer. He had attended the 'Meeting of Styles' at Lyon in April as he needed to keep in touch with artistic developments. Jeanne says he keeps saying that he wished he had known her then: there was so much brilliant art work at the meeting. At the moment he has rented a flat in Lyon. Jeanne says that he has made no secret of the fact that he has come here specifically so that he can see her. She is very flattered by that. I have never seen Jeanne so much of a dither. Jeanne is tall. She was beautiful as a teenager and indeed is still very elegant. Seeing her all a dither gives a baby-doll effect that I can imagine would get any man going. She keeps me abreast of developments by text messages as most of the time that we might otherwise see each other face to face, she is seeing Gérard.

They see 'Les Femmes Savantes' and 'Le Bourgeois Gentilhomme' at the Salle Molière, 'Balzac and the little Chinese Seamstress' with subtitles at the Pathé Bellecourt cinema and Jean-Paul Sartre's 'No Exit' at the Théatre Tète d'Or.

Then Jeanne's text messages stop. Completely. Not a word. I don't think much about that for a week and then I send her a text. There is no reply. I give her a ring. There is no answer. So having failed to make contact, I give Aurélie a buzz to see if she knows what is going on. Aurélie says that she hasn't seen Jeanne for over a week. She imagines that she has moved in with Gérard as they were getting on so well.

"Perhaps she has just lost her phone" says Aurélie.

"Yes it might well be just that, but as neither of us has heard from her in over a week, perhaps we need to check."

That proved far harder than I imagined. I didn't have the address of Gérard's flat and I didn't think Georges did. I didn't have Gérard's phone number but I imagined that Georges would have a phone number for his brother. He did but when we phoned it, there was an automatic message saying that the number was unobtainable. Georges said that he had had that number for years without using it.

Presumably, Gérard had got a new number without letting Georges know.

I am at a loss as to what to do. It seems an over-reaction to go to the police and report her as a missing person. Almost certainly there is an explanation and she is with Gérard. However, strange things do occur. If they had a row and she stomped off late in the evening, anything could happen. As is often the case with this sort of situation, I started off thinking there is nothing to worry about but then every time I think about it, I become more and more concerned. At last I had a constructive thought. I knew that Gérard did freelance work. He was bound to have a website and that would almost certainly have a method of contacting him; either phone or email. A search for Gérard Barbier (I am still finding it strange that I am Madame Barbier) does indeed take me to his website. He has some impressive examples of his work on the site and for a while I am diverted from my cause just admiring the images. Then I regain my purpose and he has in fact put a telephone number. It is an O6 number. That means it is a mobile phone so hopefully he will answer it. I ring him mid-morning from the office.

"Gérard Barbier" he answers immediately.

"Catherine" I say. "Your sister-in-law."

"Ah! My brother's lovely wife" he replies. "How are you Catherine?"

"I'm well Gérard but I'm worried about Jeanne. I haven't heard from her for well over a week and before that she was in contact every day so I'm a bit concerned. Is she with you?"

"Yes, she's fine. She's been staying at the flat I've rented here in Lyon. She left her mobile at her place. It'll no doubt be completely flat by now. Hang on a second and you can talk to her."

Thank heavens for that. Of course she was bound to be OK but that is just what everyone thinks and then there's a disaster. Jeanne comes on the phone.

"Yes I'm fine Catherine. It's sweet of you to be so worried about me. We have had a marvellous fortnight but Gérard has to go back to Limoges tomorrow. There's a meeting at the firm that he needs to attend. Also he was lucky getting this short term let because the owner is on holiday and that expires the day after any way."

I invite Jeanne round for a good chinwag the evening after Gérard leaves, Georges is at an after-work meeting. Jeanne looks the picture of health and very relaxed. We sit down with a cup of coffee. She starts to say something and I just cannot help myself.

"So he came across with it OK did he, Jeanne?" I say.

Jeanne bursts out laughing. "It's been a long time coming but I deserved that! It does seem ages ago that we were students and Jean…" she stops herself.

"It's OK Jeanne I say. Jean is well and truly buried for me now. I am so happy being with Georges. I think back to those times rather like a childhood holiday. Fond memories but well in the past."

"That's good" she says. "Gérard and I are definitely going to carry on seeing one another but it is going to be difficult, at least in the short term. He can be away from

Limoges quite a lot of the time but it is difficult to get short-term lets, hotels work out very expensive for anything much more than a night. I do not see that I can have him staying at the flat with Zoë and Aurélie. That would be a real imposition on them. The trip by car is over four hours each way and the train takes for ages." I sympathise.

One day at Bonneau Frères, Hans our chief clerk asks if he can have a few words with me in his office. A firm of notaires can be compared to a regiment in the army. The notaires themselves represent the officers. I am about a captain by now I suppose; the partners, colonels. The clerks and receptionist are the privates. The person who holds the whole regiment together, the regimental sergeant major, in a firm of notaires is the chief clerk: without a good chief clerk a firm will not function properly. In this firm that is Hans. Just as a lieutenant might not like the thought of being given a word of advice by the RSM, I was not relishing Hans having a quiet word in my ear. I remembered when I started that Monique had warned me that Hans could be a bit of a terror: that he was the one to watch out for. So it was with some trepidation that I followed him along the corridor to his office. His first words did not put me at my ease.

"Do take a seat, Catherine" he starts. "You've been with us over fifteen months now. I usually like to have a word with young notaires like yourself when they've been here about a year. Tell them how they are doing. Let them know what I think. Give them the benefit of my advice. I have been putting it off in your case. Yesterday I told myself that I really must get on and do it."

"Why have you felt that you needed to put it off, Hans?" I ask. He hesitates. Eventually he says:

"Frankly, Catherine, you're so damned good." He gives a sort of laugh. "I like to be able to give a little cautionary advice or something. In your case I have decided that there is really only one useful bit of advice that I can give you and the reason that I have hesitated is that it is not at all in this firm's interest."

"Well, what is that then Hans?"

"My bit of advice to you Catherine is that you are ready for a junior partnership. You are too good as an assistant in a firm like this. I know both the Partners here would give you a sparkling reference. They have never had anyone of your calibre before. They would be sorry to see you go but that is the nature of your present position. People come and go. Some are good, some less so. My advice to you is to look for a good firm that needs a junior partner. Any firm that appoints you is not going to be sorry."

I find that I am blushing like mad. I am fighting to hold back tears. My voice is a little croaky.

"Thank you, Hans. I shall remember what you have just said for ever." On the way back down the corridor, I pass Monique.

"What on earth is the matter, Catherine?" She asks.

"I tell you at lunch" I reply, blinking rapidly. Back in my office, I cannot stop the tears but through them I can see that the polyhedral computer screen is the most dramatic colours that most people never see.

When I get home in the evening Georges is back already. He is standing looking out of the window I go to him and give him a big hug. Then I tell him what Hans said to me. He is impressed.

"That really is an accolade. Are you going to act on it, Catherine? I know you had been thinking of waiting until you'd been there at least two years, possibly more. If you were to apply for a partnership, the fact that you are so young would not necessarily be a disadvantage if your referees say that you are ready for the post. In fact a good firm would realise that they should snap you up while they have the chance. What are your thoughts on the question?"

"I don't want to be in too much of a hurry but I can look at what comes up and wait until the right post is advertised. Georges, this involves you too because we need to both be working within a reasonable distance of where we live. Come and sit down. I want to discuss this at some length with you."

George pours us both a glass of St. Joseph, sits in a chair facing me and waits for me to start.

"My first priority is to be with you" I begin. "But as long as that would be possible, I have this dream of living in my childhood home in Écharvines, near the lake at Annecy. It is still owned by my parents or at least by my dad, I suppose, as it has been his family home for generations. At the moment it is leased on a long term rent but I know that it is coming up for review in about a year. If I were to be living at the house, there are only a few places that I could reasonably work that would have a firm of notaires that was really high-class. Annecy of course, but Albertville, Chambéry or, I'm not sure, possibly St.Julien-en-Genevois or Aix-les-Bains. Geneva is probably out because of the rush hour traffic jams. The thing is, Georges, would you be able to, want or be prepared to move from Lyon?"

"I need to think about that" says Georges. "In principle I am happy to move to wherever you would like. There is a problem at one level though. I left school without the bac. I started in the firm here at a very junior level and I have worked my way up. If I were to apply to a different firm, I think the fact that I never even took the bac might be a stumbling block to getting a comparable position. On the other hand staying within the firm I might be able to move sideways to a post in one of the places you mentioned. If I was lucky I might be able to retain the same level in the firm. I don't think that any of them has a post that is ranked higher than the one I already have but I might have a bit more autonomy because here at Lyon, one is always at the immediate beck and call of the big bosses who like to direct the way you do things and then, as like as not, take the credit for it. I certainly do not want to feel that I am holding you back and with two decent salaries coming in, I cannot see that the precise wage either of us earns will matter too much. I shall look into it: ask a few people's advice."

"OK, thanks Georges" I say. "Let's leave the subject for now. Why don't you come over here and sit on the sofa with me and perhaps we can think of something more interesting to pass the time?" He does so. Surprisingly soon, we are both thinking of exactly the same activity.

A week later Georges comes back to me about whether he might be able to move within the firm. He says that the big-brass say that it is no problem in principle but at the moment it does not look as if there is a vacancy coming up in the area that we are thinking about. They have told him that if one does, they are happy to transfer him to any comparable position without any interview or other formality. The senior post at their Geneva branch is officially more senior than his current post and would need an interview.

I have never seen Jeanne like this. She is really feeling the separation from Gérard. I hope Gérard is serious about her because as I see it if he were to give her the heave-ho, she would fall apart.

She is looking at the adverts for notaires in Limoges just to be with him. Well, if she finds a good firm, why not? But she is not only looking for junior partnerships, she is also looking at assistant positions like the one she has already. This is not good thinking. I have always imagined that Jeanne was as good as me. In the days when we were students together, we studied together a lot and tested each other. We were very much on the same level and Jeanne always seemed to have this sixth sense that led her to the correct conclusion even when she wasn't sure. Now to my mind she was not really thinking straight. Although the precise problem was different, I had had enough of my best friends having man-problems, while I was a teenager with Janine. I could not go through that again, especially without Louise to support me. There is currently no partner's post coming up in Limoges. Jeanne says she is going to apply for an assistantship.

"Don't do it Jeanne" I say. "Please don't do it." But she seems adamant; completely deaf to reason.

The next day she comes round early evening and she is furious. The senior partner at her firm, Maîtres Paillard-Montaigne, is Maître Paillard. Maître Montaigne died some time ago but the new junior partner has not yet got his name on the brasswork. She went to talk to

Maître Paillard about applying for this job in Limoges. When she told him what the job was, he apparently told her that he wouldn't give her a reference. According to Jeanne, he said 'I'm not having a young woman like you wasting her time applying for a stupid post like that. What on earth is the matter with you these days Jeanne. You're too good for that. Apply for a proper job and I'll give you a proper reference'. 'Good for Maître Paillard,' I think. You have to be a brave man to talk to Jeanne like that. I sit her down, pour her a drink and give her oodles of sympathy. She slowly calms down and then becomes a bit maudlin.

"What am I going to do Catherine?" She asks me pathetically.

"The real question here, Jeanne" I tell her, "is not what you are going to do. It is what Gérard is going to do. He was all enthusiasm initially. What does he think now? Are you due to see him? It is no good landing some useless post in Limoges if you are still not going to get together with him. What does he tell you?"

"When we talk on the phone he still seems very keen, but he just doesn't make arrangements for us to meet."

I remember how Louise helped me over a comparable crisis at a time when I didn't know Jeanne as well as I do now. Louise was so helpful. Can I see the answer in Jeanne's case?

"May be you need to make the arrangements, Jeanne. I see your point about not really being able to have Gérard stay at the flat while Zoë and Aurélie are there but things are changing. At the weekends Aurélie is spending pretty much all the time with Jacques in Annecy. If we can persuade Zoë to find somewhere to go for a weekend you could make Gérard an offer he couldn't refuse. At least if he did refuse it, it would tell you something that you didn't want to hear and clear things up. So Zoë might be the key here. She's a clerk at your work and you share a flat with her. What do you know about her that might help?"

"Her parents live abroad somewhere. She doesn't have a current boyfriend, certainly not one that she would spend a weekend with."

I get an idea. It will need Georges' co-operation, so I cannot tell Jeanne at the moment.

"Leave it with me for a day or two, Jeanne, I have the beginnings of an idea. I'll see what I can do."

Just then, with excellent timing, Georges comes home. He gives me a kiss and asks Jeanne how she is.

"Oh! I'm fine thanks Georges" she replies.

'I wish' I think to myself. When Jeanne has gone, I sit Georges down.

"Georges, I want you to do me a favour. It is on behalf of Jeanne really. She says she's fine but she isn't. She is having a problem with Gérard. If their flatmate Zoë is willing, could we have her stay with us for a weekend?"

"Sure" says Georges. "I can't see why not. If you want that Catherine, it's fine by me. Tell me about it."

So I do. Georges is very sympathetic. He rather liked the idea that his brother was dating one of my best friends and was surprised that there seemed to be a hitch.

"Would it help if I had a word with Gérard?" He asks.

"Not for the moment anyway" I reply. "Done that way I think it might annoy him."

Now, I wonder, can I arrange a weekend that Zoë comes here and that Aurélie spends with Jacques?

Oh the machinations that one gets up to, trying to help friends. To do this, I first need to have reasonable notice that Aurélie is going to spend the weekend with Jacques, then I must get Zoë to accept an invitation to stay with Georges and me early enough for Jeanne to be able to invite Gérard without it being too last minute. I do not think Aurélie will be a problem and she isn't.

"I'll tell Jacques that I'll spend the weekend with him in four weeks' time" she says. "I may have to tell him why but that doesn't matter does it? I'll do that today."

So phase one has gone all right. But I don't know Zoë very well at all. She is the replacement for me in the flat when I got married and moved in with Georges. I have only met her a couple of times. Again I need Aurélie's help. At a time when she is almost sure that Zoë will be there, she invites me over to the flat that I used to live in only a short while ago. I do my very best to be friendly to Zoë and draw her out. She is a very shy individual, obviously intelligent but far from a beauty. Her parents emigrated to Canada when she was twenty. They wanted her to go with them. She had a boyfriend at the time so decided not to go. She now regrets that decision because she fell out with the boyfriend when she found that he had a number of other girlfriends and as far as she could see, he regarded her as being about halfway down the list. By then she had her current job, clerk at Maîtres Paillard-Montaigne where Jeanne works. It didn't then seem sensible to follow her parents. She was very lonely and had jumped at the chance to share a flat with Jeanne. Aurélie leaves me to do most of the talking to Zoë but from time to time she mentions something that just happens to put Georges in a good light. Brilliant, I don't think that I would have thought of it and being his wife it wouldn't be the same coming from me. What Aurélie has realised is that it is all very well to invite Zoë to stay for a weekend but she hasn't even met Georges. As a shy person that might well put her off. So Aurélie is reducing that risk. At the end of the evening, I say how much I've enjoyed talking to her and invite her for the weekend. She is obviously a bit doubtful but I think only because she is shy. With Aurélie there it is a little difficult for her to refuse.

"Thank you Catherine" she says. "That is very kind of you. I'd like that. I'm looking forward to meeting your husband. He sounds an interesting type."

So that is phase two completed. Phase three is up to Jeanne. She is on her own. Neither Aurélie nor I can help her with that. Jeanne tells me that Gérard has accepted her suggestion of staying the weekend. 'With alacrity' was the way she put it. When she calls round a few days later, she is back to her old self. She is looking forward to what is now the next weekend but one. Having Zoë to stay is a real pleasure. She seems to be really touched that I have invited her. I hope that, if she finds out the real reason, it will not make her be angry or turn her against me. Georges is brilliant. He manages to pay her exactly the right amount of attention. Not so much she might feel he was coming on or indeed that I might get jealous but enough to make her feel very much at home. So it went well. Another advantage was that I was now a genuine friend of all the occupants of my old flat and was welcome there whenever I wanted. The reverse was equally true now that Georges knew all of them. We were a happy bunch, though as the only man, Georges may have felt outnumbered sometimes.

For the Christmas break I ask Georges if I can invite Louise to stay for a few days. I haven't really seen her for ages; not to talk to. It wasn't possible to talk to her at any length at the wedding. Georges as always is happy to comply with anything I want. I must be careful not to take this for granted. I show her around Lyon. She is rather put out by my place of work.

"This is not a very salubrious area is it Catherine? What on earth made you get a job here?"

I realise that I haven't told Louise of the scene almost exactly two years ago when I was nearly raped. It is not something that you tell someone on the phone or by email. I tell her now. She is horrified.

"You certainly thought quickly Catherine. I don't think I'd have thought of apparent acquiescence followed immediately by extreme violence. Serve the bastard right. I shall remember that if ever the occasion arises."

"The point is" I say, "that I was very vulnerable at the time and I wanted to be near Jeanne. She has become as good a friend to me as you are. We helped each other all through University. The area is a bit unsavoury but in fact the firm isn't bad at all."

In the New Year and far later than I had originally intended, I invite everyone round for the Caribbean meal based on my honeymoon experience. I give them Fricassée de Crabes and Écrevisses Étouffées. I do the Fricassée by the recipe but I modify the Écrevisses Étouffées a bit in case the original is rather too spicy for anyone. That is a bit of fine tuning. Reduce the cayenne pepper a little and increase the garlic to compensate. Yes it works. You should try it.

Then a partnership for a notaire comes up in Limoges. I cross my fingers. I hope it is a decent firm because

I know Jeanne will apply for it whatever. I don't take her word for it. I research it for myself. Thank Heavens! It is a firm with a good reputation, Maîtres Garraud-Vincent, in Avenue de la Liberation in the centre of town. Jeanne applies and she gets the job. I think 'well of course she would' but I'm sure that she would not necessarily expect to get the first partnership that she applied for. I am a little worried for her. She seems so set on Gérard and he seems rather off-hand about the relationship. At least this is a good post for her whether she has a lasting relationship with Gérard or not.

I needed to wait another three months before a possible partnership came up that I felt that I should apply for. I would have liked Annecy ideally. This vacancy is in Albertville. I discussed it with Georges and we decided that I should apply using my maiden name. In its way Albertville is rather like a mini-Lyon. It is the Prefecture of the department of Savoie and like Lyon is on the confluence of two rivers, the Isère and the smaller Arly. Although the Isère is a fair sized river, the Arly is quite small and both are only mountain streams compared with the mighty Rhône and Saône at Lyon but very pretty nonetheless.

The practice that I have applied to, Maîtres Fernand et Perrier, is on the rue Gambetta, quite close to the Town Hall. Maître Fernand is retiring but they are both present for the interviews and their chief clerk Robert Duprès is also there, making a panel of three. There are four of us who have been short-listed. The other three are men. Two are considerably older than me. The third is a tall very good-looking man maybe two or three years older than me. We are all impeccably dressed. We have been told that although they will make the decision today, we will be notified by official letter whether we are appointed or not. You never know what other candidates go through. My interview was hell. Robert Duprès never said a word but he looked very grim throughout. Maître Fernand kept asking me if I had experience of rare legal situations which at my age it was highly unlikely that I would have seen. I answered each one saying what I would do in the circumstances but had to admit every time that these were aspects that I had not yet come across. Then he would say:

"I'm not surprised, you're so young aren't you?"

It was very depressing. Then something happened that gave me a bit of hope and perked me up. Maître Perrier, who if I was appointed would be my senior partner, said: "I think we've heard enough of Catherine Diacre being so young Jean, like the rest of us she will get older."

He gave me a slight smile and asked a nice simple question on conveyancing. That was it. I was on my way out.

It was over a week before the letter came. Georges was back before me. He handed me the letter to open. I sat down and my hands were shaking as I opened it. These official letters can be stupid. There were a whole lot of conditions and caveats before it got to the main point. Somewhere toward the bottom of the page, I found that I had been given the job. Yes, I am absolutely thrilled. As by now you will expect, this gives me one of my 'hallucinations' with unbelievable shapes and colours.

"Well Catherine, Did they give it to you?"

I cannot talk. I hand Georges the letter. I am due to start in just under three months on 1st August. I contact mum and dad. They are both delighted for me. Mum, being a typical mum, asks me if I am pregnant yet. No, I am not ready for that. I ask dad about the house. I know the review is coming up soon. Is there any possibility that Georges and I might live there? He says he will look at the small print of the agreement and contact the tenants to hear their view of things. George is delighted for me but I have given us a problem. In reality it is over two hours from Lyon to Albertville so over 4 hours a day to commute. That is not realistic. I suppose it would be workable for a week or two but certainly not for long. Dad gets back to me. The rental agreement on the house ends on 31st August and the people there say they do not mind if there is no new agreement. They feel that are slightly isolated there and would sooner move into town. He says that as his only child it would come to me eventually anyway so it might as well be now as when both he and mum are dead. We can have it transferred. It is a lovely thought that I can put that in the hands of my new firm. How soon can I get the name changed to Maîtres Perrier et Diacre? As the house is over 15 years old (over 150 years old actually) it will need a full electrical check-up. I can get Jacques to do that. A lot of things are falling into place.

In the middle of July an invitation comes for Georges and me to attend the wedding of Aurélie and Jacques. That is lovely, the wedding of my cousin and my husband's best friend. It is also a marriage between a Parisel and a Diacre. A thing the family legend said would never happen. I hope it does not bring down the wrath of heaven upon their heads!

I start my new job as a partner in Fernand-Perrier on 2nd August as the official starting date of the first was a

Sunday. The chief clerk Robert Duprès, shows me to my office. He congratulates me on getting the job. He laughs as he tells me why.

"The funny thing was that Old Fernand really had it in for you. I think that he didn't want a woman. No doubt you could tell that. I saw you looking rather depressed. But the more he gave you real snorters of questions, the better you responded. To have given all the correct answers without ever having experienced those situations made both Maître Perrier and me more and more certain that you deserved the job. Not only were you the best candidate but you had all our sympathy as well. Both your referees covered the fact that you were exceptionally good for your age. I cannot say that the panel was unanimous but Louis Perrier and I were in no doubt. Let me take you round to Louis. He'll be delighted to see you've arrived."

Indeed, Louis gave every indication of being very pleased to see me. It augurs well for the rest of my career. Surely two of the most important things in life are to have a loving husband and a boss who appreciates you. I think that I am lucky enough to have both.

On 14th Aurélie and Jacques' wedding day arrives. They have attended a simple ceremony at the Town Hall and are now married. We are now at L'Hôtel Impérial. I have always said that although Aurélie and I are very alike, she is prettier than I am. If I even approach how lovely Aurélie looks on her wedding day, I must be a stunning beauty too. Most brides look beautiful. I think it is the colour in their cheeks given by the excitement of the occasion. Of course my Uncle Robert and Aunt Nicole, Aurélie's parents are here with my cousin Léo. As I look around, I can see that Jules and Marianne are still an item. Jeanne and Gérard are still an item. Guy and Eugénie that I remember from Jacques' party are still together. Georges introduces me to his uncle. He pointed him out to me at the party but I think he was too busy flirting with me to get round to actually introducing his uncle. There are a lot of people that I don't know. There is an elderly man with a rather beautiful walking stick whom I talk to for a bit. He was apparently an electrician like Jacques before he retired. Then Aurélie and Jacques are ready to depart. Nobody seems to know whether they are going on honeymoon or not, and if so where they are headed.

A couple of weeks later we can move into my childhood home in Écharvines. I get an amazing sense of returning home after a long journey. The crack in the ceiling of the living room is just as it was when I was a child. The rutted up ground running to the outhouse that we used as a garage looks completely unchanged. The view from what was my bedroom window looks as beautiful as ever but I suppose I shall have to move into the master bedroom with Georges. I don't know when that will be because no suitable job for Georges has come up in the area yet. We start to rent a place in Saint-Alban-de-Montbel on Lac d'Aiguebelette at the beginning of August when I start my new job. It is more or less halfway between Lyon and Albertville. That means that we both have a journey of around an hour each way to and from work. It also means that we need to buy a second car. I was tempted to buy an old classic like my mother's Deux Chevaux Citroën but Georges talked me out of it.

"Before you know it you'll have broken down on the A43," he says, "and then you won't find it so much fun."

He is right. I decide on a three year old Renault Mégane. I love it. It is a beautiful blue and is my pride; a real joy to drive. The journey to and from work is a real pleasure. I never thought commuting would be such fun. We have stopped paying for the ground floor flat George was renting in Lyon and now must wait until a suitable post in his firm comes up.

In November, we at last get the news that we have been waiting for. The manager at the Annecy branch of Georges' firm has been promoted to run their Geneva Office in Switzerland. That will actually happen on 10th January. So that is the appointed day for Georges to head up the Annecy branch. Jacques has completed the electrical test for the old house. As it hasn't changed hands since the 15 year rule became law, it turned out that there was quite lot that needed doing to bring the 200 year old house up to modern electrical requirements. Of course he says there will be no charge. I say we will invite him round to our house-warming. On the evening of Friday, 7th January 2005 we move into my childhood home and I go singing through the house like the child I was when I last lived here. It is so good to be home at last.

Jacques 2004–2005

We have kept it a secret from everyone. When we leave our reception at L'Hôtel Impérial, No-one knows where Aurélie and I are headed. The reason for this secrecy is that we are going to spend a fortnight in Provence. Aurélie is going to show me all the favourite places of her childhood. If anyone knew, her parents might well expect us to stay with them. We intend to give them a ring towards the end of our trip and if they invite us, spend the last couple of days there. I am very happy to have actually married Aurélie. There is a mood generally in developed countries of 'why bother?' There is no longer any social stigma to not being married; no longer any differences in tax payments. There are still some immigration problems where a marriage certificate may be necessary to allow a partner to immigrate into some countries. I like the tradition and particularly the commitment to another person that marriage represents.

I left Aurélie to book this holiday. She knew the area and she knew what she wanted to show me. She books us in to Le Moulin de Sainte Anne. It is a former olive oil mill built in the 18th century. It is an enchanting choice. It is a little outside the centre of Grasse to the west. Then she shows me round the area. In the vicinity of Grasse there are over 100 square miles of lavender fields. We are a little late in the year for the peak lavender flowering but the later varieties are still in flower. The scent is everywhere, after a while your nose adapts and it becomes less noticeable. Aurélie to my surprise rather ignores the cultivated lavender. She takes me to a plateau high above Grasse, Le Plateau de Calern. Looking down you can see wild lavender growing in profusion. This, I imagine was what the whole area was like before the perfume trade took off.

I tend to forget that my beautiful wife is far, far more than that. She is actually a high-powered doctor. She has written papers on diseases caused by nutritional disorders and a disease called Guillain-Barré syndrome that means nothing to me but apparently causes muscle weakness. She also has a Senior Neurology Post in one of the best hospitals in the country. She shows me all sorts of herbs that were commonly used as medicines a hundred years ago. They are growing wild in the mountains; Summer Balm, Lime leaves, Oregano, Thyme and Rosemary. She seems to know which of the things that they were used for worked and which probably didn't. She leaves me completely out of my depth. I do remember that she said a preparation of Lime leaves was used to treat high blood pressure but probably only worked in people who had high blood pressure because of high anxiety levels as it did have an ingredient that was calming. The old remedy that surprised me most was that an infusion of violets contained enough salicylate to be as effective for a headache as aspirin or paracetamol. I hang on her every melodic word. I could happily listen to her voice all day but I understand almost nothing. We are in the fresh air, the surroundings are beautiful and when we return to the old mill, she is once again my amazing loving wife.

She takes me to a couple of lakes that she had been to as a child. She particularly liked a little beach at Bauduen on the Lac de Sainte Croix. It looks pretty ordinary to me. She says that she once had a boyfriend in that district. Perhaps it is that fact which gives it memories. I much prefer the Lac de Cassien and the Plage du Cheion on Lac de Castillon. We also do the tourist bit of looking at the three Rubens in Grasse Cathedral. Then with three days to go, Aurélie contacts her parents and we go to stay with them for the end of our honeymoon. Robert and Nicole are delighted that we have come to visit them. They were a little disappointed, I think, that we decided to get married in Annecy and not in Grasse. This, it seems, makes it up to them. By the end of August we are back in Annecy.

Soon after we get back, Catherine asks me to check the electrical fittings of the house where she was brought up as a child. Her father has transferred it to her. I tell her I'll do it for free. Going into the house brings back vivid memories of when I was thirteen. Over there is the room where her father told me that my mother had died. Upstairs is the bedroom that I had slept in. There on the side, is the extension designed by Claude and through the window I can see the outhouse where Catherine said 'choose any one of these bicycles'. I get to work and there is going to be an awful lot to do. This house is two hundred years old. The electricity was put in, at a guess, about 1950 maybe. Things have changed. Olivier has done a brilliant job on the extension. I can pass that straight away. Nothing needs altering. What he has done, rather cleverly and I imagine to keep the costs down, is to give the extension its own fuse box. It comes separately straight off the main supply to the house. This means that he didn't have to deal with any of the old wiring at all. This has the result that there is no risk of overloading the antiquated installation to the rest of the house. Nice one Olivier! But that leaves all the work to me. There is no hurry. Catherine and Georges are not moving in for the foreseeable future. I work on it steadily between other commitments and have it all finished by the end of October.

Meanwhile, only half a mile down the road, Aurélie is deciding how to furnish our new house. The unexpected nature of the way we have come by it, that is by the original customer defaulting, has left us with hardly any money. Putting it another way, the deficit is close to the maximum that the bank will allow. Poor Aurélie is left with a bit of a dilemma. Our joint income is fine. Everything should work out fairly quickly but just now we are experiencing a cash flow problem. She is very practical.

"The only room that needs to be furnished properly at the moment is the living room" she says. "Of course we also need decent kitchen appliances. The bedroom hardly matters, apart from the bed itself, because most of the time we won't be able to see it. It'll be dark."

Even so, kitchen appliances these days come at a price. I leave it to her. I know that she will get it right. She decides that for two months we will make do with a camping stove. Then we will get a proper oven and for the moment the living room will just have two armchairs and no table.

In early January, Catherine and Georges move in to the house in Écharvines. Georges has been given the manager's position at Annecy. His place of work is in the Romains area and I find it amusing that it is only a stone's throw from where my 'studio flat' was when I first arrived in Annecy. They are having a house-warming party. Between the two houses we now have plenty of room to put friends up for the night although in our house it will mean sleeping on the floor. Catherine and Georges are having their party on a Saturday. They have invited Jules and Marianne and the all the people connected with my firm as well as their own friends. Most of the guests live fairly close but a couple of Georges' old colleagues from Lyon and Catherine's new colleagues from Albertville may want a bed for the night, as may Pierre and Nadine. It is a great occasion. Catherine is really fired up to be back in her childhood home. It is an ideal place for a party. There are no neighbours very close. The nearest house is several hundred yards away, so there is no real danger of disturbing anyone.

I am delighted to see that Jules and Marianne are very much together. That certainly suggests that Aurélie's professor when she was at Lyon, Jean-Pierre Baudouin, has done an excellent job. It is funny to think what might have been if Marianne had had that treatment a year earlier. I certainly have no regrets. It makes me feel very lucky. Aurélie is everything I have ever wished for. A post has come up in the school in Provence at which Jules teaches history. It is right up Marianne's street and she is going to apply for it. There is another thing that we need to thank Professor Baudouin for. He said Aurélie should apply for the post at Annecy. Now the things that he predicted are coming together. It looks as if the first co-operation between the hospitals at Annecy and St. Julien-en-Genevois is beginning to take place even though the new hospital for the Annecy area which is being built at Pringy does not look as if it is going to be ready for three or four years. Due to his foresight, Aurélie will end up in a very prestigious position. But from my point of view, the highlight of the evening comes when Aurélie and I are talking to a couple from Lyon. The man, Roland Bouclier, is a friend of Georges. He was actually Georges' immediate boss. He has recently been promoted to number 2 under the CEO and is looking forward to being able to do rather more work from home. His wife, Renée has a florist's shop. They are currently living in Lyon but both of them have become fed up with the big city and want to move out to the country. Renée is one of triplets who are very close but have become separated by quite a distance as a result of their marriages. Renée says that the one thing they would really like is to live next door to each other. With this in mind they persuaded their husbands last year that it would be a good idea to buy a piece of land between Pont-Évêque and Estrablin where the river Vesonne runs into the Gère, with a view to building three houses, one for each couple. It was a long term plan but the time is now right to do that.

"My parents went a bit mad, I think, when they found they had triplet baby girls. They named us Rémy, Reyne and Renée which has caused nothing but confusion ever since. Rémy lives in Chambéry. Her husband has just retired. She herself gave up her job some time ago when her arthritis got worse. Reyne and her husband live in Davézieux on the other side of the Rhône but they both work in Vienne which is only about a quarter of an hour's drive." Then Renée asks Aurélie "What do you do?"

"I'm a neurologist at the hospital in Annecy" she replies, "and Jacques is a partner in a building firm."

Aurélie has given me a good boost there. I suppose it is true that I am a partner in PRO but I would still have called myself an electrician if it had been me who was asked. This of course in view of the previous conversation is of some interest to the Boucliers. When they discover that it is also the case that Georges and I have been best mates almost since birth, Roland says:

"Well, I'll take a look at what your firm has done and get some references. If that is all good, and your quote is competitive, I expect the others would be happy if we give you the contract."

"The firm is Parisel, Rouget and Oudart" I tell him. "PRO for short."

He laughs "Clever" he says. "That certainly sends out the right message. Have you got a card on you?"

In the end, we are given that contract. Our firm, PRO, is now definitely solvent. The order book is healthy. Also because of the Boucliers, we will now become well-known over a very much larger area. Already it looks as if we will have to take on several more workers. Pierre, Guy and I give ourselves a modest rise. I suggest to Guy and Pierre that we give Roch and François a slightly bigger percentage rise than ourselves and they agree to that.

On 22nd May 2005, it is my 27th birthday. It is a Sunday. Aurélie and I invite Catherine and Georges round for lunch. It is a beautiful day. Our garden is still rough turf with the two small trees to the side. They produce just enough shade for the four of us. After lunch Georges and I are sitting with our backs against the trunks. Catherine and Aurélie are lying flat with their heads on our laps. It is idyllic. I look at our wives. They are all but identical. An idea occurs to me. It might be a bit awkward to voice my thoughts but since Diane, I have seen the benefit of sometimes saying what you think.

"Catherine" I say, "at times like this do you sometimes hear soft dreamy music?"

Catherine and George look at me in amazement. Aurélie looks very concerned, even a little annoyed.

"Not quite" says Catherine. "I do sometimes see funny shapes and strange colours."

Aurélie's expression changes in a moment. She is now seeing the benefit of me being a little outspoken. Now that we all know that both Catherine and Aurélie have this strange propensity everyone can talk about it. About how unusual it is. How Catherine and Aurélie's experiences differ. They never knew that they both had this, synaesthesia, was it Aurélie had called it? those characteristics."

When July comes, the weather is hot. I think it would be fun for Georges, Catherine, Aurélie and me to have picnic at Le Balcon au Lac. We could easily walk there from where our houses are but I want to do this with a little bit of class. When we have all agreed the day, I hire a small boat. I buy the food, all cold, from Pauvert, including two of their beautiful vegetarian quiches (I find meat at a picnic attracts the insects more than veg), a bottle of champagne and plenty of water. We take the boat to the landing place just below Le Balcon au Lac for the picnic; the spot right next to the lake where I was those years ago when Jean and Catherine were above me. After we have finished the picnic, we all ascend to Le Balcon and sit with our legs over the edge just as Catherine and I used to do fourteen years before. There is only just room for the four of us to sit side by side but that is what we do. I am so content that if I were my wife, I would be hearing soft, dreamy music from another world but all I can hear is the harsh blast of the horn on the round-the-lake ferry as it approaches Menthon St. Bernard.

Oh well, you can't have everything!